I0756281

Also by Edward Ronny Arnold

Rebecca

The Lepers

Rashida

The Ram of God

The Tenth Scroll

Plato's Dream

When does life end and death begin?
Is it possible, they are the same?

Computer Classics
Nashville

Published by
Computer Classics ®
497 Elysian Fields Road A-11
Nashville, Tennessee 37211

This is a work of fiction. Names, characters, places, and incidents are used fictitiously. Any resemblance to actual persons, living or dead, events, or locales is entirely coincidental.

Plato's Dream © is published in e-book format by Computer Classics ® on the Computer Classics ® website www.computer-classics.com.

Library of Congress Control Number: 2005900797
ISBN: 0-9748870-4-8

Printed in the United States of America

Dedication

"When a writer calls his work a romance, it need hardly be observed that he wishes to claim certain latitude, both as to its fashion and material, which he would not have felt himself entitled to assume had he professed to be writing a novel."
- **Nathanial Hawthorne** 1851.

Plato's Dream is dedicated to the Romance novel as interpreted by Nathanial Hawthorne from his preface to *The House of the Seven Gables,* published in 1851. The romance was seen as something far more than a relationship of two people. Although romance has become, in our era, defined with a love-type relationship of two people, the basic concept remains of a type of work that mingles the Marvelous as a flavor rather than as the actual substance.

The romance in *Plato's Dream* occurs when ordinary people display the most unordinary of human traits. Where those who are seen as the lowest, are transformed into the highest and in this transformation, their love goes beyond the physical. It is here, where love is believed to be non-existent, that love is discovered to be at its greatest.

Edward Ronny Arnold

Introduction

"3 And Adam lived a hundred and thirty years, and begat a son, in his own likeness, after his image; and called his name Seth:"

"4 And the days of Adam after he had begotten Seth were eight hundred years: And he begat sons and daughters:"
- **Genesis** 5.

"...either death is a state of nothingness and utter unconsciousness, or, as men say, there is a change and migration of the soul from this world to another. Now if you suppose that there is no consciousness, but a sleep like the sleep of him who is undisturbed even by the sight of dreams, death will be an unspeakable gain."
- **Plato** 360 B.C.

"Male and female differ in their essence by each having a separate ability or faculty, and anatomically by certain parts; essentially the male is that which is able to generate in another, as said above; the female is that which is able to generate in itself and out of which comes into being the offspring previously existing in the parent."
- **Aristotle** 350 B.C.

"43 He said unto them, Give place: for the maid is not dead, but sleepeth. And they laughed him to scorn."
- **Saint Matthew** A.D. 55-70.

"11 These things said he: and after that he saith unto them, our friend Lazarus sleepeth; but I go, that I may awake him out of sleep."
- **Saint John** A.D. 89-90.

"If, for instance, the seed plant has a short stem, terminal white flowers, and simply inflated pods; the pollen plant, on the other hand, a long stem, violet-red flowers distributed along the stem, and constricted pods; the hybrid resembles the seed parent only in the form of the pod; in the other characters it agrees with the pollen parent." - **Gregor Mendel** 1865.

"We realized you could copy this information if you separated the two strands. Francis said to me: 'We have discovered the secret of life' - and we had." - **James D. Watson** 1953.

Plato and Peas

Barbara was bored! She lost interest in what Professor Arnold was saying about ten minutes ago. She looked at the wall at the old clock. It was one of those clocks she remembered from high school, large with large numbers. The time was ten fifteen. Barbara attempted to look interested but she wasn't.

Professor Arnold didn't notice Barbara's boredom. He had stood and turned toward the bookcase as he was speaking. He kept talking. Frequently, he would stop speaking and look at her. He would smile, and then continued to speak.

Barbara smiled. 'He's nuts!" she thought. Why she came to see him she didn't know. She was sitting in an old office located near the shopping center. The ad in the paper read, *Dreams explained / Ten dollars for thirty minutes.* Barbara expected a psychic. She expected someone with Tarot cards that would read her palms and explain her dreams. Instead, she met a middle-aged man who claims he has a Masters in Sociology. Professor Arnold was not a psychic. He taught at a local college.

The office looked like it was seldom used. It was bare except for an old desk, two chairs and several bookcases. The bookcases covered the entire back wall. The office reminded her of the office of a college professor. There were no pictures or plants. It was bare except for books. There wasn't a computer or typewriter. Somehow she expected a mysterious person. Professor Arnold was middle-aged, pudgy, and short. He was nuts!

Plato's Dream

He began his interview talking about Plato. What did Plato have to do with her dreams? Plato was a philosopher. Barbara knew this from her Psychology classes. That was strange enough, and then he began talking about some monk growing peas. What did a monk growing peas have to do with her dreams? It was a mistake to answer the ad. She lost time and ten dollars. Barbara looked at the clock on the wall. She had about ten minutes left.

"I can prove it!" Professor Arnold said.

Barbara looked quickly toward Professor Arnold. "Prove what?" she asked.

"Have you been listening?" Professor Arnold asked, as he sat in the chair at the desk.

"Sort of," Barbara answered. "To be honest, what does a monk growing peas have to do with my dreams?"

Professor Arnold leaned forward toward Barbara. "The monk was Gregor Mendel," he answered with a slight grin. "Mendel created the basis of genetics. He published his findings in 1866. What he has to do with your dreams is simple." He leaned closer toward Barbara. "They are not dreams."

Barbara was startled. "How do you know anything about my dreams? She asked. "You don't know anything about them! You have no idea what my dreams are."

Professor Arnold smiled. "Do you mind if I smoke?" he asked.

Barbara nodded. Professor Arnold opened a desk drawer and he removed a small box of cigars. He removed the wrapper on one of the cigars and he lit it with a match. "Your dreams started about one year ago," he said. "At first, you didn't pay much attention. Then, they appeared like a story. There were bits and pieces of the story but it didn't seem," Professor Arnold paused, as he puffed on the cigar, "to be joined or make any sense."

He stood and looked at Barbara. "The dreams were different each time," he added. "There were events like ordinary life; walking on the street; eating a meal with several people at the table; a holiday like Christmas or a birthday. Then one dream kept occurring. The one dream seems to play over and over. Each time you have the dream, there is a little more."

Barbara narrowed her eyes. "Yes!" she said, "That is pretty much what has happened. Do you know anything else?"

Professor Arnold puffed on the cigar. "The one dream that keeps occurring is sexual in nature," he answered.

Barbara blushed.

"The person in the dreams is not you!" he added.

Barbara's eyes widened. "That's right!" she said excited, "The person in my dreams is not me! I have had many dreams and in those dreams, it's me. Some have been strange and some are simple and made no sense. In all of those dreams, it was me. The dreams I have been having are not me. It's someone else!"

'Now were getting somewhere," she thought. "Who is it?" Barbara asked.

Professor Arnold smiled. "I told you!" he answered. "I think you weren't listening,"

Barbara looked confused. "You didn't say anything except lecturing me on Plato and the monk Mendel. You kept talking about Mendel growing peas. What do peas have to do with my dreams?"

Professor Arnold grinned. He puffed on the cigar then he placed it in the ashtray. He sat in his chair looking at Barbara. "It appears you weren't listening," he said, "Your dreams are real! They are not dreams."

Barbara was confused. "They're dreams! Nothing more than dreams! Who is the woman in my dreams? Why am I having them? What do they mean?"

Professor Arnold smiled. He looked at the desk and he picked up a black marker lying on the desk. "This marker is a child's marker," he said, as he looked at the black marker. "It belongs to my neighbor's four year-old daughter. The ink is easily erased and it has a flavored smell." He handed the marker to Barbara. "Look at it! Feel it! Smell it!"

Barbara took the black marker and she smelled it. "Its licorice!" she answered.

He opened a drawer in the desk and removed two markers. One was yellow and one was red. He handed the two markers to Barbara. "Look at them!" he said, "Feel them! Smell them! They are children's markers. Each has a scented smell."

Barbara placed the black marker on the desk. She picked up the two markers and smelled them. "The yellow is lemon and the red is cherry."

"You just used several of your senses," Professor Arnold said, as he grinned "You touched the markers; you could feel them. You looked at them; you could see them. You smelled them; you associated the smells with licorice, lemons, and cherries."

Barbara's eyes narrowed.

Professor Arnold leaned forward on the desk and he placed his elbow on the desk. He leaned his chin forward and rested his chin on his hand. "Plato had a theory of consciousness," he said. "He believed a person's conscious was contained in the entire body. He did not believe a person's conscious was contained in the brain or the heart. Plato also believed that a person's conscious was based upon the consciousness of others. Consciousness was an act of nature. It was not an act of supernatural means. It was a plan whereby one person passed their consciousness to another."

"His pupil, Aristotle, believed the male contributed the plan to the female. The female contributed the raw material. Aristotle wrote *The Generation of Animals* about 350 B.C. In Aristotle's writings, the theory of Plato was contained in the plan."

He looked at Barbara closely. "Gregor Mendel used their theories to develop one of his own. There was a theory that environment caused change in plants and animals and humans. Mendel planted different plants beside each other. In every case, the plants produced seeds that were like the original plant. One plant did not affect another plant. He grew peas and recorded physical traits carried from one generation to another. His theory was of genetic inheritance. He proved that one pea's characteristics can show up in another generation."

Barbara's eyes widened.

Professor Arnold leaned backward in the chair and he crossed his arms on his chest. He looked at Barbara. She was about thirty years old and attractive with long brown hair. Her eyes were green. She was wearing a gray suit. The suit was not expensive but attractive. When she entered his office, he noticed her body. She was thin and about five feet four inches tall and she appeared to exercise regularly. "Do you have children?" he asked.

Barbara lowered her head. She did not like the question. Hell, she heard it enough at work and at church. She raised her head. "No," she answered. Her eyes were narrowed as she looked at Professor Arnold. "My husband Brad and I are trying. We have been married seven years. Our first goal was to establish ourselves a career. Then, we wanted to purchase a home." Barbara lowered her head and sighed. "We placed children at the bottom of our list."

She raised her head and looked at Professor Arnold. Her eyes were watering. "Brad and I are the only children. We now realize the one thing we really wanted, the one thing that really mattered was placed on hold. We made a decision to delay children." Barbara smiled slightly. "We made the wrong decision."

Professor Arnold smiled. He knew her feelings. One of the classes he taught was Marriage and Family. This was one of the most common concerns from the students, the decision was made to obtain material possessions first; children were an after thought. He stood and walked to the bookcase where he removed a large white packet. The packet was used in his Marriage and Family class. He smiled as he handed the packet to Barbara. "This will help," he said, "There are suggestions for relaxation and charts on fertility. Also, there is a list of several doctors."

Barbara took the packet and placed it on the floor. "We have considered adoption."

Professor Arnold frowned. "That should be a last resort," he said abruptly. "That is a decision that should not be taken lightly and it requires much discussion."

"Why?" Barbara asked. She didn't like the tone of Professor Arnold's voice. He sounded like he was condemning her.

"Adoption is a great thing!" he said. "If you and your husband wish to adopt a child it is wonderful. If your decision is to replace something you can not have, your decision has far reaching consequences. Every adoptive parent is looking for a blonde-haired blue-eyed newborn boy or a blonde-haired sweet newborn girl. It is unfortunate that such children are rare to adopt. Most of the children, available for adoption, have emotional scars that may never heal."

Barbara narrowed her eyes. She didn't like him. She didn't like his attitude or his comments. If she and Brad wanted to adopt, it was none of his business. "That's not true," Barbara answered. "Adoptive children are very loving. I know of several couples in my church that have adopted. There are no problems."

"Did you read about the newborn girl discovered in a garbage dumpster?" he asked.

Barbara nodded her head. "I can't believe a mother, any mother, would do such a thing!" she said.

"How do you think the young girl will accept it when she is told the truth?" he asked.

"Not very well," Barbara answered. "Her adoptive parents will love her! I am sure the young girl will learn to forget what happened."

Professor Arnold laughed. "How naive you are!" he chuckled.

"I am not!" Barbara answered irritated. She didn't like him. Barbara didn't like Professor Arnold one damn bit! He was an arrogant bastard.

Professor Arnold leaned forward toward Barbara and cocked his head slightly. "How do you forget that your mother left you in a pile of garbage to die?" he asked. "How do you forget that your mother left you on the street to starve while she partied? How do you forget that your mother's boyfriend used you as a sex-toy? How do you forget that your mother and father beat you and shamed you?"

Barbara lowered her head.

"All of these children are damaged!" he added. "There are events in their lives we can not comprehend and there are events they can not forget. They should not forget."

Barbara smiled softly. "Perhaps so, but a parent's love can help to mend the pain and suffering," she answered.

"If you adopt a child, you are not their parent!" he said abruptly, as he sat in his chair. "Only by law are you their caregiver. You are not their parent. There is no history. If you decide to adopt because you want to help the child and to provide a good safe home, that is a very good thing. If you and your husband want to adopt to fill a void in your life and make the child as your flesh and blood that is different."

"Why are you anti-adoption?" Barbara asked.

"I'm not!" he answered. "I am for adoption. I am against the so called adoption parties where prospective parents review children eligible for adoption. It is like a cattle auction! Adoption is a great thing for the child and the adoptive parents if the adoption is for the child not the adoptive parents."

Barbara lowered her head. She knew what he was talking about. As a social worker, she had attended many adoption parties. The children were treated like cattle. The prospective parents looked at them and judged them like buying a pet. The children were hopeful someone would select them. There were always tears when it was over. The children felt rejected because they were not selected. One or more of the prospective adoptive parents always asked the same question, 'Is this all there is?'

Barbara raised her head. "Do you have children?" she asked defiantly.

"My wife and I adopted two boys," Professor Arnold answered. He stood and walked toward the bookcase where he removed a photograph of two young boys. He turned and pointed the photograph toward Barbara. "James was three and John was two when we adopted them. Their mother left them in a parked car with the windows rolled up while she went drinking on Broad Street. It was June and very hot. They were screaming for someone to help them."

He walked to the desk and sat down. Professor Arnold handed the photograph to Barbara. "It was noontime and more than one hundred people walked past the parked car," he added. "James and John were screaming for help but everyone ignored them." Professor Arnold's eyes began to water. "Two women were seated in a restaurant. From where they sat, they could see them yelling in the car. James told the police the two women looked at them but ignored them. The two women were friends who had met for lunch."

Barbara's eyes began to water. "Perhaps they couldn't hear the two boys," she said as she shrugged her shoulders.

"Perhaps," Professor Arnold said. "Officer Nicholas Young heard them! He was on patrol and he heard their yells above the sound of his motorcycle. As he broke the windows of the hot car with his nightstick, the two women were watching him. They heard the young boys and they saw them."

"You adopted them?" Barbara asked, surprised.

"Yes!" he answered. "My wife is unable to have children. We contacted the state agency and told them we wanted to adopt siblings. It didn't matter if they were boys or girls. Three days later, we met James and John."

"How many other children did you meet?" she asked.

"None!" he answered. "Our goal was to provide a safe, secure home for children. It didn't matter if they were special needs or of a different race. Our goal was to adopt to help the needs of the children not our needs. We accepted the first choice given. "

Barbara moved in her seat. She was suddenly interested in what Professor Arnold was saying. All of a sudden, he wasn't a bastard. He was very wise and sincere. She suddenly liked him because everything he said made sense. So many adoptive parents adopt for the wrong reasons. "How are James and John doing?" she asked.

"Very well," he answered. "James is currently attending Middle Tennessee State in Criminal Justice. He wants to be a policeman. John attends the University of Tennessee. John hasn't selected a major as he tends to drift. He is on the fourth string football team. We attend every home game."

"How did things work out?" she asked.

"Years of therapy," he answered. "James was oldest and he understood more than John. For many years, James did not trust obese white women."

Barbara narrowed her eyes. "Was their mother obese?" she asked.

"No," Professor Arnold answered. "The two women who watched them as they yelled for help were white and obese. James remembered them looking at him as he yelled for help. The two women ignored them. James and John were afraid, hungry and thirsty. The two women sat watching them. They casually ate their lunch while James and John were close to death from the heat of the car."

Barbara narrowed her eyes. "How is John?" she asked.

"Wonderful!" Professor Arnold answered. "We attend every home game. He always hugs his adoptive mother and me. John is doing very well."

Barbara decided to change the conversation. "What does my having children have to do with my dreams?"

Professor Arnold smiled. "I had hoped to present something closer to yourself that you could more easily relate to," he answered. "As you know, James and John are adopted. They are not related and neither boy looks like their adoptive parents. From which parent did you get your hair color?"

Barbara smiled. "Neither," she answered, "my mother's hair is a reddish blond. My father's hair is black."

Professor Arnold smiled. "From which parent did you get your eye color?" he asked.

"Neither!" Barbara answered. "My father's eyes are brown! My mother's eyes are blue!"

Professor Arnold smiled as he reached for his cigar. He picked it up, lit it, and he puffed on his cigar. "Who do you look like?" he asked.

Barbara smiled. "I look more like my grandmother's sister Marlene. She has brown hair," she answered.

He smiled. "Who do you look like?" he asked again.

Barbara shrugged her shoulders. "I look like my grandmother's sister Marlene," she answered again.

"Is she petite and short?" he asked.

"No," Barbara answered. "She is tall and heavy."

"Has your grandmother's sister always been heavy?" he asked.

"Yes! She was fat as a little girl. She has always been fat," Barbara answered with a puzzled look on her face.

Professor Arnold stood. "Is there anyway you can check on another relative?" he asked, as he placed his cigar in the ashtray. "Perhaps, your great-grandmother on either side?"

"I don't know. Why?" Barbara asked as she narrowed her eyes.

He leaned toward the desk. "Plato believed consciousness resided in the entire body," he said as he stared at Barbara. "Aristotle believed the male and female passed the consciousness of one person to another at the moment of conception. The male sperm contained the combined consciousness and the female egg contained the raw material and the current female's consciousness. Mendel proved that the characteristics of a pea would show in subsequent generations. Recent discoveries in DNA have shown that physical traits are contained in the DNA of every cell in the body. Recessive genes can appear in later generations in the form of eye color and body type. Twins may appear in subsequent generations. Many times, an illness such as diabetes and cancer will appear. Each person contains, within their DNA, the characteristics of relatives. These characteristics are passed from generation to generation."

Professor Arnold sat in his chair and leaned backward. "Just as you received the hair color of your grandmother's sister, you received even more from another relative," he continued. "Your basic physical characteristics are from a female relative. As you used your senses to feel, look, and smell the children's markers, your consciousness recorded the information. It is possible that this experience is recorded in the DNA of one or more cells in your body. Mrs. Parker, this is called Plato's Dream! In addition to hair color, eye color, and body type, you received something else from your distant relative. You received their consciousness! Your dreams are not dreams! You are experiencing the actual consciousness of a relative!"

Barbara stood quickly. "What the hell are you talking about?" she asked. "You think I am possessed by the spirit of a dead relative?"

"No!" Professor Arnold answered, "This has nothing to do with spirits or ghosts. It is based in nature. Plato believed the consciousness of a person was built upon the consciousness of a previous person such as the mother and father. Each generation passed their consciousness to another generation. Just as the genes of hair color and eye color were passed, he believed the consciousness was passed."

"How can a person's consciousness be passed?" Barbara asked excitedly. "When a person dies, there is no consciousness. They are dead!"

"The consciousness is passed at birth, when the fetus is developing," Professor Arnold answered. "Only those experiences prior to birth are passed. If a person lived twenty years beyond the birth of a child, those twenty years are not present. They are yet to occur. There is no way to pass the consciousness. Only those experiences, from childhood to the birth are passed. Consciousness of previous generations is also passed at birth. Aristotle believed the consciousness was passed in the sperm. At your birth, your DNA contained the consciousness of your mother and father and other relatives."

"This is crazy!" Barbara said laughing. "How can I be experiencing the consciousness of a dead relative?"

"That's the puzzle!" Professor Arnold answered. "We have not yet discovered why certain genes are activated and others are not. I have a friend whose wife delivered a healthy baby boy. Two years later, she delivered a baby girl. The girl was born with glaucoma in both eyes. This rare defect occurs in one of one hundred thousand births. Somewhere in past generations, this defect occurred. One of the parents, or perhaps both of them, had the defective gene. It has been passed to their son and daughter. No one knows why it occurred in the girl but not the boy. Sometime in the far future, in a future generation, it will occur again."

Barbara laughed, "I understand that! But consciousness?"

Professor Arnold shrugged his shoulders. "Why not?"

Barbara smiled as she looked at the clock on the wall. The time was ten thirty-five. "I'm running over," Barbara said, as she opened her purse. She removed a ten-dollar bill and handed it to Professor Arnold.

"You are the only person I am seeing today," Professor Arnold said, as he took the money. He pointed toward the chair. "Sit. We will continue at no additional charge."

Barbara sat in the chair. "They are so real! It is like I am actually living them."

"They are real!" Professor Arnold said, with a serious look on his face. "You are experiencing the same sensations, visual, auditory, tactile, and smell one of your relatives experienced."

"Why?" Barbara asked. "I have never had anything like this happen. Why now? Why have they just occurred?"

Professor Arnold stood. "Something you have done or seen triggered them," he said. "They are there in all of us but never surface. Plato believed everything we knew was based on the consciousness of others. I have the consciousness of perhaps all of my relatives. It is possible that sometimes the consciousness is not passed, or if it is, it may somehow be defective."

Barbara laughed. "So this is where past life regression comes in? Someone is hypnotized and they believe they were some princess in a previous life."

Professor Arnold laughed. "Exactly!" he answered. "If you believe Plato, Aristotle, and Mendel, the person actually lived that life. In a previous generation, that person existed. Somehow, that person's consciousness was activated. They see, hear, feel, and smell what the person experienced."

Barbara smiled and blushed. "I read a lot of romance books," she said. "The most current theme is for a person to visit an old castle or building. When they enter the building, they are somehow transported backward into time. There they meet a handsome man. The man is usually misunderstood and a romance develops. The romance is called a time-travel romance." She blushed.

Professor Arnold smiled and nodded his head. "If you believe Plato, Aristotle, and Mendel, it actually happened," he said. "The place the person visited triggered the consciousness of a previous relative."

Barbara giggled. "Well it appears Plato, Aristotle, and Mendel were wrong!" she said smiling. "The time-travel romances go both ways. Most occur in the past. Some occur in the future. Plato, Aristotle, and Mendel are wrong! How can you experience the consciousness of a person that hasn't been born?"

Professor Arnold leaned forward toward Barbara. He was irritated at her question. "Mrs. Parker it appears you were not listening," he said as he narrowed his eyes. "Do you not recall anything I said about Plato's Dream?"

"I'm sorry! I wasn't listening," she answered, as she nodded her head. "I tuned you out when you began talking about peas."

He nodded and stood. "If you accept Plato's theory, each person holds the consciousness of their prior generations," he said. "You hold the consciousness of generations going back hundreds perhaps thousands of years. Do you know the approximate time period of the woman in your dreams?"

Barbara shrugged her shoulders. "I am not sure. They appear to be in the late 1800's."

Professor Arnold nodded. "Let's assume the person in your dreams lived in the year 1820," he said. "Within your DNA you hold the consciousness of that person and every person you are directly related to." He paused. "You have a new set of DNA consciousness every thirty years. It is possible that you can tap into the consciousness of the woman in 1820 and a relative in the year 1960. To the consciousness of the woman in 1820, 1960 is the future. In actuality, it is the past. It is your past but her future."

Barbara looked confused. How can it be the future if it is the past? How can they mix?" she asked.

"You really weren't listening," Professor Arnold said, as he leaned toward Barbara. "The big problem with Plato's Dream is his conclusion. The only way a person can tap into one or more of the prior sets of consciousnesses is when they are dead!"

Barbara stood quickly. "Dead! You're saying I am dead?" she asked with a surprised look on her face.

"No!" Professor Arnold answered. "I just answered your question about time-travel romances where the romance occurs in the future not the past. In Plato's Dream, there is no future. Plato did not believe in the future as it is yet to occur. I call the experience related-conscious. What is experienced is a far past which looking forward, is the future."

Barbara looked confused. "I don't understand," she said sheepishly.

"Mrs. Parker lets imagine for a few minutes," Professor Arnold said, as he frowned. "Let's pretend that anything is possible and Plato is correct. Your dreams are real! You are actually experiencing the consciousness of a woman who lived in the year 1820. The current year is 2001."

Barbara nodded her head. "I'm with you so far," she said as she smiled and sat down.

He smiled and nodded his head. "The actual date is not 2001," he said grinning. "The actual date is 2076. You are a young girl and you are asleep. In your sleep, you experience the actual consciousness of Mrs. Barbara Parker. Mrs. Parker is a distant relative that lived in the year 2001."

Barbara's eyes narrowed. "You're saying I am actually a young girl living in the year 2076?" she asked. "I have somehow tapped into the consciousness of a woman that lived in the year 2001."

"No," he answered, "I am saying Plato believed a person's consciousness was passed to future generations. Just as you have tapped into the consciousness of a relative that lived in the year 1820, it is possible that the actual year is 4024. A far distant relative has somehow tapped into the consciousness of a relative that lived in 2001. The dates are irrelevant!"

Barbara's eyes narrowed. "What you are saying is that God does not exist!" Barbara said, as she stood. "Everything is based on biology."

"On the contrary, what I am saying proves the existence of God!" Professor Arnold said quickly. "Plato's Dream proves God exists."

Barbara slowly sat down. "How does this prove God exists?" she asked with a puzzled look on her face.

Professor Arnold walked from the back of the desk to the front and he sat on the edge facing Barbara. "If you assume Plato was correct, this is not an accident," he answered. "In fact, it proves a great love of man from God."

"What love?" Barbara asked.

"If Plato was correct, we all have something in us. We all have a great gift from God," Professor Arnold said. "If consciousness is passed from generation to generation, it is not an accident. Steven Hawking wouldn't attempt to calculate the odds that a strike of lightening hitting primordial soup could create such a thing."

Professor Arnold paused. He looked at Barbara. She was looking intently at him. "Mrs. Parker," he continued, "If Plato was correct and Mendel's pea experiments are accurate, we all contain within our DNA the consciousness of the first man and woman."

Barbara stood very quickly. "We have the consciousness of Adam and Eve?" she asked excited.

"Yes!" Professor Arnold answered, "And within that consciousness is their experiences with God."

"That can't be proved!" she said excitedly.

"It already has been to a point," Professor Arnold answered. He stood and walked to the bookcase where he removed a book and he turned to look at Barbara. "Do you remember in 1994 that a man was discovered frozen in a glacier in Italy?"

"I think so," Barbara answered. "He was like a caveman and he had been frozen for four or five thousand years."

Professor Arnold held the book upward. "Dr. Brian Sykes examined the remains," he said. "He is an authority on DNA. Dr. Sykes was able to trace, through the Ice Man's DNA, an ancestor living in England." Professor Arnold thumbed through several pages of the book. "He discovered something else. Dr. Sykes discovered that all peoples from Europe can be traced, by their DNA, to seven women. He called the seven women The Seven Daughters of Eve. This is his book! It was released in July."

Barbara smiled and shook her head. "Seven women are not Eve," she chuckled.

Professor Arnold smiled. "Perhaps so, Dr. Sykes has named them Ursula, Xenia, Helena, Velda, Tara, Katrine, and Jasmine," he said. "A friend of mine took a DNA test. The test results show he is descended from Velda. Velda is from the region we know as Spain."

Barbara's curiosity was raised. "How could he do it?" she asked.

"It appears that there is a mitochondrial gene which passes down the maternal line undiluted," he answered. "The gene doesn't change. It has not changed in more than seventeen thousand years."

Barbara's eyes narrowed. "How is it possible?"

"It appears DNA has many secrets to reveal," Professor Arnold answered. "Dr. Sykes can only show seven women. It is believed everyone is descended from a single woman named African Eve. Perhaps, in a few years, the seven women will narrow to four and then one." Professor Arnold replaced the book and he removed another book from the bookcase. "You said you read time-travel romances. Have you ever read, *The Search for Omm Sety: Reincarnation and Eternal Love* by Jonathan Cott?" he asked as he turned toward Barbara.

Barbara nodded her head. "I have heard of it but I have never read it," she answered. "I was told it was a mystical book about magic."

Professor Arnold shrugged his shoulders. "The book has a very basic premise," he added. "It is about the life of a woman named Dorothy Eady. She was born in England in 1904. At the age of three, she suffered a fall that almost killed her. When she recovered from the fall, she could read Egyptian hieroglyphics."

"Read Egyptian hieroglyphics?" Barbara asked. "How can a three year-old girl read Egyptian?"

Professor Arnold smiled. "Strange isn't it?" he asked, as he looked at the book. "Dorothy not only could read Egyptian, she claimed, at the age of six, her real home was at the ancient city of Abydos, Upper Egypt." Professor Arnold returned the book to the case. "She claimed she was a virgin priestess named Bentreshyt at the temple of Sety I. At the age of fourteen, she met fifty-three year old Sety I. They had an affair where a child was born. To keep the true secret of their child, she committed suicide. In the book, they keep meeting in many different lives. She claimed she kept seeing him and speaking to him. She died in 1981."

"That sounds more like reincarnation than a time-travel romance," Barbara said smiling. "In a time-travel romance the person goes backward or forward in time, and then returns to the present day. This lady seemed to be stuck in the past reliving a dream."

"Exactly!" Professor Arnold said. "Bentreshyt lived about three thousand years ago. The Ice Man had been frozen for an estimated five thousand years. Dorothy was the first woman ever hired by the Egyptian Department of Antiquities to work as a draftsman. She worked at Abydos at the Temple of Sety I. She seemed to have an uncanny knowledge of ancient Egypt. She worked very hard to restore the temple."

Barbara narrowed her eyes.

"She even fed the cobra at the temple," he added, with a grin.

"That is not proof that consciousness can be passed," Barbara said smiling.

Napoleone Buonaparte

Professor Arnold smiled. He walked to his chair and sat down. "Have you ever taken a Psychology course in college?" he asked, as he leaned backward in the chair.

"Yes," Barbara answered. "I have a degree in social work. Several Psychology classes were required."

"Have you ever heard a professor make a comment about someone being crazy and thinking they are Napoleon?" he asked.

Barbara giggled. "One of my professors in Abnormal Psychology spoke of it," she answered. "He would stand and place his right hand in his coat like the painting."

"Do you know where the story originated?" Professor Arnold asked.

Barbara nodded her head.

Professor Arnold stood. He looked at Barbara and smiled. "The story originated in the early 1900's," he said. "A man lived in New York. He became ill with a fever. When he recovered, he believed he was Napoleon."

Barbara shrugged her shoulders. "Lots of people believe they are Napoleon," she answered. "If I remember my Abnormal Psychology class, it has something to do with an inferiority complex. The person wants to be someone important. Napoleon was a great leader and he conquered most of Europe. He would have succeeded but he was defeated at the Battle of Waterloo."

Professor Arnold sat down. "Have you ever heard of a crazy person that believed they were Napoleon who could speak Corsican?" he asked.

Barbara nodded her head.

"Have you ever heard of a crazy person that believed they were Napoleon who could name every battle Napoleon fought?" he asked.

Barbara nodded her head.

"Have you ever heard of a crazy person that believed they were Napoleon who could name every general under their command?" he asked.

Barbara narrowed her eyes. "What are you getting at?" she asked.

"The man that believed he was Napoleon knew everything about him," Professor Arnold answered. "He knew the battles, the people under his command and every battle except Waterloo." Professor Arnold leaned toward Barbara. "He knew nothing about Waterloo."

"He was crazy!" Barbara answered. "He believed he was Napoleon. His facts were mixed up!"

Professor Arnold stood. "The man that believed he was Napoleon was alleged to be descended from Napoleon," he said. "It appears Napoleon was not as dedicated to Josephine as history tells us. According to the man's family history, Napoleon had a brief fling with one of the locals. The fling occurred about seven months before the battle of Waterloo. The man, who believed he was Napoleon, could tell you anything about him except for Waterloo. He knew nothing about Napoleon beginning about seven months prior to the battle. The man had no knowledge of Napoleon's defeat and exile."

Professor Arnold placed his hands on the desk and he leaned forward toward Barbara. "He knew everything about Napoleon except Waterloo and how he died," he added.

Barbara shrugged her shoulders. "The man read a lot of books," she said. "He was fascinated with Napoleon. Perhaps the story of him being related set him off. He went crazy!"

"It's possible," Professor Arnold answered. "He read everything he could on Napoleon. He read books written in French and he studied every battle Napoleon fought."

Professor Arnold sat in his chair. "He traveled to the island of Corsica and learned the dialects," he continued. "The man studied the plans for Versailles so he could answer any question about the palace." Professor Arnold blushed. "Somewhere, he discovered secret writings concerning Josephine. He could describe her body including the mole near her left armpit."

Professor Arnold leaned forward toward Barbara. "He knew everything about Napoleon except Waterloo," he added.

"So what is the big deal?" Barbara asked. "A man studies Napoleon and he gets fixated. The man was crazy! He thought he was Napoleon! He refused to accept Napoleon's defeat at Waterloo." Barbara shrugged her shoulders. "It is classic Psychology."

"Perhaps," Professor Arnold answered. "The man was strange. He believed he was Napoleon. He knew nothing about Napoleon until his fever. He even knew that Napoleon changed the spelling of his name."

Barbara was puzzled. "Changed the spelling of his name?" she asked. "I have never heard of that."

"Neither had a lot of people," Professor Arnold answered. "Napoleon's last name was originally Buonaparte. He changed the spelling by dropping the u to Bonaparte. Napoleon's first name ended in an e. He changed the spelling of his name to appear French. If you believe in Numerology, the original spelling of Buonaparte gave a number of one which represented power and victory. The new spelling is a four which represents defeat."

Barbara laughed. "The man really was crazy!" she said. "Why would someone spend months or even years studying Napoleon? He must have read hundreds of books."

"Perhaps so," Professor Arnold said. He leaned backward in his chair and crossed his arms. "I forgot to mention that the man was blind. He was blind from birth."

Barbara's eyes widened. "That is not proof that consciousness can be passed," she said quickly.

"You are correct!" Professor Arnold answered. "Plato created his theory in the year 360 B.C. His pupil Aristotle created his theory in the year 350 B.C. Mendel published his findings on genetics in the year 1866. DNA was not discovered until the year 1953. It has only been in the last ten years that the true nature of DNA is being discovered. Only a few animals have been successfully cloned from the DNA of adult animals. Those animals experienced the illnesses of the adult animal. Their DNA carried old genes and new genes. A newborn sheep had arthritis."

"Mrs. Parker, you are correct! There is no proof that Plato's Dream is accurate. It took more than two thousand sixteen years before Mendel's theory of genetics. His theory was based on Plato and Aristotle. It took eighty-seven years for James Watson, Francis Crick, and Rosalind Franklin to prove Mendel's theories with their discovery of DNA. No one has proved or disproved Plato's theory, yet!"

Barbara turned her head toward the wall. "What did you say about death?" she asked, almost in a whisper.

"Plato's Dream is that a person doesn't die when the brain dies," Professor Arnold answered. "A person dies when every cell of their body has died. Within one or more cells is the consciousness of that person and others. It is possible that the person experiences more than one consciousness at the event of death. The event could take minutes, hours, or days. Plato believed the conscious ceased when every part of the body was dead."

Barbara turned toward Professor Arnold and smiled. "So this means that when a person dies they are not really dead," she said quietly. She walked toward the door and turned. "They can experience the consciousness of their life and past generations. This means that if I were to die, I could experience the consciousness of my mother and father and my grandparents."

Barbara smiled. "It is possible that the experiences would go backward," she said in a short laugh, as she smiled at Professor Arnold. "They would begin with the most recent and go backward."

"Yes," he answered. "They could go backward to the end or the beginning."

Barbara laughed and smiled. "The last consciousness we would experience would be the first," she said as she raised her eyebrows. "We would experience what Adam and Eve experienced in the Garden of Eden. We would end up where we began. We would be with God in the Garden of Eden."

"It is possible we are dead already," Professor Arnold remarked, as he shrugged his shoulders. He waved his right hand in the air. "Everything we are experiencing, the temperature; the smells; the sounds were all recorded in our DNA and passed to a future generation and they are being played back. It is possible the year is 4074 and a distant relative has just died. We are that relative experiencing the consciousness of Edward Arnold and Barbara Parker. The relative is experiencing what we experienced on September 3, 2001."

Barbara nodded her head. "Our distant relative is reliving our life?" she asked.

"No," Professor Arnold answered. "Our distant relative is not reliving anything. There is nothing to relive. They are dead and we are dead. At their death, they have tapped into our consciousness. They are experiencing everything we experienced. It is like a tape being replayed. It never changes. It can't be altered."

"If that is possible," Barbara said, as she lowered her head. "There is no death! Life and death are the same. You can't tell what life is and what death is. You can't tell the difference because there is no difference."

Professor Arnold nodded his head in agreement.

Barbara raised her head. "At our death we could experience all of the good parts and fast forward over the bad parts," she added. "If we were good, and we had a good positive life, the experiences are good. If we were bad, we could get stuck on all the bad parts. There would be a heaven and a hell."

"Plato didn't address that issue," Professor Arnold answered. He shrugged his shoulders. "It is only a theory but it seems to make sense. It combines science and religion. It presents the best and the worst of mankind. If you believe Plato, your dreams are real. Somehow you tapped into the consciousness of a woman who is a relative that lived sometime during the 1800's. I call it relative-conscious."

Professor Arnold lowered his head. "As I told you, my wife is unable to have children," he said quietly. "My wife and I are the only children and we have no natural children. If you believe Plato, Aristotle, and Mendel, the line of consciousness ends with both of us." He raised his head. "James and John are adopted. There is no way to pass our consciousness to them. If they have children, they will pass the consciousness of their natural parents. Ours will not be included." He smiled. "However, we provided them with a safe, secure home. Their experiences with their adoptive parents were positive and these experiences will be passed to future generations. While our past has ended with us, James and John carry within their consciousness the positive experiences of their adoptive parents. In a way, the line has not been completely broken; it has been slightly bent."

Barbara nodded her head. She understood what he had said.

Jenny's Letter

Barbara walked quickly to the chair and she sat down. "What was it?" she asked. "What triggered these dreams?"

Professor Arnold picked up the cigar in the ashtray but he didn't light it. He placed it in his mouth. "Did anything unusual happen in the last year?" he asked. "Has something happened such as an event or have you visited the home of a distant relative?"

Barbara shrugged her shoulders. "No," she answered. "I work for the state as a social worker and my husband and I attend the First Baptist Church on Broadway. We attend church every Sunday and I visit the elderly on Friday and Saturday nights." She paused, thinking. "We used to visit the elderly in the nursing homes but someone suggested we visit the elderly in their homes, before they needed constant care. Last year, I began visiting an elderly woman. I visit every Friday night and I read to her."

She suddenly stood. "I know what it is! I know what triggered the dreams," she said excitedly. "It makes sense! Everything makes sense! It began when we compiled the list of the elderly. There was a name that looked familiar. The name was Beverly Maston. She lives in an old home off Riverside Drive. Somehow, the name seemed familiar. Her husband worked for the railroad. He died about twenty years ago and Beverly stayed in the house."

Barbara leaned toward Professor Arnold. "Her husband loved to read," she said smiling. "He had a small library full of books. Most of the books are poetry. I was reading from an old book of poetry by Keats." She paused. "In the book was a letter. It was a page from a letter." Barbara turned her head toward the wall. "The letter was not complete. It looked like the last page of a letter with several pages. What was written was simple - *I leave you now with my love, a love for you that I will always cherish. Love Jenny."*

Professor Arnold shrugged his shoulders. He bit a piece of the cigar, in his mouth, and placed it in the ashtray. "I don't think that's it. Are you related to Jenny?" he asked. "Do you know who she is?"

Barbara sat down. "No," she answered. "I am not related as far as I know. There is no one in my family tree with the name Jenny, Jennifer, or anything like it. For some reason, I feel I know Beverly. She is eighty-two years old and still cooks and cleans. Beverly was born around 1917, I think. She said the letter was from her husband's great-grandmother to his great-grandfather. He had kept it in the book of poetry."

"Is there anything else you can think of?" Professor Arnold asked.

"No," Barbara answered. A big smile came on her face. "That's it!" she said. She looked at Professor Arnold with a big smile on her face. "What triggered the dreams was the letter. Jenny's letter triggered the dreams!"

"I don't think so," Professor Arnold answered. "It is unlikely simple words could do it. You don't think you are related. Jenny means nothing to you. A simple letter wouldn't trigger a distant relative's consciousness."

Barbara smiled. "It wasn't the letter it was what was on it that triggered the dreams!" she said "They began that night! I dreamed the most exciting erotic dream. Then other dreams occurred. They were simple dreams, nothing special. Every Friday night I visit Beverly. We spent a great deal of time talking about Jenny's letter and her husband's great-grandparents."

Barbara stood quickly. "The erotic dreams occur every Friday night. They occur when I come home. It's the letter! It's Jenny's letter!"

Professor Arnold stood. He removed the cigar from his mouth and he placed it in the ashtray. "I don't think so," he said smiling.

"No! That's it!" Barbara said smiling. "It's not the words on the letter, it's the perfume! There is a perfume on the letter. It smells like lilacs. I have never smelled such a perfume. It is very sweet. I will read the letter and sniff it. The perfume is very strong! I began having the erotic dreams when I touched Jenny's letter. The smell was on my hands for several days."

Professor Arnold's eyes widened. "Smell is one of the strongest senses," he said thoughtfully. "A certain smell can bring back memories and emotions." He quickly sat in his chair. "That is what happened to me!"

Barbara looked at Professor Arnold. "You have had dreams too?" she asked.

"Yes! Only once," he answered. "They began when I was about twelve years old and lasted about one week. They were horrible dreams! I was in war. The dreams were so real I awoke shaking and screaming. My mother and father were very concerned. In my dreams, I was in war. I was in a muddy trench fighting the German army."

Professor Arnold sat in his chair and he looked at Barbara. "It was horrible!" he added. 'I was fighting for my life. The German soldiers came over the barrier into the trench. I shot a German soldier in the chest and I began to beat him with my gun. More German soldiers came into the trench. Many others and I fought them with our bayonets. Everyone was screaming and yelling. The German soldiers kept coming into the muddy trench. We killed them as they crawled in. One of the British soldiers held an axe."

Professor Arnold turned his head toward the wall and he spoke very softly, "He chopped several of the German soldiers to pieces as they climbed into the trench. We fought in the mud. The dream ended the same. I was shot in my right leg."

He turned his head and he looked at Barbara. "I know what triggered it!" he said with a surprised look on his face. "The school visited the city museum. We were in the section on World War I and the guide told us about the medicine the soldiers used. He opened a packet actually used by the soldiers. It was a paper laced with medicine. The paper was soaked in water and placed on the wound. The guide poured water on the paper and he passed it around. It smelled horrible! My dreams began that night! The smell tapped into the consciousness of my grandfather. He was in World War I and he fought in the battle of Argonne Forrest. It was the deadliest battle of trench warfare. The battle lasted three days and my grandfather was shot in his right leg. My mother was conceived after he returned."

Barbara's eyes were widely opened.

Professor Arnold stood. "I know how to stop them!" he said excited. "I know how to close the consciousness of your relative! Don't touch the letter! Don't smell it! If you don't smell it, the dreams will stop! What was tapped into will close."

Barbara leaned toward Professor Arnold. "You don't understand!" she shouted. "These erotic dreams are fantastic! They are wonderful! I didn't come here to find out how to stop them I came here to learn how to increase them! I don't want them to stop!"

Barbara quickly stood. "I want more!" she shouted.

Professor Arnold's eyes narrowed. "Mrs. Parker, you do not understand," he said sternly. "If smelling the perfume triggered the consciousness of a distant relative, you have tapped into everything! You have tapped into the good and the bad. You have access to every emotion, every feeling, every sound they experienced."

Barbara smiled and laughed. "You mean there is more?" she asked.

"Yes!" Professor Arnold answered. "But what you have experienced will not last! They will disappear. One day, they will not be there. One day, they will never return!"

Barbara frowned. She turned toward the door. "The first dream was sexual," she said softly. "I was with a man in a type of parlor." She turned and looked at Professor Arnold. "He was very handsome. He was very tall with dark brown hair and brown eyes. He came to me and picked me up in his arms. I could feel his arms. He was strong and very muscular." Barbara walked to the chair and sat down. "He carried me to the sofa and gently placed me on it. Then, he removed his coat and shirt. His chest was dark and hairy. He leaned toward me and kissed me gently. I could smell his breath there was a light scent of rum. Then, he made passionate love to me."

She quickly stood. "I awoke breathing heavily. I awoke my husband and ravished him," she added.

Professor Arnold's eyes narrowed. "What were the other dreams like?" he asked. "Do you feel comfortable discussing them?"

"Yes," she answered smiling. "That dream occurred on a Friday night. The dream Saturday night was different. I was riding in a carriage with an elderly woman sitting across from me. I was wearing a very pretty dress. It was white with blue edging. I held a bonnet and a parasol. We talked about the weather and then I looked out the window to see a large home. There were many people standing and talking."

Barbara sat in the chair. "I emerged from the carriage and walked toward the porch," she said slowly. "There were several young women I greeted." Barbara smiled. "We exchanged hugs and I walked to the porch. It was there, I saw him. The man, that made passionate love to me, approached me and smiled. I held my hand outward and he kissed it. When he kissed my hand, I became very wet and I awoke."

Professor Arnold's eyes widened.

Barbara stood. "Sunday night's dream was horrible!" she said, as she placed her hands to her face, "The man was asleep on the sofa. He was naked. I looked at his body. It was lean and strong. I was naked!"

Barbara lowered her hands and she turned toward the wall and spoke softly, "I walked to a chair where his coat was draped. I reached into the breast pocket and I removed a pistol." Barbara turned toward Professor Arnold and she held her hand outward. "I could feel the pistol. It was heavy and cold. I walked softly toward him and placed the barrel near his left temple. I could feel the trigger as I pulled it. The trigger was heavy. The gun made a pop sound when I pulled the trigger."

Professor Arnold's eyes were widely opened.

Barbara had a very sad look on her face. "His body jerked once," she said slowly. "His eyes didn't open. A small red hole appeared about one half inch from his ear as a small trickle of blood began to come from the hole. As I watched, the blood flowed down the side of his face to the sofa and then it dripped to the floor. I sat on the floor, naked, weeping. Then, I awoke."

Barbara sat down. "The next dreams were different," she continued. "I was sitting at a table. The man was opposite me and we were playing a card game. He would lose and remove a part of his clothing. He lost a lot. Then, I lost. I was in my pantaloons. Again, he picked me up in his strong arms and carried me to the sofa. He made passionate love to me." Barbara shrugged her shoulders. "Then, I awoke panting and horny. I ravished my husband."

Professor Arnold shook his head slowly. "Mrs. Parker, it seems you have indeed tapped into the consciousness of a relative. This love relationship appears very strong. If Plato is correct, you witnessed a murder! Your relative killed someone. You witnessed it because she did it!" he said.

Barbara spoke softly, "I want to know who he is or was. I want to know what happened."

"Are you sure?" he answered. "They appear very intense! You have tapped into the good and the bad."

Barbara lowered her head. "Yes! I am sure," she answered. She raised her head. "Professor Arnold, I am very religious and

I love my husband very much. If a murder did occur, perhaps this has happened to solve it." Barbara suddenly laughed. "It seems Plato, Aristotle, and Mendel were correct! If our love produced a child, I received something from him."

"What?" Professor Arnold asked excited, as he sat on the edge of the desk.

Barbara stood and laughed. "I have a gift!" she giggled. "In my dreams, the man seems to know a lot about cards. In my dream, he lost on purpose." Barbara laughed. "Cards! No one can beat me at cards! All my life when I played cards, no one could beat me! We had a casino night at the church last year and I was a blackjack dealer. No one could beat me! I let people win on purpose. It seems I know what card is coming next or which card has been played."

Barbara laughed very hard. "I can play any card game and win!" she chuckled. "My husband wants to take me to Las Vegas but we don't gamble."

Professor Arnold smiled. "It's possible," he said grinning. "There is a belief that distant generations pass such gifts as intelligence and music ability. There are families where one child is very intelligent and another child is not. Identical twins share almost the same exact interests." He paused and cocked his head slightly. "It is possible that when you play cards you tap into his consciousness. It is also possible, that she was not so nice. You are nice because she wasn't."

Barbara stood. "Professor Arnold that was the best ten-dollars I ever spent!" she said smiling "My first task is to determine if such a woman did exist. If I can find that, I may be able to determine what happened." She shook Professor Arnold's hand and quickly left the office.

Plato's Dream

Sarah Evans

Barbara walked quickly to her car and entered. She opened her purse and removed her cellular telephone. She quickly dialed her mother's number.

Beep! Beep! Beep! "Hello," Barbara's mother answered.

"Mom, its Barbara. I have a question to ask," Barbara said excitedly.

"Honey, is something wrong?" Barbara's mother asked.

"No mom. I have been speaking to a man about heredity. I know I look like grandma's sister Marlene, is there another relative I look like? Is there someone I really look like?" Barbara asked.

There was a pause on the telephone. "Honey, why are you asking this question?" Barbara's mother asked.

"I want to know," Barbara, answered. "I want to know if there is a female relative I really look like. Is there someone I don't know or someone you know?"

There was a pause on the telephone. "I guess you are old enough," Barbara's mother answered. "It is not something we talk about in the family but you look exactly like your great-grandmother Sarah Evans. She lived in the 1800's in Lexington, Kentucky."

"I don't recall hearing about her," Barbara said.

There was a pause on the telephone. "Your great-grandmother was sort of wild. Her first child was illegitimate," Barbara's mother said softly. "She was a good girl but she met a man. According to the stories, they fell in love at first sight. He was not very wealthy but he traded in horses. She met him at a horse race."

Barbara paused. "Did anything unusual happen in the relationship?" Barbara asked quietly.

"Yes. He was a gambler," Barbara's mother answered softly. "He gambled on horses. According to the stories, Sarah and he were to be married but someone killed him. He was shot while he was sleeping,"

Barbara's voice became very low. "Was Sarah, I mean great-grandma, there when he was killed?" she asked.

"No," Barbara's mother answered. "She was in Lexington at the time. He owned a horse farm outside of town. There was to be a horse race the next day and she was at home. He was murdered in his office. He had an office in the stables. Someone sneaked in while he was sleeping and shot him. They never discovered who did it."

"Mom," Barbara said softly. "Was he naked when they found him?"

There was a pause on the telephone. "What a question?" Barbara's mother answered. "He was killed as he slept on the sofa. He was not in the bath or in his bed. He had his clothes on. He had visited the horses and he returned to his office. He fell asleep on the sofa and someone shot him. They shot him in the head with his own gun. It was not suicide because his gun was found outside the office. Someone shot him in the head and threw the gun outside on the ground."

"Barbara, these are strange questions and I don't want to talk anymore about it!" Barbara's mother said, in a sharp tone. "When you come over I will show you a picture of your great-grandmother. You look exactly like her! Is there anything else you want to know?"

Barbara paused. "Do you know his name? Are you sure it was his child?" she asked quietly.

"I have to go!" Barbara's mother said quickly. "When you come over I will show you her picture. You look just like her! You have her hair, eyes, face, body, and temperament."

"What temperament?" Barbara asked.

"Barbara, sometimes you seem wild like your great-grandmother," Barbara's mother answered irritated. "His name is not important but if you insist his name was Morgan Wade. He was a horse breeder and he gambled on horses. Your great-grandmother met him and she had a torrid love affair. He was murdered!"

"Your grandmother Brenda was born out of wedlock," she continued. "Sarah married a very nice man and he took your grandmother in. He gave her the name Owen and Sarah had two more children. You look exactly like your great-grandmother Sarah Evans. You look like your grandmother's sister Marlene Owen. I am sure he is in there somewhere. I have to go! Bye!"

The telephone clicked and Barbara sat holding the cellular telephone. 'I look exactly like my great-grandmother," she thought. 'The dreams can't be real because I saw Sarah murder Morgan. They can't be real because he was not naked when they found him."

Barbara laughed as she looked toward the mall where Professor Arnold's office was located. "What a crock," she said. "He is a nut and I fell for his story of DNA and peas. He took my ten dollars without doing anything."

She started the car and drove her car from the parking lot. As she drove, she laughed, "What an idiot I am! I paid him ten dollars for nothing."

She drove her car toward the corner where the light turned red. As she waited for the light to change, she changed her turn signal from right to left. When the light changed to green, she turned left. Barbara drove to the home of Beverly Maston.

Plato's Dream

Relative-Conscious

Barbara sat on the couch watching television. She was not paying attention to what was on. She sat on the couch thinking. Her husband, Brad, had already retired to bed. He had to go to work early. Barbara looked at the clock. The time was 11:12 P.M. Barbara reached to the telephone stand where a small book was sitting. She picked up the book and opened it. Inside was an old sheet of paper. It was Jenny's letter! Barbara had borrowed the book and letter from Beverly.

Barbara lay on the couch and held the book upward. She looked at the book. 'Keats," she thought. She held the letter and sniffed it. It smelled like lilacs. The smell was sweet. She attempted to remember if she had ever smelled anything like it. She hadn't. She visited her grandmother's sister Marlene many times before she died. She did not recall the smell. It was different.

She laid the book on the floor and sniffed the letter again. 'If Professor Arnold is correct, the smell will cause a dream to occur. I will tap into the consciousness of Sarah Evans," she thought. 'Perhaps I may dream of Morgan."

Barbara looked at the clock. The time was 11:12 P.M. She stretched her legs outward on the couch and closed her eyes as she sniffed the letter. Then, she seemed to drift off to sleep.

"I love you!" Morgan said, as he bent downward.

Sarah was busy shuffling the cards. She placed several of the cards on the desk as Morgan bent downward. He placed his right hand over the cards and kissed her softly on her neck.

Sarah smiled as she moved his right hand from the cards. "Do you cheat?" she asked softly.

Morgan was standing behind Sarah. He placed his right hand on the cards again. "No. I just count the cards. It is not difficult," he answered.

Sarah smiled. She looked upward and turned her head toward Morgan. He was handsome! He had the rugged looks of a dangerous man! Dangerous in love! His eyes were dark brown and his long brown hair just touched his shoulders. "Are you sure?" she asked coyly.

Morgan looked into Sarah's eyes. They were a beautiful green. Her long, brown hair fell over her shoulders and covered her small breasts. He kissed her on her neck again. "Just because you lost doesn't mean I cheated," he laughed quietly.

Sarah pushed the chair backward and stood. She held to Morgan. "If you cheated, I may get angry!" she said smiling.

Morgan placed his arms around her and held her tightly. She could feel his muscles and his hairy chest. The hair on his chest was short and dark brown. Sarah felt his hairy chest against her bare breasts. It made her tingle all over.

"Why would I cheat you?" Morgan smiled as he placed his hands on her hips. He moved his hands to locate the slit in the rear of her chemise. He smiled as he slowly reached his hands inward to caress her buttocks.

"I don't know," Sarah replied. She looked toward the desk where money was lying on top. There were many coins and paper bills. "Did you cheat them?" she asked as she looked at the money.

Morgan smiled. "No. I don't cheat. I count the cards and I know what the possibilities are. I have worked with horses all my life. I can tell which horse will win and which one will lose," he answered. Morgan removed his right hand from her buttock and turned her head toward him. He kissed her gently on the lips.

Sarah tingled all over! She opened her mouth, pressed her tongue into Morgan's mouth, and tasted the rum. It tasted good. She closed her eyes as she kissed him.

Morgan held tightly to Sarah. He pushed the chair backward and turned her toward the desk. He bent her forward and kissed her on her neck. Sarah tingled all over. She moved her hips backward, as Morgan entered her.

The passion was fast. Sarah moaned quietly and Morgan grunted. She moved backward and forward. Her body was sweating as she moaned. The lovemaking was soft and gentle, intense. It seemed like hours before she fell forward onto the desk.

Morgan picked up her limp body and he carried her to the sofa. Then, the lovemaking began again. The lovemaking was fast, then slow. Sarah clung to Morgan kissing his neck and his lips. She could smell the rum. It smelled good!

"I have to go," Sarah said, softly.

"I know," Morgan, answered. He kissed her gently on her lips and slowly stood. Morgan walked to the desk and he picked up their clothes. He began to dress as Sarah watched. He was tall and strong. Morgan had the look of a field hand with the manners of a prince. He was charming and gentle. However, Sarah knew he could be rough.

Morgan dressed very quickly and then he brought Sarah's clothes to her. He watched as she dressed. Her body was small and petite. He liked the curve of her hips and her small waist. Her buttocks were small and firm. His hands easily covered each one. Morgan could place his whole hand on her buttock. She liked it when he gently squeezed them.

Sarah quickly dressed and brushed her hair. She walked to Morgan and kissed him softly. "Mr. Wade," she said smiling. "I enjoyed the tour of the stables and I hope your horse, Gentleman's Gin, wins tomorrow. However, I do not gamble and I feel your offer of one hundred dollars to win is too much."

Morgan laughed. "I am sorry Miss. Evans that you have no faith in Gin. He has been trained well! If you bet one hundred dollars, your winnings will exceed five hundred dollars. If you lose, I will personally repay the money."

Sarah turned quickly. "With what Mr. Wade?" she asked. "If you loose, you will have no money to repay me."

Morgan reached to Sarah and he turned her toward him. "Miss. Evans, I will think of something. I am sure a lady, like you, will accept something from me," he laughed softly.

Sarah laughed as Morgan walked her to the door. He kissed her gently then she opened the door and walked toward the house. As she walked toward the house, she turned and smiled.

Barbara awakened slowly. She smiled and stretched, looking at the clock. The time was 11:18 P.M. She reached to the floor and picked up the small notebook. Barbara placed Jenny's letter in the book and placed the book on the telephone stand. She sat on the couch and held the notebook in her lap and she began to write what she had experienced.

Barbara smiled as she wrote sex. She attempted to remember, how many times she and Morgan had sex. She quickly wrote office, stable, apple orchard, and creek.

Barbara paused. There were several meals. Only two times was Morgan present. Most of the meals she ate with Mary Grace. Barbara wrote, lunch, breakfast, dinner, picnic, and brunch before Gentleman's Gin's race. There were four horse races. The main race was on Saturday. Gentleman's Gin won! She should have bet the one hundred dollars. She had the money but she was afraid someone would discover she had spent it. She wrote main race Saturday. One race was on Wednesday, Thursday, and Friday.

Barbara marked through Thursday. There were two races that day! She sat with Mary Grace, Elizabeth, and Carrie. She smiled. Carrie screamed and screamed when her horse came in last. There were a total of five races not four.

She placed the pen down and thought. So much happened! Most of what happened was boring. She lost count of the conversations with Mary Grace's mother. She liked her but she seemed to talk for hours. Carrie's father was funny. He was a typical dirty old man. She reached toward her right buttock where he kept pinching her.

Barbara remembered the baths. They were nice! She really liked the large tub at Mary Grace's home. The water was warm and the soap smelled nice. It was very pleasant to relax in the tub before dinner. She picked up the pen and wrote six baths.

'How many different people did I meet?" she thought to herself. There was only one young girl she didn't know. Most of the older people were not important, except for James. James was one of the jockeys. He was too old to ride anymore so he trained the horses. He was very funny at the dance. Barbara wrote James Maston and Martha June Breyer.

She thought a minute and then added Robert. Robert was one of the horse owners. She spoke to him before the Saturday race. He kept telling her that his horse, Colonel Sam, would win. He didn't. Colonel Sam came in a slow fourth.

Clothes! Barbara had a small trunk with her. There were four dresses and two shifts. She brought one cuirass bodice and three bonnets. She had one gown that she wore to sleep. The young girls shared the beds. She and Mary Grace slept in the big bed. Barbara smiled. They were typical girls, always talking about the men. She and Mary Grace would lie in the bed talking. They talked very late Friday night. It was almost dawn before they went to sleep.

The mattress was wonderful! She couldn't remember when she had slept so well. Her own bed was smaller. She shared a room and bed with her older sister Martha. Martha married last spring and Sarah had the bed to herself. Still, the bed at Mary Grace's home was the best.

Barbara laughed. She liked Mary Grace. She had known her for two years and they became friends the minute they met. Mary Grace was one year younger than Sarah was. They met at a picnic for July 4th. Mary Grace's family had just moved to Lexington. Her father was in horses and he bred them. Mary Grace was taller than Sarah was and pretty. She was funny! She laughed as she remembered what Mary Grace had said when Carrie's father, Adam, approached them, 'Watch your butt!'"

She placed the notebook on the floor and looked at the clock. The time was 11:27 P.M. Barbara paused. 'The clock stopped!" she thought. She stood and walked to the wall to look closer at the clock. The second hand was moving. 'Strange!" she thought. The time was 11:12 P.M. when she drifted to sleep and 11:18 P.M. when she awoke. Barbara looked at her watch. The time was 11:26 P.M. She turned and walked into the bedroom where Brad was asleep. She looked at the clock on the dresser. The time was 11:29 P.M. The clock in the bedroom was about two minutes fast. 'Strange," she thought.

Barbara returned to the couch and she picked up the notebook. She didn't write down many events. There was her sister's wedding. She didn't write it down. In all, there was about two years. Barbara looked at the time. She must have been asleep three to four minutes. In that time, she experienced almost two years! 'Impossible," she thought. 'I spent most of Wednesday with Morgan at the creek." They went fishing. Morgan came for Mary Grace and her before sunrise. They walked to the creek and toward 9:00 A.M., Mary Grace slipped away leaving them alone. She returned about one hour later. While she was gone, Sarah and Morgan went swimming in the creek naked and made love on one of the blankets. The three returned to the house about 3:00 P.M. That time alone was more than nine hours. She couldn't have experience nine hours in less than five minutes. She couldn't experience almost two years in less than five minutes.

Barbara stood and she walked to the television cabinet where her purse lay. She opened her purse, removed Professor Arnold's card, and called him on her cellular telephone.

Beep! Beep! Beep! "Thank you for calling," she heard Professor Arnold's voice. It was an answering machine. "I am currently away from my office. Please leave a message at the beep. Press nine when you have left your message."

Beep!

"Professor Arnold, it's Barbara Parker," Barbara answered. "Something very strange has happened. Can you call me?" She asked. Then she pressed nine on her cellular telephone.

Click! Humm!

Plato's Dream

Battle in the Trenches

Professor Arnold was in the bathroom when he heard the telephone ring and the answering machine turn on in his study. He heard Barbara's voice and he shrugged his shoulders. He looked at the package. It was a medical pack used during World War I. He purchased it at an Army surplus store. The cost was cheap, one dollar. He opened the brown paper package. Inside was a folded piece of grayish paper. He smelled it! The smell was like a mixture of boric acid and iodine. The smell was very strong.

The instructions were to dampen the paper and place the paper on the wound. It was suggested to use fresh, boiled water to dampen the paper. If fresh, boiled water was not available, the instructions suggested rainwater or drinking water. There was a warning on the package – not for internal use. In case of a stomach wound, do not use. If no water is available, use fresh urine.

Professor Arnold winced! The idea of urine made his stomach queasy. Still, it was designed for war and combat conditions. Urine was preferable to death. He placed the grayish paper near the sink and he walked to the bedroom. His wife was asleep. He walked quickly to the guest bedroom and turned the covers down. Then, he returned to the bathroom.

He turned the hot water on and smelled the paper. It smelled strong but not like, he remembered as a young boy. The smell had made him feel queasy and light-headed. He remembered he felt ill the remainder of the day. That night, the horrible dream occurred. He felt the water, it was very hot. When he placed the paper in the stream of water, it fizzed! The paper looked like mixing vinegar and baking soda.

The smell made him gag!

Professor Arnold bent over from the smell. It was as he remembered it; it was strong! The paper felt like potter's clay. The surface was slick. Then, it began to congeal. The paper stuck to his hands like adhesive. The smell was horrible! It stunk! He walked to the toilet and threw up. The smell made him feel weak and he kneeled in front of the toilet. He heaved from the smell. Then, his forehead broke out in a cold sweat.

He took the paper and threw it in the toilet. When the paper entered the toilet, the water in the toilet made the paper fizz. Then, the water turned a grayish color. Professor Arnold looked at the paper, it was a bright white. The water had removed the chemicals. The smell was strong. He heaved one last time, and flushed the toilet.

His head felt light and his body was in a cold sweat. He walked slowly to the guest bedroom. Once, he almost fell. The smell was in his nostrils and the chemicals were on his hands. He felt very ill as he lay on the bed.

The clock beside the bed read 11:57 P.M. Professor Arnold's body began to ache as he looked at the clock. Then, he drifted to sleep.

"Take his gun and bayonet," Sergeant Walker said, as he looked at Private Cline.

Private Rooks carefully removed the bayonet from Private Cline's belt. He was dead. He died from a chest wound. Private Rooks placed the bayonet with the others and he pulled the blanket from him and carefully picked him up. He carried him to the rear of the dugout with the others. Seventeen were dead.

He returned quickly to change a medicine patch. Private Rooks opened the packet and dipped it in the hot water. He held it as it fizzed. Then, he placed it on Private Marlin's shoulder. "Leave it! I'll change it tomorrow," he said. "It smells like hell but the medicine will stop the bleeding and help to keep infection down."

Private Bill Marlin winced as Private Rooks placed the medicine patch on his shoulder. The medicine stung and the smell was strong.

Captain Anderson walked into the dugout. "The rain has stopped and the sun has almost set. We can expect a charge when the sun sets," he said. "I want every soldier to have two bayonets! You will only have time to fire one round."

Captain Anderson held two bayonets. One was in each hand. "Push one toward his face! When he moves his head backward, lunge the second one in his chest area!" he said as he held the two bayonets upward. "Don't attempt any heroics! We want to wound them so they can't fight! Kick their gun away from them."

"I have this!" Private Malcolm Benson said laughing, as he held upward a two-edged axe.

"A woodsman's chopper?" one of the American soldiers laughed. "Leave it to the British, very innovative in a desperate need!"

The men laughed at Malcolm.

Malcolm stood. "Why not? If it can fell a tree, it can fell a man," he laughed.

Captain Anderson laughed, "Leave it! That's an order! I can't have you striking one of us!"

Malcolm laughed. He walked to the opening of the dugout and he placed the axe near the door.

Captain Anderson pointed to Private Rooks. "You will stay here and protect the wounded." He pointed to three others. "Stay by the door. Two soldiers will reload while one-soldier shoots. Fire as many rounds as you can."

He looked to the men. "Our orders are to hold this trench at all cost. We can't desert the Argonne Forest! We must hold the Meuse!"

As Captain Anderson turned, a shout was heard," They're coming!" a sentry yelled. "They have already crossed No-Man's Land." Several shots were fired.

Private Rooks looked outward, as many German soldiers began to climb down the parapet. As they rolled in the mud to stand, many guns were fired. Then, the allied soldiers attacked them with their bayonets. As the soldiers ran from the dugout, the German soldiers met them in the muddy trench. They began to push them backward. Private Rooks fired two rounds when Malcolm came running toward him. "The chopper! Throw me the chopper!" he yelled.

One of the soldiers at the door fired one round. Then, he picked up the axe and pitched it to Malcolm. Malcolm was running toward the doorway. Behind him, a German soldier followed. In the German soldier's hands was his rifle with the bayonet fixed.

Malcolm caught the axe handle halfway toward the blade in his right hand. He turned quickly to face the German soldier. The axe blade struck the German soldier near his neck. The German soldier fell as Malcolm continued to strike him with the axe.

Malcolm went crazy!

He was screaming as he began to swing the axe. A German soldier ran toward Malcolm. Malcolm dropped to his knees in the mud and swung the axe upward. The German soldier was struck near his neck. Malcolm stood and struck the fallen soldier more than six times.

Private Rooks was looking at Malcolm when something struck him in the chest. He was pushed backward and he fell onto the dirt floor. Something heavy fell on top of him as a muddy fist struck him in the face. Private Rooks reached for his bayonet, he couldn't reach it! The German soldier struck him in the face and chest again. Private Rooks struggled to strike the German soldier but he couldn't. Suddenly, the German soldier was pushed on top of Private Rooks. The German soldier struggled then his body went limp. He pushed the German soldier off him to see Malcolm standing with the axe.

Malcolm turned quickly and ran toward the parapet. He was screaming and swinging the axe. Everything seemed to stop! Everyone seemed frozen except for Malcolm.

The German soldiers stopped fighting when they heard Malcolm scream. He was chopping the German soldiers into pieces. The allied soldiers stopped fighting when they heard Malcolm scream. A German soldier was climbing into the trench as Malcolm struck him with the axe. Everyone watched as Malcolm screamed and chopped the German soldier into pieces with the axe. Malcolm turned to face the German soldiers. He was covered with blood and his eyes were widely opened as he screamed and swung the axe. Then, the German soldiers began to run. They were afraid! They had never faced a British soldier with an axe. The German soldiers ran as Malcolm chased them. He chopped them! He chopped them into pieces as they ran. He swung the axe at them. One German soldier fell in the mud. Malcolm struck him with the axe about his face, as he screamed.

Malcolm chased the German soldiers and slipped in the mud. He struggled to stand as the German soldiers climbed over the parapet. Then, he dropped the axe and wept. Everyone was silent. They watched Malcolm weeping in the mud.

Then, he stood. Captain Anderson was standing near. Malcolm walked to Captain Anderson and he saluted. "Private Malcolm Benson reporting for punishment!" he said forcibly.

Captain Anderson was stunned! Everyone was stunned!

"Punishment?" Captain Anderson asked quietly.

Malcolm stood straight. "I was ordered not to use the woodsman's chopper! I disobeyed a direct order!" He saluted Captain Anderson. "Private Malcolm Benson reporting for punishment," he said quietly.

Captain Anderson turned quickly. "What are the casualties?" he yelled.

A Corporal stepped forward and saluted. "Seventeen dead and twelve wounded," he answered.

"How many of them?" Captain Anderson asked quietly.

"Thirty to forty," the Corporal answered.

"How many did Private Benson kill?" Captain Anderson asked.

The Corporal paused. "I don't know?" he answered.

Captain Anderson snapped at the Corporal, "Take a guess?" he asked.

"More than half," the Corporal answered.

The men were stunned. They looked about in the mud. Many German soldiers lay dead. Many were missing arms, legs, and heads.

Private Rooks stood near. He reached for his face where the German soldier had struck him. He turned and looked toward the mud floor at the dead German soldier. The dead soldier was struck several times in his back with an axe. Malcolm killed him!

Captain Anderson turned toward the men. "They will be back! They expected us but they didn't expect Private Benson. How many woodsmen's choppers do we have?" he asked laughing.

The Corporal smiled. "Ten maybe fifteen," he answered.

Captain Anderson turned toward Malcolm. "At ease Private!" he yelled. "It seems I was not aware of the defensive value of a chopper. There is no punishment! You reacted accordingly! Our orders are to hold this trench at all cost!"

Professor Arnold awoke. He slowly raised and shook his head. The nausea was gone. He looked at the clock. The time was 12:09 A.M. His eyes narrowed as he looked at the clock. "Impossible," he said. "I couldn't have been asleep for only twelve minutes! I saw and felt everything! The boat trip from New York to London took two weeks."

He swung his feet to the floor and sat thinking. 'Impossible! Totally and completely impossible!" he thought. 'I experienced more than seven years in twelve minutes."

Professor Arnold stood and he walked to the bedroom. His wife was still asleep. It appears he didn't scream or yell as he slept. He walked to the living room and sat in the easy chair. He paused, thinking. 'They came before dawn. The sunset and sunrise would show their silhouette. They began to come into the trench before sunrise. We were waiting! We allowed them to enter the trench. Captain Anderson divided the men with axes. They worked in teams of two. The battle was brutal as the soldiers fought with bayonets and axes."

He placed his hand on his right leg and felt where he was shot.

The German soldier fired his rifle from the parapet. He was struck in his right leg above the knee. He looked to his right hand. He could feel the cane. It was cut from one of the trees. He held it as he carried Mathew's coffin from the train. 'Train!" he thought. He remembered the parade going to war and returning. He remembered the train arriving home. His wife was yelling and screaming as the men disembarked from the train.

The band was playing as the men lined up beside the train. The crowds were held back until the coffins were unloaded. As the coffins were unloaded, the band began to play a slow dirge as the people wept. He wept. They brought four coffins with them. They returned Matthew, Calib, John, and Harrison.

He stood quickly. The funeral of his grandfather! It was cold! The snow was not deep but it was cold. He was six years old when he attended his grandfather's funeral. He attended school at Atkin.

'Atkin!" he thought. He sat in the desk on the second row toward the door. Robert Kane and Steven Jameson sat in the desks beside him. Matthew Lawrence sat two seats behind him. His sixth grade teacher was Mrs. Fentress.

He lowered his head. 'Mrs. Fentress was a widow," he thought. Her husband, Gary, drowned in the flood. Mr. Stevens' horses were trapped on a high spot. Mr. Fentress and several of the men attempted to rescue them. As they were leading the horses to safety, one of the horses panicked. Mr. Fentress was trapped between two of the horses. He drowned attempting to rescue the trapped animals.

Professor Arnold walked toward the television set. He remembered his marriage and the funeral of his mother and his father. He remembered! "My God!" Professor Arnold said. "I experienced everything! I felt everything! I didn't experience seven years in twelve minutes! I experienced my grandfather's entire life! I experienced more than twenty-seven years in twelve minutes!"

Professor Arnold walked to the chair. He sat and he wept. He experienced everything!

Love and Tragedy

Barbara sat on the couch. She reached for the book, slowly opened it, and removed Jenny's letter. She sniffed it! The perfume smell was sweet. It smelled like lilacs. She laid the letter on the floor and lay backward. Barbara didn't look at the clock. She smiled slowly as she drifted to sleep.

"What a fool I was," Sarah said. She turned toward Morgan. He was asleep on the sofa. In her hands, she held a letter she found in the breast pocket of his coat. She smelled the letter. There was perfume on it. It was expensive, from New York. It was Midnight Dew. The perfume cost more than twenty dollars for a small bottle. The letter reeked of the smell. 'She must have bathed in it. Morgan probably purchased a gallon and she bathed in it!" she thought.

She opened the letter. There was only one page. "I leave you now with my love, a love for you that I will always cherish. Love Jenny," Sarah read. She replaced the letter in Morgan's coat pocket and removed the pistol.

Sarah walked softly toward the sofa, as not to awaken Morgan. She looked at him. He was naked. His body was lean and strong. He slept soundly. She watched his stomach move as he breathed softly. Sarah bent downward and kissed him softly on the forehead. She held the gun to her back as she cocked it. "I wasn't your first love but I will be your last," Sarah said softly. She placed the barrel of the gun to his left temple. The sound was not loud. There was a pop sound as she pulled the trigger. Morgan jerked once. She watched the blood trickle from the small hole in his temple.

She sat on the floor and cried bitterly. Sarah loved Morgan but she could not believe he loved her. His promise of love and marriage were a game! He really loved Jenny.

Sarah slowly stood and walked slowly to the desk. She picked up Morgan's clothes and returned to the sofa. The blood had dripped to the floor. Sarah placed a cloth near his head, to slow the flow of blood, and she dressed him. Then, she returned to the desk and picked up her clothes. She dressed and brushed her hair.

Before she left the office, Sarah removed the cloth from Morgan's head. She watched the blood slowly trickle to the floor. As she walked out the door, she threw the pistol and bloody cloth to the ground. Sarah walked slowly to the house and undressed for bed.

Mary Grace was not asleep. She watched Sarah undress and place her nightgown on. She sniffed as Sarah pulled the covers down and climbed into bed. "Midnight Dew," she said. "I haven't smelled that in a long time."

Sarah pulled the covers upward and looked at Mary Grace. "I must have been near someone that was wearing it," she answered.

"Who?" Mary Grace asked, as she sat upward in the bed. "A lot of people have it but they won't wear it."

Sarah narrowed her eyes. "Why not?" she asked.

"Jenny," Mary Grace answered.

Sarah sat upward in the bed. "You know about Jenny?" she asked surprised.

"Of course!" Mary Grace answered. "Everyone knows about Jenny but no one will talk about her because of Morgan."

Sarah's eyes narrowed. "You know about Jenny and Morgan?" she asked softly.

"It's really sad," Mary Grace said. She leaned upward to look at Sarah. "You have probably noticed how the older women are so nice to Morgan. No one really cared for him until Jenny came. The older women couldn't believe a man could love a woman as much as Morgan loved Jenny."

'Why is she telling me this?" Sarah asked herself. 'She must know about us."

Mary Grace continued, "Morgan took Jenny everywhere. He took her to the races and all the dances. Everyone was surprised when he took her to New York. Morgan sold everything he owned. He even sold Gentleman's Gin."

Mary Grace smiled. "Morgan took Jenny everywhere in New York. They went to the plays and ate in the best restaurants. She saw the perfume in an expensive store in Washington. She liked the scent and Morgan bought her every bottle in the store."

Sarah turned her head from Mary Grace. 'She must have bathed in it," she thought. Sarah was beginning to get angry with Mary Grace. She didn't care about Jenny or Morgan. It was over! Morgan would never make love to another woman. Jenny was a widow without the marriage vows.

Mary Grace laughed, "When she was very ill, Morgan brought Gentleman's Gin into her room. He brought Gin through the front door, up the stairs, to her room."

Sarah turned quickly toward Mary Grace. "Jenny's ill?" she asked quickly.

Mary Grace narrowed her eyes. "Jenny's dead! She died more than two years ago," she answered.

Sarah had a puzzled look on her face. 'If she is dead, why did Morgan have the letter? Why is he still in love with her?" she thought.

"What was she like?" Sarah asked quietly.

Mary Grace shrugged her shoulders. "I don't like to talk about the dead but she was nothing special!" she answered. "She wasn't pretty and she really didn't have a personality. When Morgan took her to the dances, he danced almost every dance with her. I think he either paid or threatened the men to dance with her."

Mary Grace leaned close to Sarah. "You may have noticed that James Maston, the jockey, won't come near Morgan," she whispered. "James liked her but Morgan wouldn't let him near her. One night, they got into a fight and Morgan beat James up. After the fight, James wouldn't come near Jenny." Mary Grace shrugged her shoulders. "I think Jenny liked James but Morgan didn't like James."

Sarah looked at Mary Grace. "Morgan fought over Jenny?" she asked, surprised.

"Yes! Many times," Mary Grace answered. "There is a rumor that Morgan killed a man in New York. The man said something to Jenny and Morgan went into a rage. They went to a play in New York. During the intermission, a man leaned toward Jenny and said something to her. Morgan had left his seat to get Jenny a punch." Mary Grace leaned closer to Sarah. "When Morgan returned, Jenny was crying. She told him what the man said. He went into a rage and they fought in the seats. During the fight, the man pulled a gun. Morgan pulled his gun. Morgan shot him dead in the theatre."

Sarah's eyes widened.

"Morgan took Jenny to Washington! He arranged for the President to meet her," Mary Grace said, excitedly.

Sarah seemed bewildered. 'Why is she telling me this? Doesn't she know?" she thought.

"Morgan took Jenny to the gates of the White House. He said something to one of the guards and handed him a package. A few minutes later, the President himself came to greet them. He took Jenny for a personal tour of the White House," Mary Grace whispered. "Many people believe Morgan had more than five thousand dollars in the package. He paid the President to give Jenny a personal tour."

Sarah turned her head. She was angry! Morgan never did anything like that for her. He kept their affair a secret. She suspected Mary Grace knew but it appears she did not know. Morgan told her he loved her but he really loved Jenny.

"When did Jenny die? What was wrong with her?" Sarah asked softly.

"She died in the spring two years ago. No one really knows what was wrong with her. It was some type of illness where

your body stops working," Mary Grace answered. "At first she fell for no reason. It was when Morgan was told she would die that he sold everything he owned. He sold Gentleman's Gin. He took the money and he and Jenny went to New York. The rumor is he went into debt."

"Jenny died a slow death. It was sad to watch as her body slowly stopped working. She couldn't walk and eventually lost movement in her arms. Morgan stayed by her bedside day and night. When she died, he wept," Mary Grace added.

Sarah turned to look at Mary Grace. "Morgan sold Gentleman's Gin? Morgan wept?" she asked surprised.

Mary Grace looked downward. "It was so sad! At her funeral, Morgan read a letter she had written to him. I remember it - I leave you now with my love, a love for you that I will always cherish. Love Jenny," Mary Grace said softly.

Sarah's eyes glared with anger.

Mary Grace continued to look downward. "Morgan poured the Midnight Dew on the letter as a reminder. No one will wear the perfume out of respect for Morgan," she said softly.

Sarah's eyes were filled with anger. "Did you go to the funeral?" Sarah asked sharply.

"Everyone went," Mary Grace, answered. "It was very sad." She looked upward at Sarah. Sarah's eyes were filled with rage.

"What's wrong?" Mary Grace asked. "It is a beautiful story. Morgan loved Jenny very much. He sold everything he had to make her last day's good ones. He has the letter she wrote him and he carries it with him at all times."

Sarah turned her head. "If he loved her so much, why didn't he marry her!" she snapped.

"Marry her?" Mary Grace asked surprised.

Sarah turned toward Mary Grace. "What was wrong? Was she married already? Did Morgan make false promises of love? Did he buy her then feel guilty when she became ill?" she snapped.

"Sarah, Jenny was Morgan's sister!" Mary Grace answered.

Sarah's eyes widened.

"Sarah, no one has told you about Jenny?" Mary Grace asked, surprised. "James Maston tried to court her! He believed if he married her, he would get Morgan's money and control the horses. He didn't love Jenny! He attempted to use her! That is why Morgan fought him. That is why Morgan kept him away from her!"

"All those meetings with my mother. I thought she told you. Everyone was hoping you and Morgan would fall in love! Everyone has been waiting to see if you are the one!"

"One what?" Sarah asked.

"The one woman Morgan would love!" Mary Grace answered. "We all tried. I tried but Morgan wasn't interested in me! He wasn't interested in anyone! Morgan was devoted to his sister."

Mary Grace bent forward and whispered, "When my mother first met you, she told everyone that you were the one woman Morgan could love. She said you had fire and spirit! Not a lot but enough to keep Morgan interested."

Sarah turned her head. She remembered the first time she was alone with Morgan. He was talking about Gentleman's Gin and she asked if she could see him. Morgan laughed and he took her to the stables. He was a beautiful horse! She petted him and asked if she could ride him. Morgan laughed. He asked her when and she said now. Morgan picked her up and placed her on Gin's back. As he picked her up, his hand was under her dress between her legs. She became excited when she felt his strong hand against her privates.

Morgan laughed, as she sat on Gin. "You are the first woman I have met that really wanted to see Gin," he said. "Most women are afraid of him. You have spirit and you interest me."' Morgan leaned upward to look into Sarah's eyes. "You are the first woman I have ever met that didn't bore me."

Mary Grace nudged Sarah. "Haven't you noticed that everyone leaves you two alone? Everyone is hoping you and Morgan will fall in love! I left the creek to give you time to talk." Mary Grace leaned closer. "Did he say anything?" She giggled. "Did Morgan hold your hand?"

Sarah's eyes widened. 'Hold my hand," she thought. 'The first time we made love was in the stable. We made love the first time we were alone. Morgan reached upward and kissed me as I sat on Gin. Then, he pulled me down from Gin and pleasured me! We had made love more than twelve times before we went to the creek."

Sarah turned slowly to Mary Grace. "Morgan doesn't have a girlfriend?" she asked softly.

"Heavens no! Everyone has tried but he wasn't interested. His sister had been ill as a young girl and Morgan protected her. He treated her like a queen!" Mary Grace answered. She lowered her head. "When I told my mother I was interested in Morgan, she laughed. She said I didn't have spirit! Morgan is not interested in a person's looks, he is interested in their personality."

Mary Grace looked upward. "Morgan loved his sister very much. He sold everything he had to make her last days happy. He sold Gentleman's Gin to take her to New York. She became very ill in New York and he brought her back to Lexington. She loved Gin and Morgan gambled to get him back," she added.

Sarah shrugged her shoulders. "He cheated to get him back," she remarked.

"No! No!" Mary Grace said, surprised. "Morgan doesn't cheat! He remembers the cards. He remembers every card that has been played. We tested him once! We played several hands, he told us which cards had been played, and the order they were played. When he gambled for Gentleman's Gin, many people watched the game. Morgan doesn't cheat!"

Sarah lowered her head. 'The first time she played cards with Morgan he lost almost every hand. He was almost naked, then, he began to win," she thought. 'It didn't take long before she was completely naked. Then, they drew cards. If he drew the high card, they would make love. If she drew the high card, she would dress and return to the house. She drew the four of Clubs. He drew the Ace of Hearts."

"Why does everyone like him?" Sarah asked quietly.

Mary Grace laughed, "He has everything! He's handsome and charming. People couldn't believe it when he gambled to win Gentleman's Gin for Jenny. He wagered two years of his life to train horses if he lost. When he won, he took Gin to the house. He kept him on the porch and he went to Jenny's room. In his hand, he held carrots. He wanted Jenny to feed Gin. She didn't like his joke because she couldn't walk. She could barely use her hands. Morgan laughed and he left her room. When he returned, he was leading Gin! He brought him into the house and up the stairs to Jenny's room!"

Mary Grace paused and she laughed loudly, "Jenny fed Gin from her bed!"

She giggled. "Whoever captures Morgan's heart is the luckiest woman in the world," Mary Grace said smiling. "My mother thinks it will be you! Morgan was devoted to his sister. Whoever he marries will have a handsome man to love. Whoever marries Morgan will have a devoted husband."

Mary Grace nudged Sarah. "Has anything happened? Has Morgan said anything or done anything that indicates he may like you," she asked quietly.

Sarah turned her head. 'Yes, if you consider making love more than twenty times a good sign," she thought. 'He has told me that he loved me and he wanted to marry me. He told me that he would never cheat on me or betray me."

"How do you know Morgan has no girlfriend?" Sarah asked softly. "Is it possible that he is in love with someone? Carrie is very pretty."

"Heavens no," Mary Grace answered. "Morgan is the best catch in the state. I don't think any woman could keep a secret like that. Carrie would tell everyone if Morgan even looked like he was interested. Morgan has no one. If he did, my mother

would know. If she knew, everyone would know. She plans to speak to you tomorrow. My mother is hoping something has happened. She wants you and Morgan to marry."

"Marry?" Sarah asked surprised. She turned quickly to face Mary Grace. "Your mother wants Morgan and me to marry?"

"Of course! She thinks your wedding will be the social event of the year. My mother believes you and Morgan were made for each other," Mary Grace snickered. "I think she has already written the guest list! She is waiting for something to happen. She is waiting for some sign from you or Morgan that there is an interest."

Mary Grace nudged Sarah. "Tell me? Has Morgan said anything that indicates he is interested?" she asked.

Sarah turned her head. 'Tonight we made love in his office. He asked me to marry him and I began to cry," she thought. 'Morgan and I were on the sofa naked and he stood. He went to his coat to get his handkerchief. When he dried my eyes, I smelled the perfume! It wasn't mine! He said he would make the announcement tomorrow. He said he would tell everyone he had found his true love."

Sarah lowered her head. 'When he went to sleep, I returned his handkerchief to his coat. I found the letter and his gun!" she thought. 'Everything made sense. He used me! He cheated on me like he cheated at cards. I was a diversion for him. I was something to keep him interested until he could be with Jenny."

Sarah spoke softly, "We mainly talk about horses."

Mary Grace frowned. "It is a start! He never said anything to me except, 'Hello'. He was polite to Carrie. He has never shown interest in anyone. If he is talking to you, it is a good sign." Mary Grace laughed as she nudged Sarah. "Maybe the talk of horses will change. Maybe he will hold your hand and kiss your hand!"

'Kiss my hand?" Sarah thought. 'That's the only part of my body he hasn't kissed."

Mary Grace smiled. "I hope I didn't upset you with all the talk of marriage? I hope I didn't get your hopes up that Morgan may be interested in you. It's late. Let's get some sleep," Mary Grace said.

They both lay down to sleep. Sarah couldn't sleep. It was close to dawn when there was a light knock on the door. Mary Grace's mother entered slowly. She was upset. "Wake up Sarah," she said softly. "You have to go!"

Sarah sat upward in the bed. Her eyes narrowed. "Go where?" she asked softly.

"Mother, what's wrong?" Mary Grace asked, as she sat upward.

"All the young ladies are leaving," Mary Grace's mother, answered, as she opened Sarah's trunk. She looked through the clothes and pulled a dress and chemise from the trunk. "This will do."

She walked to the bed and laid the clothes on the cover. "Hurry and dress. A carriage is waiting to take you home," she said quietly to Sarah.

"Mother, what's wrong? Why are the young girls leaving?" Mary Grace asked.

Mary Grace's mother sat on the edge of the bed. "Listen to me," she said quietly. "All of the young girls left two days ago. They went to the home of Mrs. Abrams. They weren't here last night or the night before."

She stood quickly. "Hurry Sarah!" she said softly. "The carriages are waiting. Your trunk will be sent later. You must leave as quickly as possible!"

Sarah stood and she removed her gown and pulled the chemise and dress on. "What's wrong Mrs. Anderson? Why are we leaving?" Sarah asked.

Mary Grace's mother looked at Sarah. "You were never here the last two days," she answered softly. "The driver has a letter explaining everything. He will give it to your mother. If anyone asks, you were at the home of Mrs. Abrams the last two days."

Mary Grace's mother sat on the edge of the bed. She had tears in her eyes and she wiped her eyes with a handkerchief.

"Something terrible has happened! We don't want any of you young ladies involved," she sobbed.

She looked at Mary Grace. "Stay in your room today," she said sobbing. "Mr. Morgan Wade has been murdered."

Sarah's eyes widened. She looked quickly at the door, as a light knock was heard at the door. The door opened slowly as Mrs. Thomas looked into the room. "The carriages are waiting," she said quietly.

Sarah hugged Mary Grace and Mrs. Anderson and then she followed Mrs. Thomas to the front porch. Several young ladies were waiting on the porch as the carriages were being loaded.

She stood beside Carrie as James Matson, the jockey, walked quickly to them. "You must leave quickly," he whispered. He motioned for a carriage when he sniffed the air. He had a puzzled look on his face as he sniffed the air. He looked at Carrie and sniffed the air; nothing. Then, he looked at Sarah and sniffed the air; his eyes widened. He leaned toward her and sniffed again. His eyes widened!

"Quickly!" he said, as he took Sarah's hand and led her to a waiting carriage. He opened the door for her to enter and motioned for the driver. "Drive to the front gates and stop!" he ordered the driver. James opened the carriage door and quickly sat inside.

The driver drove the carriage slowly from the front porch toward the front gates. James sat in the opposite seat staring at Sarah. "Where is it?" he demanded, as he leaned toward her.

"Where is what?" Sarah asked.

James reached forward and he grabbed her right hand. He sniffed her right hand then he grabbed her left hand and sniffed it. "Where is it?" he demanded.

Sarah became frightened. She pulled her left hand from James. "I don't know what you are talking about," she said.

"Fool!" James said, as he reached into his coat pocket. He removed a small metal flask and he removed his handkerchief. He placed his handkerchief on his lap as he opened the flask. Sarah could smell rum. James poured rum on the handkerchief,

soaking it. Then, he grabbed Sarah's hands and quickly wiped her hands with the rum soaked cloth.

"What are you doing?" Sarah asked quickly.

"Fool!" James said as he grabbed her hands. He sniffed them then he poured more rum on the handkerchief and wiped her hands again.

Sarah looked at her hands and sniffed them. All she could smell was rum. She narrowed her eyes and looked at James.

"It's mine!" James said quickly. "Jenny wrote the letter to me not to Morgan! Where is it?"

Sarah's eyes widened.

"Give it to me!" James demanded. "It's mine!"

"I don't understand," Sarah said quietly.

"You touched it and it is not in Morgan's coat pocket," James said quickly. "You are the only one that could have it! It's mine, Jenny's letter is mine!"

James raised his hand as he was to strike Sarah. "It's mine! Give it to me!" he threatened.

Sarah was frightened. Her eyes widened as she slowly lifted her dress. She reached into her chemise and slowly removed Jenny's letter. She held it outward to James and he quickly took the letter, then he lowered his head and he began to weep.

Sarah cocked her head as James held the letter and wept.

"I loved her!" he sobbed.

"Why?" Sarah asked, surprised. "She wasn't pretty and she didn't have a personality. She was ill."

James raised his head. "That didn't matter," he sobbed. "I loved her and she loved me. This letter is mine! She wrote it to me."

"All you wanted was Morgan's money!" Sarah snapped.

James laughed, "Morgan has no money! He is in debt! There is no money!"

Sarah leaned closer toward James. "If there is no money, why did you love Jenny?" she asked surprised.

James lowered his head. "You are too young to understand," he answered. He sniffed the letter and carefully folded it. He placed it in his coat pocket and drank from the flask. "When you are old, like me, you will understand."

Sarah narrowed her eyes.

"The stories are not true," James said, as he wiped his eyes with the rum soaked handkerchief. "I fell in love with Jenny when I first met her." He looked at Sarah as he sipped from the flask. "To me, she was the most beautiful woman in the world!"

"She was ill," Sarah said softly. "How could you love her?"

James smiled. "It didn't matter," he said softly. "I think I loved her more when she was ill." He sipped from the flask.

"She could not walk, or talk or do other things," Sarah whispered.

James laughed, "Sex isn't everything!"

Sarah cocked her head slightly. "How do I know you loved her?" she asked. "Perhaps you hated Morgan?"

James lowered his head. "Are you referring to Miss. Jenny Wade or are you referring to Mrs. Jenny Matson?" he asked grinning. James raised his head. "We were married two weeks before she died."

Sarah's eyes widened.

James removed the letter from his pocket and he held it toward Sarah. "Jenny wrote this letter to me when she had use of her hands," he said softly. "Mrs. Anderson knows the truth! She arranged for our very quiet and discrete wedding."

James stood and leaned out the window of the carriage. "Stop here!" he yelled to the driver.

The driver stopped the carriage and James opened the door and quickly stepped outside. He leaned inward toward Sarah and he handed her the rum soaked handkerchief and the flask. "Use all of it," he said quietly, as he looked around. He smiled and waved as two carriages were driven quickly past him.

James placed Jenny's letter in his coat pocket as he slowly closed the carriage door. "Your secret is safe," he whispered.

"What secret?" Sarah asked defiantly. She smelled her hands. All she could smell was rum.

James laughed. "When I smelled the Midnight Dew on your dress, I knew you had the letter," he said quietly.

Sarah had a puzzled look on her face. "Why did you wipe my hands with rum?" she asked.

James smiled. "Morgan's gun was mine," he answered. "I made it special and I lost it to Morgan in a card game. The breech has been widened so the sound is like a pop when it is fired. When the gun is fired, gunpowder is blown backward onto the hands. I smelled the gunpowder!"

Sarah's eyes widened. She quickly grabbed the rum soaked handkerchief and wiped her hands.

James laughed. "I was cheated of my love and Morgan was cheated of his love," he giggled. "Your secret is safe. My secret is safe."

"Go!" James yelled to the driver.

The driver began to drive the carriage quickly. As the carriage was driven from the home of Mrs. Anderson, Sarah lowered her head and wept bitterly.

Barbara awoke slowly. She sat on the edge of the couch thinking. 'It was a big mistake," she thought. 'Sarah must have loved him very much to kill him."

Barbara stood. 'What am I thinking about? She murdered him!" she thought.

Barbara reached for the letter and she smelled it. 'Midnight Dew," she thought. 'I wonder if it is still available." She stretched out on the couch and she attempted to sleep. The television was on and she watched an old movie until she drifted to sleep.

"Wake up," Brad said, as he gently nudged Barbara. "You fell asleep watching TV."

He picked up the letter on the floor and read it. "Nice love letter," he said. "Where did you get it?"

Barbara slowly stood. "It was in an old book Mrs. Matson has," she answered. "I borrowed the book and the letter. It's very old. It's gone!"

"Mrs. Matson is gone?" Brad asked. "When did she die?"

"No, Mrs. Matson isn't dead," Barbara answered softly. "Something else is gone."

"How is she doing?" Brad asked, puzzled.

"OK. She has a series of tests scheduled next week," Barbara answered.

"Good," Brad said. He kissed Barbara on the cheek. When he kissed her, Barbara grabbed him. "Let's make love," she said smiling.

Barbara was wearing a large T-shirt and panties. She quickly pulled the shirt from her and removed the panties. Then, she began to unbuckle Brad's belt.

"Now?" Brad asked, excited.

"Now!" Barbara answered, as she began to unbutton Brad's shirt. "Life is very short. I love you more than anything. One day, we will be too old or one of us may be ill." She lay on the couch and pulled Brad on top of her.

Brad began to kiss her. She held to him tightly and kissed him. She placed her hands in his hair and kissed his lips very hard. She pushed her tongue into his mouth and tasted coffee. Brad began to kiss her neck. Barbara could smell his hair. There was a faint smell of Midnight Dew on his hair. The smell came from her hands where she had touched the letter. The smell was in his hair from where she had placed her hands in his hair. Barbara smelled the perfume and she remembered the many times Sarah and Morgan made love. She began to pant very heavy. She remembered the many times.

Professor Arnold opened the packet and placed it in the stream of hot water. The chemicals began to fizz as the water soaked the paper. The smell was very strong but he did not get nauseated. He smelled the paper; nothing! He did not feel ill. He threw the packet into the toilet and flushed it. Then, he opened another one. He opened six packets. The smell was strong but he did not feel ill.

"It's gone," he said sadly.

Plato's Dream

6:32 A.M. – September 4, 2001

Marcy fell backward on the couch as she was struck on the face. “You heard me!” one of the three boys said. “When Leon comes, yell for us!”

She rubbed her cheek. “He don’t owe but fifty dollars and he’s good for it,” she answered.

“Weed is weed! Money is money,” one of the three boys said. “You heard me! When Leon comes, yell for us!” The three boys turned and walked out of the room.

Marcy held to a pillow on the couch and she began to cry.

7:00 A.M. – September 4, 2001

Leon stood on the corner watching the kids walk toward school. They lived in an apartment on Second Avenue on the second floor. He was born in the city hospital and this was the only home he had known. The apartment was cold in the winter and hot in the summer. He lived with his mother and his younger sister Charlotte. This was the only home Charlotte had known.

He stood watching the children. He watched Charlotte leave the front door of the apartment. He watched her as she walked toward him.

"Aren't you coming to school?" Charlotte asked Leon.

Leon shrugged his shoulders. "School is a waste! Life is too short to spend it sitting in a classroom. There is nothing there for me," he answered.

"How are you going to make anything of yourself if you don't go to school and learn?" Charlotte asked.

"What have you learned?" Leon asked. "You make D's and F's."

"I go. There is no way I am going to get out of this hell hole if I don't," she answered.

Leon lowered his head. "There is no way out of this hell hole. There are no jobs. The only thing to do is to enjoy life," he said softly.

"Playing B ball ain't life! Selling weed is only going to get you into trouble. Jail ain't fun," Charlotte answered.

Leon raised his head and smiled. "You go to school and make something of yourself," he said as he placed his hand on Charlotte's shoulder. "Me, I am going to enjoy myself."

"Where are you going?" Charlotte asked.

Leon smiled. "I am going to see Marcy and then play some B ball," he answered.

"Marcy is trouble," Charlotte said. "I think that girl has taken every drug made. She hangs with a rough crowd. One of these days, you're going to get hurt."

Leon smiled. "Marcy is OK! I am going to get some weed to sell and make some money," he said.

Charlotte shrugged her shoulders. "Leon, you are all we got! You will never get anywhere selling weed. You are going to wind up like papa!" she said.

"No I'm not!" Leon yelled. "Papa didn't care about anybody! He didn't care about momma, you, or me! If he did, we wouldn't live in this hell hole! All we have is each other!"

"That's right! All we have is each other. I love you Leon!" Charlotte said. "All we have is each other. Come to school and make something of yourself."

"It's too late for me," Leon said. "I done gave up. I'm going to enjoy myself. Life is too short to waste it sitting in a school."

Charlotte turned and walked toward the corner. Leon watched her walk to the corner and cross the street. Then, he turned. Leon walked quickly to the street corner. He turned left and walked to the third building. Marcy lived on the second floor. He opened the front door of the apartment building and walked quickly up the stairs. He knocked very softly. "Marcy, it's Leon," he whispered.

The voice sounded muffled. "Come in."

Leon smiled as he opened the door. Marcy was sitting on a couch with her face in a pillow. "Hay babe, I need a pound of weed!" Leon said.

Marcy moved the pillow and she looked upward. There were bruises on her face. "No more weed! You owe me for the last bunch," she said softly.

Leon walked quickly toward her. "Hay babe, I'm good! Give me some weed to sell. I'll bring you the money tomorrow," he said, as he held his right hand toward her.

Marcy stood quickly and she grabbed Leon's arm. "He's here!" she yelled.

"Shut up!" Leon said quietly. "What's wrong?"

"He's here!" Marcy yelled.

Leon attempted to push Marcy from him. She held onto him as he attempted to push her away. "He's here!" Marcy yelled, as she held to Leon's arm.

Leon pushed Marcy backward. He pushed her toward the couch and they both fell onto the couch. She acted like she was high. He pushed her away from him and quickly stood.

"He's here!" Marcy yelled.

Leon ran for the door and he pushed it open. Then, he bolted for the stairs. He jumped downward toward the first landing.

"He's here!" Marcy screamed. She had run to the opened door and she stood in the hallway yelling.

Leon looked upward at Marcy. "He's here!" Marcy screamed.

Plato's Dream

7:34 A.M. – September 4, 2001

He grabbed for the rail and jumped toward the door. Leon reached for the door when he saw many flashes of light. The flashes were so quick and intense he could not count them. It seemed like thousands and thousands of light flashes went off in front of him. The flashes of light were bright and intense.

He felt his left side become numb. It was numb, and then, it wasn't there. Leon felt nothing to his left side. He could feel his right side. There was a feeling to his right side.

Leon did not know where he was. He wasn't hot or cold. There was no noise. He attempted to speak but his mouth did not move. He listened for a sound, any sound. There was no sound. He wasn't in pain. Leon felt no pain. In fact, he felt nothing. There was a sensation to his right side. He could feel a sensation on his right side.

He attempted to move his arms but they didn't move. He attempted to move his legs and his feet but they wouldn't move. His eyes were open because he could see. He could see flashes. There were many more flashes, and then there was a street lamp. It was daytime and he was looking at a street lamp. That is all he could see, a street lamp.

The flashes came again. They came very quickly. He saw colors. There were red and blue flashes. Then, the flashes stopped. Leon was looking at the street lamp.

He attempted to move his head to the right but his head would not move. Leon felt no pain. He wasn't hot or cold. Leon was looking at a street lamp.

He attempted to yell but his mouth would not move. The flashes came again. They were very intense this time. They didn't hurt his eyes. He saw flashes of intense white light. Then, the flashes stopped. Leon was looking at the street lamp.

It was daytime and he was looking at a street lamp. The lamp was made of metal and the bulb looked broken. He could see the sky. The sky was blue and there was a cloud in the distance. Leon paused. He attempted to look upward but he couldn't. He attempted to look downward but he couldn't. He attempted to look to the right and left. His head wouldn't move. He was looking at a street lamp.

The flashes came again. They were very intense. The street lamp kept flashing in front of him. Then, the flashes stopped. Leon was looking at something. He didn't know what it was. It looked like a stick standing straight up.

9:02 A.M. – September 4, 2001

"Which bullet killed him?" the detective asked the policeman.

"Take your pick," the policeman answered, as he pointed to Leon's body. Leon was kneeled down near the door. The door was partially pushed open and Leon's left arm was partially outside the door opening. "One bullet struck him behind the left ear. It took part of the skull and brain. One bullet struck him at the base of his neck. It looks like it shattered part of his spine."

The policeman leaned forward and pointed toward Leon's left leg. "That's where all the blood came from. The bullet caught an artery. He probably has less than one pint in him."

"Did the shots come from the same gun?" the detective asked.

"No," the policeman answered. "The bullet that struck his head looks like a 9 mm. The bullet that struck his neck looks like a 45 caliber." The policeman pointed toward Leon's leg. "I know for certain what that is." He turned and looked at the detective. "That is a deer slug from a 410 gauge shotgun."

The detective shrugged his shoulders and wrote on a small notepad. "Any suspects?" he asked.

"We have a young girl who appears strung out," the policeman answered. "She had a 9mm Glock hidden under a pillow on the couch." He pointed upward toward the stairs. "She was in room 215."

The detective looked upward toward the stairs. "Did she fire one of the shots?" he asked.

"No," the policeman answered. "The gun hadn't been fired."

The detective wrote on a small notepad. "Are you finished?" he asked the photographer.

"Yes," the photographer answered, as he bent downward and placed the camera in the bag.

The detective shrugged his shoulders. "Take him!" he said.

4:25 P.M. – September 4, 2001

"Homicide subject is African male age 16," the doctor said. He moved toward the side of the table. "Victim's name is Leon Charles Martin. He was shot three times at close range." The doctor looked upward toward the microphone. "It can't be determined which shot killed him."

The doctor turned the electric bone saw on. He leaned forward and cut the left side of Leon's head with the saw. He carefully removed the skull section and placed it in a bowl. The doctor looked upward toward the microphone and he paused. "One bullet entered approximately one inch behind the left ear. The bullet entered the lateral fissure and partially separated the temporal lobe. The lower section of the brain was destroyed. The bullet separated the brain near the spine." The doctor looked at Leon's back. He picked up a scalpel and began to dig into Leon's neck. "One bullet entered at the base of the neck severing the spine."

Leon looked at the stick in front of him. He didn't know what it was. He thought he had seen it before but he couldn't remember. He attempted to speak but his mouth would not open. He attempted to move his arms and legs but they would not move. Leon paused. He attempted to remember who he was. He didn't know.

He attempted to speak. His mouth didn't open. He didn't hurt anywhere. There was a sensation on his right side. He attempted to look toward his right, his head wouldn't move. Leon was looking at the stick in front of him. There was sky and a cloud. Then, there were many flashes. The flashes came very quickly. When they stopped, he was at home.

Leon attempted to smile but his cheeks wouldn't move. He was at home looking at the television set. The set was old and it didn't work. It was the only one they had. His mother purchased it for five dollars from a neighbor. The cabinet was made of wood and the set was not color. It worked for about five years before it broke. Leon attempted to smile. He would sit for hours watching the television. It wasn't safe for him to go outside. His mother wouldn't let him go outside.

When the television set stopped working, he continued to sit and watch it. He would pretend he was watching cartoons. He would spend many hours looking at the broken television. Many times he looked out the window. They lived on the second floor of an older apartment building. He could see the street lamp from the window. The glass was broken where someone had busted it. The street lamp was old and made of metal. There were several buildings that had been demolished. He would stand on his toes to look out the window. He could see the street lamp and the sky. The sky was blue and there were big clouds behind the street lamp.

Leon looked closely at the television screen. It was daytime and the sun was shining through the window. He could see a reflection in the blank screen. It was him! He could see his reflection in the television screen. He was six years old and he was wearing a blue denim jumper and a light colored shirt. Leon looked closely at the image. He wasn't moving!

"Mom!" Leon attempted to yell. His mouth wouldn't move. The image seemed frozen. Nothing was moving. 'That's strange!" Leon thought. 'Where is everybody? What's wrong?"

11:00 A.M. – September 7, 2001

Leon's casket was pushed toward the front of the church. The funeral director and one of the salesmen pushed it. The casket was moved near the pulpit. The funeral director turned to the salesman and whispered, "Don't leave! Tell the others I need them to carry the casket to the grave."

The salesman nodded. He turned toward the benches. Leon's mother and sister sat on the first bench. He looked toward the back, there was no one there! The only people here were Leon's mother and sister.

The salesman smiled briefly at Leon's mother. He nodded and walked quickly toward the back. He stood near the door with four other salespeople.

Reverend Andrews spoke softly, "We are gathered here today to pay our last respects to Leon; a young boy whose life was taken far too early, a young boy who was deeply religious."

Leon's mother and sister sat on the first row of the First Baptist Church. Leon's casket was near the pulpit and they wept. They were the only ones there. Leon's four friends didn't show. Mr. Camery, Leon's English teacher, came to the funeral home but he didn't attend the funeral.

The funeral was short. Reverend Andrews spoke about ten minutes. When the service was concluded, the funeral director and one of the salesmen pushed the casket from the church to the van. They loaded the casket in the van and drove the van slowly to the City Cemetery. Leon's mother and sister rode to the cemetery in the car of one of the salesmen.

Leon was buried in the City Cemetery in the pauper's section. The casket was a simple metal one, provided by the city. There was no graveside service. The salesmen carried the casket to the opened grave and two of the workmen lowered it. The workman quickly placed the dirt on top. Leon's mother and sister sat in metal folding chairs as they watched the workmen cover the casket with dirt. They stayed until Leon was buried and the grave was completely covered with dirt.

The funeral director placed a large flower cascade on top. He smiled and walked slowly toward the van.

Leon's mother and sister stayed by Leon's grave for about one hour. Then, Leon's mother walked to another grave in the cemetery. She kneeled by the grave and wept very loudly. They left the cemetery about three o'clock.

Leon continued to look at the television set. He could see his image reflected on the blank screen. The image didn't move. Leon attempted to listen for any noise. There was no noise.

2:34 A.M. – September 8, 2001

The brown Chevrolet drove quickly to the gates of the City Cemetery. The car stopped in the parking lot and five young boys emerged slowly. In their hands, they held cans of beer. One of the boys walked toward the gates and urinated. The gates were locked and a stone wall surrounded the cemetery. The stone wall was old and not tall. The boys walked toward the rear of the cemetery, to the alley, where a portion of the stone wall had collapsed. They stepped over the broken stones into the cemetery.

"Where is he?" one of the boys asked, as he sipped his beer.

"Toward the front," one of the boys answered.

"How do you know?" one of the boys asked.

"I picked up Charlotte and Leon's mother about three o'clock," the boy answered.

The five boys walked toward the front of the cemetery. They stopped to look at the graves. They were looking for a freshly dug grave. They walked toward the front where a new grave had been dug. There was a cascade of flowers on top of the grave.

"Is this it?" Bubba asked.

One of the boys nodded.

"Get up Leon! What the hell is matter with you?" Bubba yelled. Two of the boys laughed.

"He's dead!" Jackson yelled. "Leon's dead! He ain't never gonna play B ball again!"

Bubba walked to the dirt and he kicked it. "You stupid!" he said. "We told you to stay away from those people! They don't play games."

"Let's go!" Jackson said. Four of the boys drank their beer and threw the empty cans on the dirt.

"Oh man! Show some respect he's dead," Jackson said.

"What respect! Who are we going to get to play guard?" Bubba asked, as he kicked the dirt.

The five boys walked toward the front of the cemetery to the gates. They climbed over the stone wall. When they neared the car, one of the boys walked to the trunk and opened it. He reached inside the trunk and opened a cooler and removed a six pack of beer. He popped a top on one of the beers and looked at the other boys. "Take a drink! Be somebody!" he said, laughing. The four boys laughed as he passed the beer to them.

They opened the car doors and sat inside the car. The driver turned the ignition key and placed a cassette tape in the tape player. He began to push several buttons.

"Turn that damn thing off!" Jackson yelled.

"What's wrong with you?" the driver asked, as he pressed the off button.

"Don't you feel anything man?" Jackson asked. "Leon's dead! We won't ever see him again!"

"So!" the driver said. "We all die!"

Bubba was sitting in the front seat. He turned to look at Jackson. "You got religion?" he asked.

"No!" Jackson answered. "Leon's dead."

Bubba smiled. "Where do you think he is?" Bubba asked, as he looked to his right. "There he is!"

One of the boys giggled.

"Show some respect," Jackson said.

Bubba drank from the beer can. "Nothing happens when you die! There's nothing," he said, as he turned to look at Jackson.

"Don't you believe in God?" Jackson asked.

Bubba smiled. "God!" he smirked. "Where was God when Sally was shot in that drive-by? If there was a God she wouldn't be dead." He looked forward.

Jackson lowered his head. "I don't know," he answered.

Bubba turned quickly toward Jackson. "I don't know! I don't know!" he said. "You sound like those church volunteers. When Sally was killed, they were all over the neighborhood talking to people. They came to our house and I asked them why God allowed Sally to die." Bubba smiled and sipped his beer. "They gave the same answer, I don't know."

Mark was sitting in the back seat. "Don't disrespect them!" he said quickly. "They are OK. They helped momma with the back rent."

Bubba looked toward Mark then he looked at Jackson. "There is no God! If there was a God, Sally would not have died! She was nine years-old. Sally was just standing in the yard. If there was a God, Sally would be living!"

Jackson frowned.

"What's wrong with you?" Bubba yelled at Jackson. "Do you think Sally is somewhere playing hopscotch wearing wings? Nothing happens when you die! Sally is dead! Those boys who fired the shots will never be punished! There is no heaven or hell! There is no God!"

Bubba looked at Mark and he frowned. "Church volunteers," he snickered. "A few bucks here and there and they think they own you. What did they ever do for any of us?"

Mark leaned forward. "They helped Mrs. Allison get a job," he said.

"Some job," Bubba said, as he drank from the beer can. "She works in a department store downtown making minimum wage."

"It's a job. She didn't have anything until they helped her," Jackson added.

"What did they do to help Leon?" Bubba asked with a smirk on his face.

"Enough!" the driver, interrupted. "Leon was cool! He was OK! I have known him for about six years. What happened won't bring him back."

"Who killed him?" Jackson asked.

Bubba shrugged his shoulders. "I don't know and I don't care!" he answered. He sipped his beer and looked at Jackson. "He knew what he was getting into! If you want to play your gonna pay!"

"He didn't do anything but sell some weed," Jackson said.

"Weed is weed," Bubba said, with a big smile on his face. "Money is money!" He finished his beer and threw the empty can out the opened car window. "Let's go."

The driver turned the ignition on and slowly drove the car from the parking lot. When he got to the street, he gunned the engine and popped the clutch. The tires squealed as he turned to the right.

Leon watched the television set. He could see himself in the reflection of the blank screen.

9:13 A.M. – September 20, 2001

The riding mower hummed as the caretaker followed the line of the grass. He drove the mower slowly over Leon's grave, as the dirt was soft. He stopped the mower and started the gas trimmer. The trimmer string made a loud buzzing sound as it cut the young grass near the concrete. A form had been placed to support the headstone. The concrete had been poured and it was wet. The caretaker trimmed the grass carefully around the wet concrete.

Leon watched the television set. There were several quick flashes. The flashes were not as intense as the others were. These came very slowly. The television set seemed to fade then it returned. The television set was not the same. The image was faded! Leon could see a reflection on the blank screen but the reflection wasn't clear. The reflection looked like him but it wasn't the same. The image had faded.

Plato's Dream

4:30 P.M. – September 26, 2001

"Hello Leon!" Leon's mother said. "It looks real good!" She began to weep.

"Now everybody will know who you are," Charlotte said. "Let me read it to you, LEON CHARLES MARTIN BORN 1985 DIED 2001."

Charlotte began to weep. "They caught the guys that killed you," she said. "They're in jail and they have been charged with murder. One of the guys is Bubba! But you know that. You're in Heaven and I guess you know everything."

"I got an A in English and I think I may graduate next year. Mr. Camery asked about you. He asked how we were doing."

Leon watched the television set. He attempted to make out the image on the blank screen, it was faded. The entire image was faded. There were several flashes. These flashes were very slow. The image faded very badly. Leon couldn't see the image. It was blurred. Then, there were several quick, intense flashes. He was looking at the street lamp. The image was sharp and clear! Leon could see the rust on the metal pole and broken glass on the lamp. The sky was a deep blue. In the background was a white cloud.

Plato's Dream

1:38 P.M. – December 22, 2001

"Oh Holy Night! The stars are brightly shining," the loudspeaker blared.

"Merry Christmas, Leon!" Charlotte said, as she placed the small Christmas tree on top of the marker.

"We are doing real well! Mom got a job at the clinic! She's a filer! She couldn't come because she had to work." Charlotte kneeled toward the marker. "We got a new TV. We threw that old one away that didn't work. School is real good! I am making C's and B's. Next year, I will graduate."

Charlotte stood. She looked at the people in the cemetery. It was a Christmas gathering for the people buried there. There were many people walking among the graves. Many of the graves were not marked. Church volunteers had placed small Christmas trees and crosses on the graves.

"I have to go," Charlotte said. "I will try to come on your birthday. It is lonely without you. Those boys got off. They were charged with your murder but they got off."

Leon looked at the street lamp. He looked toward the white cloud that didn't move. He wondered where the wind was. If the wind was blowing, the cloud should move. It didn't. The sky never got dark. It seemed like he had been watching the sky for several hours. Leon wondered when it would get dark. He attempted to move his legs and arms but he couldn't. All he could do was look at the street lamp.

'When will dinner be ready?" Leon thought to himself. He hadn't eaten in a while. He wasn't hungry or thirsty. He

remembered the taste of a soft drink. Leon attempted to lick his lips but his tongue wouldn't move. He couldn't feel his left side. It wasn't there. He could feel something on his right side. There was a sensation but he didn't know what it was.

There were several flashes of bright light. The street lamp dimmed then there was a color of blue. Everything was blue! Leon looked at the blue. There was nothing there but blue.

3:38 P.M. – June 22, 2002

"Miss. Charlotte Angelina Martin!" the principal shouted into the microphone. There was much applause as Charlotte walked toward the principal. She shook his hand and took her high school diploma. She raised the diploma high into the air, "This is for Leon!" she shouted. The crowd clapped softly.

Leon's mother was in the audience and she wept. "I am so proud of my baby!" she said.

The blue color didn't change. Leon watched the blue. There was nothing there. He attempted to look into the blue. 'Perhaps there was something there," he thought. There wasn't. The flashes came very quickly. The flashes were to his right side. He felt them! There was a sensation to his right. Then, the flashes stopped.

Leon attempted to turn his head to his right. He couldn't. He felt the sensation to his right. Then, something happened! Leon could not feel the sensation toward his leg. He could feel the sensation on his right arm and shoulder. 'That is where my right arm and shoulder should be. I can't feel anything toward my leg," he thought. The flashes came again and the sensation was back. He could feel something on his right side.

Leon looked toward the blue. 'I wonder if it means anything?" he asked himself.

6:45 A.M. – December 21, 2002

The maintenance workers walked quickly over the graves. They were preparing for the Christmas gathering. They picked up discarded flowers and trash from the graves. One of the workers walked to Leon's grave. There was a small Christmas tree near the marker. The wind had blown it over and pushed it toward the side. The maintenance worker quickly picked it up and placed it in a plastic garbage bag.

Leon looked toward the blue. 'I wonder if it means anything?" he asked himself.

Plato's Dream

4:00 P.M. – December 21, 2002

"We missed one!" the church volunteer said, as she looked at Leon's grave. "Do we have any left?" she asked.

"Yes!" one of the volunteers, answered. He walked quickly to Leon's grave and he placed a small cross near the marker.

"Are all the Christmas trees gone?" she asked.

"Yes! All we have left is crosses," he answered.

"It looks beautiful," the church volunteer said as she sipped a cup of hot chocolate. "My name is Barbara Parker. What is your name?"

"Tommy Davidson! Is this your first year?" Tommy asked. He smiled. "Are you Brad Parker's wife?"

"Yes," Barbara answered.

Tommy laughed very hard. "I went to college with Brad. I met you at casino night last year! How did you learn how to play cards?" he asked.

Barbara smiled. "I just do. I think I may have inherited the gift from my great-grandfather."

Tommy laughed. "It was great fun. Is Brad here?" he asked, as he looked around the cemetery.

"No," Barbara answered, as she sipped the hot chocolate. "He had to work tonight but he wanted to come."

"I feel sad for them," she added.

"Yes!" Tommy said. "We will come back in a few days and remove the trees and crosses." He looked toward Leon's grave.

"This one is different! Most don't have a marker. Perhaps a relative will come later."

"No! All of the people are gone," Barbara answered. "If they haven't come by now they won't show. Perhaps next year someone will come."

Leon looked at the blue. It seemed to brighten and fade. He thought there was a pattern but there wasn't. It was just blue.

7:22 A.M. – March 14, 2004

The flashes came quickly and were intense. Leon could see them in front of him. He felt the sensation on his right side come and go. The flashes kept coming. Then, they stopped. There was a face in front of him. Leon didn't know whose face it was. It was a young woman. The face was in front of him, and then it was gone. There was a car! It was a beat-up 1976 Camero. Leon recognized it! He attempted to repair it.

The car was abandoned in the neighborhood. He and several of the boys pushed it toward the alley and hid it. Leon attempted to repair it. He couldn't.

The car was cool! Leon would sit inside for hours and pretend it ran. The seats were torn and the paint faded but he loved the car. He looked closely at the back fender. A softball had struck the fender. Leon attempted to smile but his mouth wouldn't move.

The flashes came quickly. There were a lot of flashes. When they stopped, Leon was looking at the television set. The image was very clear. He looked to the reflection on the blank screen and could see himself. The image was very clear. He was six years old and sitting in front of the television. The bright sun reflected his reflection on the blank screen.

1:34 P.M. – May 12, 2004

"This was your uncle Leon," Charlotte said, as she held the infant child toward Leon's marker. "He would be very proud of you."

A man leaned downward and placed a small bouquet of flowers on the headstone.

"Leon! I am married! I got married a year ago," Charlotte said smiling. "His name is Jerry and we love each other very much."

"Is this it?" Jerry asked, as he pointed toward a grave near Leon's.

"Yes!" Charlotte answered.

They walked from Leon's grave to a grave near his.

"This was your grandmother Marcella," Charlotte said, as she held the infant child toward her mother's grave. "She would be very proud of you."

Jerry leaned downward and he placed a small bouquet of flowers on the grave.

Charlotte lowered her head. "I'm sorry I haven't been to visit but Jerry and I have been very busy," she said quietly. "I wanted to show you your granddaughter. I named her Susan! She just turned one!"

"Let's go," Jerry said.

"Bye Momma," Charlotte said, "We will come back Christmas to place a tree on your grave. Everything is going OK! We bought a new car. Jerry and I have had some problems but we are working them out. Don't worry about me. You and

Leon are in Heaven with God! I know everything is good. One day, I will see you."

"Mmmm. Da ta. Mmmmm," Leon's mother hummed. She watched Leon sleeping on the bed. In her arms, she held Charlotte. She attempted to smile but her cheeks didn't move. She looked toward Leon. There was only one bed and she and Leon slept together. Near the bed was a new bassinet. One of the church volunteers had given it to her when Charlotte was born.

She looked to her lower left. She could see Charlotte's face as she held her in her arms. Charlotte was asleep. She looked toward the bed to Leon. He was asleep. Charlotte was three days old and Leon was two.

"Mumm. Da ta. Mummm," she hummed.

She looked toward the pillow on the bed. There was a fly on the pillow. She attempted to stand to brush it away, but her legs didn't move. The fly was on the pillow near Leon's face. She looked to his face and saw beads of sweat. 'Is he sick?" she thought. She looked to her right toward the window. A slight breeze had moved the curtain. It was summer.

Charlotte was born July 19th and it was hot. The window fan was broken and a slight breeze entered the room. She could see the window curtain where the breeze moved it. Leon's mother looked to her lower left. She could see small beads of sweat on Charlotte's brow. She attempted to move her right hand to wipe her brow. Her hand didn't move.

She wondered why they were sweating. It wasn't hot. She didn't feel hot or cold. She didn't feel anything.

The fly on the pillow was very still. Leon's mother wondered why the fly didn't move. It just sat on the pillow. She watched Leon sleep. When he awakens, she will fix lunch. Leon liked macaroni and cheese. They received the food stamps and there was food. One of the church volunteers brought her some new cloth diapers for Charlotte. Leon's mother attempted to smile but her face didn't move.

"Mumm. Da ta. Mummm," she hummed. When Leon awakened she would fix lunch and wash diapers.

She was sitting in the rocking chair but it didn't move. Leon's mother attempted to rock Charlotte but her legs wouldn't push the rocker. She looked to her lower left at Charlotte. She was asleep in her arms. There were small beads of sweat on her face from the heat.

"Mumm. Da ta. Mummm," she hummed. She looked toward the bed to Leon. The fly was on the pillow near his face. She looked toward the window to the curtain that had been blown by the wind. The curtain didn't move. She looked at the curtain waiting for another breeze. It didn't matter! One of the church volunteers was bringing her a new window fan so the baby wouldn't get hot.

"Mumm. Da ta. Mummm," she hummed. When Leon wakes up she will fix him some macaroni and cheese and wash diapers.

Leon continued to look at the television set. He could see himself in the reflection. Leon wished the television had been color. He attempted to remember if they ever owned a color television set. He couldn't remember.

4:30 P.M. – December 17, 2005

"Silent Night, Holy Night," the music stopped quickly as one of the church volunteers stopped the tape. The people began to slowly walk toward the parking area. "It was beautiful!" an elderly woman said, as she walked through the metal gates. "Thank you!" Barbara answered. It was cold and she shivered.

"You have done a wonderful job!" the Mayor said.

Barbara blushed. "Thank you! Is this your first visit?" she asked.

The Mayor smiled. "Yes! I had planned to come last year but there were some last minute details I had to work on." He looked toward the small cemetery. The graves were adorned with small Christmas trees and white crosses. "Who is in charge?"

Barbara smiled and waved toward Tommy. "Tommy Davidson is in charge," she answered quickly.

Tommy saw Barbara speaking to the Mayor and he walked quickly to the gates. He approached the Mayor and nodded. "It is an honor to have you visit."

"The honor is all mine," the Mayor said, as he shook Tommy's hand. "I had heard about the cemetery last year and I wanted to visit." He looked toward the cemetery and the parking lot. "How many people came this year?"

Barbara looked at her hand counter. "We had seven hundred and twenty-two," she answered.

"Amazing!" the Mayor, said. He turned and looked at Tommy. "Is there anything I can do?"

Tommy smiled. He pointed toward the back of the cemetery. There was a portion of the stone wall that had fallen. The stone wall was near an alley and a street light was near the wall. The street light was not working and the rear of the cemetery was very dark. "It's real dark at the rear," Tommy answered. "There are many older graves there but I have noticed the people do not go toward the back." He looked toward the Mayor and lowered his head. "Is it possible to get the street lamp fixed?"

The Mayor looked toward the rear of the cemetery and he began to walk toward it. Barbara and Tommy followed him. He walked to the rear where the stone wall had fallen. He looked at the street lamp and the damaged wall. He turned and looked toward the front gates. "How many graves are here?" he asked.

Tommy looked toward the cemetery. "We don't know for sure. I think as many as twelve hundred. People are still being buried here," he answered.

The Mayor looked at Tommy. "Do they all have markers?"

Tommy lowered his head. "No. Some do. Most of the people buried here can't afford them."

"They don't have to anymore," the Mayor said smiling. "I will make sure that anyone buried here has a marker." He looked toward the stone wall. "We'll fix it and place new street lamps around the edges." The Mayor looked at Tommy. "You and the church volunteers have done an excellent job bringing public notice to the cemetery. Just because a person is poor, they don't have to lie in an unmarked grave."

Tommy and Barbara smiled as they walked past the unmarked graves toward the front gates. As they walked toward the front gates, they passed an unmarked grave. The Mayor stopped and looked at the grave. "This one looks recent," he said.

"Yes!" Barbara answered. "Twelve people have been buried here in the last two years. This lady died last year."

The Mayor nodded his head. He looked at the grave and then began to walk toward the front gates.

When they approached the front gates, Brad was waiting for Barbara. In his arms, he held their infant child, Morgan.

"He looks just like you!" Tommy said, as he looked at Brad.

"Pretty baby," the Mayor said, as he looked at the child in Brad's arms. "Everything will be taken care of." He smiled at Tommy and walked to his car in the parking lot.

"You missed the show," Tommy said to Brad.

"It's OK, there will be another year," Brad answered.

Barbara smiled. "Tommy this is the first time you have seen Morgan. He is two years-old. Morgan was born December 12, 2003," she said proudly.

"Happy Birthday," Tommy said as he lightly touched Morgan's face. "He looks just like Brad. Why did you select the name Morgan?"

Brad smiled. "Barbara picked it out," he answered. "At first, I didn't like the name but then it began to grow on me. I like it!"

"Mmmm. Da ta. Mmmmm," Leon's mother hummed. She watched Leon sleeping on the bed. In her arms, she held Charlotte. She attempted to smile but her cheeks didn't move. She attempted to push the rocker but her legs wouldn't move. She looked toward Leon. Near the bed was a new bassinet. She looked toward the pillow Leon was sleeping on. There was a fly on the pillow.

"Mmmm. Da ta. Mmmmm," Leon's mother hummed

Plato’s Dream

6:00 A.M. – January 9, 2006

The workmen began arriving before 6:00 A.M. Tommy was waiting for them at the front gates as they arrived. The main trucks drove to the back near the stone wall and the workmen began to replace the old street lamp. He watched them as they dug into the ground to place the new street lamps. The section of the stone wall, that had collapsed, was slowly dismantled. The stones were cleaned and stacked near the wall. The men who were to repair the wall would not come until next week.

Several new lights were placed at the front of the pauper's section near the gates. Tommy watched the workmen dig the holes and place the lamps. The lamps were made of metal and closely matched the style of the gates.

One of the two gates was damaged by weather. A portion of the top hinge had rusted and the metal broke from the stone wall. A workman attempted to push the damaged gate open; the gate made a loud screech noise when he pushed it open. The workman looked at the hinge. "We can't repair it," the workman told Tommy. "This whole section will need to be removed. I had hoped we could do something to temporarily repair it but we can't."

Tommy nodded his head.

The workman looked at the damaged gate. "It looks like the whole thing was made as one piece," the workman said. "Both gates will need to be removed and reworked to make them both open correctly." He looked at the sides and the top of the gates. "Beautiful! I have never seen such craftsmanship!"

"They were made in New York in 1822," Tommy remarked.

"Beautiful!" the workman said. He turned and looked at Tommy. "Four different companies quoted a price to repair them. The lowest bid was ten thousand dollars. The council will consider it next year."

"Why so high?" Tommy asked.

The workman moved backward and pointed at the gates. "Look at them!" he said proudly. "I have never seen such craftsmanship! It appears as both gates were made from one solid piece of metal." He pointed toward the top of the gates. "It is difficult to see from the weathering and the black paint but those bumps are not bumps."

Tommy walked closer to see. He looked at the top of the damaged gate. There appeared to be many small bumps along the top and the sides. "What are they?" Tommy asked.

"Carvings!" the workman answered. "The gates can't be sandblasted because the process will damage them. The carvings are not welded, they appear to have been carved or molded as the bars were made." He turned and looked at Tommy. "One of the bidders thinks the gates were made from one solid piece of metal. The carvings were dug into the metal first and the bars machined by hand."

Tommy scrunched his eyes.

"It's like a statue!" the workman said. "The artist starts with a solid piece of stone. The stone is slowly chipped away to reveal the finished work. The gates may have been made the same way."

"What are the carvings?" Tommy asked.

"Angels! The carvings are the faces of angels," the workman answered.

Tommy looked closer at the bumps. They looked like small faces carved into metal. The faces were raised about one inch above the bars.

"There is something else," the workman said. He motioned for Tommy to step inside the cemetery. Tommy stepped inside the pauper's section, then, he began to close the gates. As he closed the damaged gate, it made a loud screech noise.

"You can't see it unless you're on the other side and the gates are closed. One of the bidders noticed it," the workman said.

When the gates were closed, Tommy could see the words. He had not noticed them before. One gate was always opened while the other gate was closed. The top of the gates had been painted black and the paint had filled the openings of the words. The words were carved into the metal at the top and they spanned both gates. TODAY SHALT THOU BE WITH ME IN PARADISE, he read.

Tommy smiled. "The words are from the book of St. Luke. They are from chapter twenty-three verse forty-three. They are the words Jesus spoke to one of the criminals as they were crucified," he said as he looked at the workman.

"It's the Resurrection," the workman said. He pointed toward the graves. "Graveyards are designed so the feet of the buried are facing east. The head is toward the west. The belief is that the dead will be resurrected and facing east."

"Every grave is perfectly aligned so the feet of the deceased are pointing east," he added.

The workman walked to the closed gates and pointed upward. "Beautiful!" he said. "Every letter is perfectly aligned. The letters are carved into the metal."

Tommy looked at the gates. "Aren't they on the wrong side?" he asked.

"No," the workman answered. He pointed toward the graves. "They are for them, not for us! It will be the first thing they see when the Resurrection occurs." He pointed toward the main section of the cemetery. "They really messed up! The whole section is twenty degrees off. The feet are pointed twenty degrees toward the north."

Tommy looked through the closed gates to the main section.

The workman looked at Tommy. "One grave is really messed up," he said. He pointed toward the back of the main section of the cemetery to a large monument. "The wording is on all four sides of the monument and the inscription is something about a woman of noble character." He smiled. "The body is placed behind the monument! The head is pointed toward the monument which is toward the east and the feet are pointing toward the west. When the Resurrection occurs, she will be looking in the wrong direction!"

The workman pushed the gates opened. The damaged gate made a screeching sound when he pushed it open. He and Tommy stepped through the opened gates into the main section of the cemetery. "I appreciate everything the council has done," Tommy said. "Perhaps next year, the council will approve their repair."

The workman smiled and shrugged his shoulders. "Sorry we can't do anything about the gates," he said. "The stone wall was built around them and it will be necessary to remove a portion of the wall to remove them."

The workman stepped backward and looked at the walls. "Beautiful!" he said. "Each stone was carefully cut to fit beside the other." He pointed toward the bottom and he looked at Tommy. "The base is solid granite. The wall is perfectly level."

"Why did the wall collapse?" Tommy asked.

"A car struck it," the workman answered. "We found pieces of the headlight among the stones."

The workman pointed toward the main gates of the City Cemetery. "Junk! Nothing but junk!" he said. "The bars were spot welded and bolted in several places. The paint covers the bolts."

"This was the original cemetery," Tommy said, as he pointed toward the pauper's section. "This section was added in 1823."

"Whoever built it did a piss poor job," the workman said, as he shook his head. "The main gates have been repaired more than five times that I know of and the walls are made of poured cement blocks. There isn't a level spot I could find."

The workman laughed.

"What's funny?" Tommy asked.

"If I had my choice, I would be buried there," the workman answered as he pointed toward the pauper's section. "Beautiful!"

The workman smiled and nodded as he walked to one of the trucks. Tommy looked at the gates as he waited for the markers to arrive.

At 10:30 A.M., the markers arrived. They were made of white marble with the name and dates cut into the stone. Tommy held the map where they would be placed. Several of the markers were loaded onto a wheelbarrow and a workman followed Tommy. They walked to one of the unmarked graves. Tommy looked at his list. "Marcella June Martin," he read.

The workman looked at the markers and he removed one. The soil on the grave had been dug down so the marker would be flush with the soil. He carefully placed the marker in the indent. He looked at the marker. MARCELLA JUNE MARTIN BORN 1969 DIED 2004, he read. "She was young. How did she die?" the workman asked.

"Apartment fire," Tommy answered. "She lived in that dump near Second Avenue." He looked at his map. "Her daughter is buried over here."

Tommy walked to a grave toward the rear. The grave was about seven graves away from Marcella's. He looked at his map. "Cassie Renee Martin," he read.

The workman walked to the wheelbarrow and he removed a marker. He walked to the grave and he carefully placed it in the recess. He looked at the marker. CASSIE RENEE MARTIN BORN 1984 DIED 1984 SIX MONTHS, he read.

"How did she die?" the workman asked.

"Pneumonia," Tommy answered. "They lived in that rat trap on Second Avenue."

"Didn't they have anybody?" the workman asked.

Tommy was looking at the map and he looked upward. "Marcella had another daughter. When she died, we tried to contact her but she had moved away. She had a son that got into some sort of trouble. He is buried over there." Tommy pointed to a grave that was near. Then, he looked at his map. He looked toward the left and he walked two graves over. "Unknown," he read.

"We have a lot of those," the workman said. "Does it make a difference?"

"On some," Tommy answered. "This one is Unknown Male Died 1957."

The workman walked to the wheelbarrow and he removed the correct marker. He placed it carefully in the recess.

"Mmmm. Da ta. Mmmmm," Leon's mother hummed.

Leon looked at the Camero. He looked at the wheels. The tires and the rims were missing and the Camero was sitting on bricks. The tires and rims meant something. He couldn't remember.

There were several quick flashes. The Camero faded, and then returned. Leon remembered. He attempted to smile but his face wouldn't move. He and Charlotte stripped the car! They sold the tires and rims. Leon attempted to smile and to laugh. His face wouldn't move. His mother was sick. She had a real bad cough and she needed cough syrup. Their welfare money was spent. He and Charlotte stripped the Camero! They sold the tires and the rims for twenty dollars. Leon attempted to laugh but he couldn't. The tires were too heavy for him to push alone. He was twelve years old and Charlotte was ten. He and Charlotte had to push the tires one at a time.

He attempted to laugh. He cut his left thumb on one of the steel rims. Leon attempted to look at his left hand. There was nothing there! He couldn't see his left hand. There was nothing to his left.

There were several quick flashes. The Camero faded, and then returned. Leon was looking at something. He didn't know what it was. It looked like an old, beat-up car. The tires and rims were missing. There was a large dent in the back fender. Leon was looking at an old beat-up car. He didn't know what it was.

7:30 P.M. – July 8, 2006

The music from the tape player was loud in the car as the three boys were sitting in their car. The car was parked in the rear of the First Baptist Church parking lot. Bubba, James, and Carl were sitting very quite. They sipped beer as they listened to the music.

Carl sat on the right front side and James was sitting in the driver's side. Bubba sat in the back seat. His eyes were closed as he listened to the music. Carl was nodding his head to the music as he looked in the rear view mirror. His eyes widened as he noticed a movement behind their car. "Run!" Carl yelled, as he pushed opened the car door. In the rear view mirror, he saw police sneaking toward their car.

Bubba kicked opened the rear door and he dove for the parking lot. He looked backward to see several policemen running toward the car. Bubba rolled quickly to stand, and then he ran toward the church. Three policemen ran after him.

Bubba ran as fast as he could. He turned the corner of the parking lot toward the front of the church. Quickly, he ran up the front steps toward the front door. He grabbed for the door handle but the door was locked.

"Face down and spread them!" one of the three policemen, yelled.

Bubba held his arms outward as he slowly turned toward the police. There were three policemen at the bottom of the steps. They had their guns drawn and pointed at him. Two of the policemen were black. One was white.

"Give me a break?" Bubba smiled, as he looked at one of the black policemen. "I'm a brother!" he said, with a grin on his face.

"Face down and spread them!" one of the three policemen yelled.

Bubba smiled as he held his arms outward. "You can't arrest me!" he said, "They dropped the charges! I had no part in killing Leon!"

"This isn't about Leon Martin!" one of the policemen yelled. "You're under arrest for the murder of nine year-old Sally Cain in a drive-by shooting!"

Bubba's eyes widened. He screamed as he turned quickly toward the door. As he turned, he reached for the gun in his pants pocket. He crouched as he pulled the gun and he continued to turn. He turned a complete circle to face the three policemen. In his right hand he held a 9 mm Beretta semi-automatic pistol. The gun was turned sideward pointed toward the three policemen.

Bubba saw three flashes of light. The flashes came from the barrels of the policemen's pistols.

Bubba was frightened!

He looked at Gabe and the six others. They stood with their guns in their hands. He looked at Gabe. There was a smile on Gabe's face.

He was in the park near the railroad trestle. Bubba was kneeled on the ground looking toward them. He could see the trestle toward the rear and the river was on his right. He wondered if he could make it. Bubba wondered who had drawn the low card.

Gabe smiled but he didn't speak. Bubba became terrified! He had stolen money from Gabe and this was his punishment. Each had drawn a card. The one with the lowest card would shoot first. He attempted to look toward his knees but his head wouldn't move. The knees were shot first then the feet. If Bubba could crawl to the trestle, they would stop shooting.

Bubba looked at Sam. Sam's head was cocked backward. He looked like he was laughing. In Sam's hand was his gun. Sam carried a Colt 38 short barrel. Sam never missed.

Bubba attempted to cry but his face wouldn't move. This is the same thing that happened to Burke! Burke messed over Gabe and they took Burke to the railroad trestle. Bubba drew the seven of hearts. He fired the third shot. Burke begged for mercy as he crawled toward the trestle. He was shot in the right knee then the left foot. Burke begged for his life as he crawled toward the railroad tracks. Bubba shot him in the back as he crawled.

Something was wrong! Bubba looked at the seven boys. Burke was with them! 'What?" Bubba thought to himself. 'Burke is dead! We killed him!"

Burke was killed two years ago! Bubba fired the last shot. When he was dead, they pushed his body into the river. A fisherman found his body three weeks later.

Bubba looked at the seven boys. They were standing with their guns drawn. They were laughing. He could see the smiles on their faces. It looked like the time he was initiated in the clan. Burke was alive then. They took him to the trestle and they acted like they were going to kill him. They did this to frighten him. That was six years ago! Burke was dead! They killed him two years ago! Burke couldn't be alive! He was dead! Bubba fired the last shot!

It couldn't be that time! It occurred six years ago! Leon was dead and Burke was dead!

Bubba was confused. 'What is happening?" he thought. He attempted to speak but his mouth wouldn't move. Bubba attempted to stand. He couldn't feel his legs! He couldn't feel anything. He looked at the seven boys. They weren't moving. Their heads were cocked backward laughing with their guns drawn.

He was terrified!

They were going to kill him! They would shoot his knees and his feet. If he could crawl to the railroad tracks they would stop shooting. 'Why is Burke here? He was killed two years ago!" Bubba thought.

It looked like his initiation in the clan. It couldn't be! That was six years ago! Smith drew the low card and he shot into the ground. Burke was there and he fired the second shot! Bubba began to crawl toward the railroad tracks as they shot into the ground laughing. It was a test! They tested him to see if he would beg for his life. Bubba didn't beg! He crawled toward the railroad tracks. When he reached the tracks, they stopped shooting. He was never shot. They fired their weapons toward the ground.

Leon was dead and Burke was dead!

Bubba was terrified! They were going to kill him! Gabe knew about the money he had stolen. He looked toward the railroad tracks. If he could crawl to the railroad tracks they would stop shooting.

'Who drew the low card? Who would shoot first?" Bubba thought to himself, as he looked at their faces. Their heads were cocked backward laughing. Their guns were drawn. They weren't moving!

Bubba was terrified!

He looked toward the railroad trestle. He couldn't start crawling until the first shot was fired. If he attempted to run, they would all shoot him. He had to wait! Bubba had to wait until the first shot was fired before he began to crawl. He looked at Burke. Burke knew Bubba had fired the last shot.

'Who drew the low card," Bubba thought. He looked at the seven boys. 'Who will shoot first? Is it Gabe? Is it Sam? Is it Burke or Smith?"

He looked at their faces. Their heads were cocked backward laughing and their guns were drawn. They weren't moving!

Bubba was terrified!

'What game is this? What are they waiting for? Shoot! Somebody shoot so I can start crawling! Please someone shoot so I can start crawling!" Bubba thought.

8:45 P.M. – November 2, 2006

The flashes of light were quick and intense. The television set flashed very quickly. Leon saw bright flashes of blue and green. The television set would fade and then become very bright. At one time, he could almost see the expression of his face in the reflection. Then, the television set dimmed.

The flashes were fast and furious. He felt many sensations on his right side. The sensations were strong then weak. The television set was very clear, and then it dimmed. Leon didn't know what was happening. The flashes were fast and very intense. Then, there was nothing.

Plato's Dream

5:30 P.M. – December 23, 2006

"Hurry up before the people come in!" Barbara yelled, as she bent downward to light the candle on Leon's grave. She lit the candle then ran to another grave to light the candle.

"Brumm! Brumm! Brumm!" The young boy beat softly upon the drum.

"Come they told me, pa rum pum pum pum. A newborn king to see, pa rum pum pum pum. Our finest gifts we bring, pa rum pum pum pum. To lay before the King, pa rum pum pum pum, rum pum pum pum, rum pum pum pum," the combined choirs of the First Baptist, First Presbyterian, and Holy Name churches sang. There were more than forty members of the combined choir. They stood near the front gates dressed in white robes.

Four men and two women began to play their acoustic guitars as a young woman began to play the electric organ. The people stood at the front gates of the City Cemetery listening to the choir. Near the gates, the twelve-member ensemble of the Charlton School of Music waited. Beside them, a young girl walked and smiled. She was next! She and the entire band and choir would sing "Oh Holy Night." The young girl would sing the high notes.

The parking lot was full of cars as policemen directed traffic on the street. The cars were parked along the street for more than twelve city blocks. Near the entrance to the parking lot, the wives of the City Council members sold hot chocolate and hot cider. A sign on the stand stated that all proceeds were for the

Christmas dinner for the homeless. A man walked to the stand and he picked up two hot chocolates. "One dollar," the lady said. "Keep the change," the man replied, as he handed her a ten-dollar bill.

"Thank you for coming," the Mayor said, as he walked through the crowd. As he walked through the crowd, he shook the hands of the people waiting.

"It's beautiful!" a young girl said smiling. The Mayor bent downward toward her and smiled. "Thank you for coming" he said, as he shook the young girl's hand.

"We're ready!" Tommy yelled, "Let them in!"

The candles were all lit and the gates were opened. The people began to walk toward the graves. Each grave had been adorned with a white paper bag with a lit candle inside. The sun was setting as the many people began to walk among the graves looking at the candles. From a distance, the graveyard was beautiful. The small lights lit up the graves.

"It's beautiful!" many of the people said, as they walked among the graves.

"Where is it?" Charles asked, as he and Charlotte walked toward the grave of Charlotte's mother.

"Over here, I think!" Charlotte responded. She held to two small children as she looked at the headstones. "It has been a while since I have been here. I used to come every Christmas and place a tree on mommy's grave."

They looked at several graves. Charles walked looking. "Where is your brother buried?" Charles asked Charlotte.

"Somewhere near momma," Charlotte answered.

"Here it is!" Charlotte said. She kneeled toward her mother's grave. "Hello momma! Things didn't work out with Jerry and me. Your granddaughter is somewhere in foster care. I don't know where she is. They won't let me see her. I brought you something better!" she said, as she pushed the two young children toward the grave. "This is Brandy and Earl! They are Charles' two children but we plan to marry next year."

Charlotte smiled. "Now you have three grandchildren. You know that! You and Leon are in heaven with God! I know you are well."

"Let's go," Charles said, as he tapped Charlotte on her shoulder.

"Bye momma! I will come and see you on your birthday," Charlotte said.

They walked toward the front gate of the City Cemetery toward the parking area. They walked past Leon's grave to the parking lot. The lot was full and they had parked on the street. Charlotte and Charles walked quickly to their car. They placed the two children in the backseat and quickly drove away.

The people walked among the graves reading the headstones and markers. They looked upward when they heard the trumpets. The violins began to play and the combined choir began to hum softly. "Oh Holy Night, the stars are brightly shining. It is the night of our dear Savior's birth," the young girl began to sing.

The crowd stopped looking at the headstones and they stopped to listen to the young girl sing. The crowd began to softly clap. When the song was finished, there were cheers and screams. The people continued to walk among the graves. They looked at the white paper bags and the headstones.

The candle on Leon's grave burned brightly as the people walked among the graves looking at the lights. They walked toward the back of the cemetery where there were many streetlights. The stone wall had been rebuilt. Barbara and Tommy stood at the gate of the pauper's section watching the people. The cemetery was beautiful! Several people gathered in front of Tommy and Barbara. They waited until ten people had gathered together. "Thank you for coming!" Tommy said, as he smiled. "This is the original City Cemetery."

"Mmmm. Da ta. Mmmmm," Leon's mother hummed. She watched Leon sleeping on the bed. In her arms, she held Charlotte. There was a fly, on the pillow, near Leon's head. When Leon wakes up, she will fix him lunch. Leon likes

macaroni and cheese. When he wakes up, she will fix him macaroni and cheese and wash diapers.

"Mmmm. Da ta. Mmmmm," Leon's mother hummed. She watched Leon sleeping on the bed.

9:47 P.M. – December 23, 2006

The church volunteers walked quickly among the graves. They stepped on the white paper bags to extinguish the candle burning inside. Tommy walked quickly from grave to grave stepping on the paper bags. Barbara followed Tommy. She was carrying a garbage bag and she picked up the squashed white bags. Tommy walked to Leon's grave and stepped on the white bag. Barbara leaned downward to pick it up. When she picked it up, she saw the stone marker underneath. She stopped and quickly read the marker, LEON CHARLES MARTIN BORN 1985 DIED 2001. Barbara placed the squashed white bag in the garbage bag. She walked quickly to the next grave.

The corpse of Leon Charles Martin lay six feet below the stone marker. He died November 2, 2006 at 8:45:02 P.M.

2:42 P.M. – April 12, 2007

"Mmmm. Da ta. Mmmmm," Leon's mother hummed. She watched Leon sleeping on the bed. In her arms, she held Charlotte.

The flashes came very quickly. It was dark, then light. She saw the image brighten and then fade. The image disappeared. Then, it returned. She was looking at Leon lying on the bed. On the pillow, near his face, a fly was standing. She looked at the fly. Slowly, the fly began to fade.

The whole image began to fade. The colors seemed to slowly blend together. She watched the curtain slowly blend into the wall. She looked at Charlotte. She could not see the outline of her eyes and nose.

There was a quick flash. The image was sharp and clear. She looked at Charlotte. She could see her eyes and nose. On her forehead were several small beads of sweat. The image began to slowly fade. As she looked at Charlotte, her face seemed to fade together. She could not see the outline of her eyes and nose.

The image slowly faded. Leon's mother could not see the bed and the bassinet. Everything had faded to a cream color. There was a flash and the image was bright and clear.

The image began to slowly fade. Leon's mother watched as the bed and curtain faded into a cream color. She looked at Charlotte. Charlotte had faded into a cream color. Everything was the same color, cream. Then, the cream color began to darken.

Plato's Dream

The cream color slowly darkened to a brown. The brown slowly darkened to a black. Then, there was nothing.

1:00 P.M. – December 20, 2007

"Each tour will last about thirty-five minutes," Mrs. Ray Barkley said, as she handed the maps to the volunteers. She pointed toward the City Cemetery. "There are six stops." She smiled and pointed toward herself. "I am the first stop! I will portray Caroline Brown Harrison, the wife of the Mayor of the city."

The people standing smiled and lightly clapped their hands.

Tommy looked at the map. "Excuse me," he said, "There is a mistake! The pauper section is not on the list of stops."

Mrs. Barkley smiled politely. "There is not enough time," she said grinning. "We expect many people and they are mainly interested in seeing the graves of the most important people buried here!"

Tommy frowned. "The purpose of the tours was to educate people about the poor who are buried here," he said. "Our goal was to present an awareness of the poor at Christmas."

Mrs. Barkley pointed toward the main section of the cemetery. "Mr. Davidson, people will be paying five dollars each to see the important people buried here. They are not interested in the poor," she snarled.

"Five dollars!" Tommy said surprised. "We never charged anybody. There was no charge last year."

"I am in charge! The City Council voted me in charge!" Mrs. Barkley responded. She was irritated at Tommy's remark.

"I know," Tommy answered. "It is that the purpose of the tours was to educate people on the poor. There should be at least one stop."

Mrs. Barkley was irritated. "Mr. Davidson, we will not stop anybody from visiting the poor section." She pointed toward the gates of the poor section. "If anyone wants to visit, they are more than welcome." She turned toward the people standing. "Every stop has five minutes. Since my husband and I will portray the first couple, we will have ten minutes."

"Excuse me," Tommy said. "There are many unknown graves toward the rear. It is believed that several bodies were returned from World War I. Surely, these people are consideration for a stop."

Mrs. Barkley was irritated. "Take it up with the council!" she shouted.

Tommy started to speak when he was interrupted. "We do not have time for a stop at the poor section," Mrs. Barkley snapped at Tommy. "I don't know of anyone who would want to portray a drunk or a prostitute." She looked toward the small group of people. "My son, Ray Jr., will portray Captain Steven English. He is the man who saved our city from the Indians."

Tommy lowered his head. "Their only crime was that they were poor. What will you do with the money?" Tommy asked.

"Expenses!" Mrs. Barkley said, with a frown. "There will be a party after the tour for all of the tour guides and performers." She looked toward the gates to the poor section. "The council took care of them! They all have headstones and the wall was repaired. In a few years, we may repair the gates."

Tommy lowered his head.

Mrs. Barkley smiled. "Now that that has been taken care of," she grinned. She looked at the people standing. "Follow me! It is important that we keep the crowds moving. Last year, we had more than twelve hundred visitors. We want to give them their monies worth so they will come next year."

She turned and walked toward a grave near the center.

Tommy stood looking at the map. All of the stops were in the main section of the cemetery. Only one stop was even near the gates. The tour began toward the rear where the Mayor and his wife were buried. He walked slowly behind the small group of guides.

Plato's Dream

5:30 P.M. – December 23, 2007

The cars began arriving at 4:30 P.M. The workers came earlier and setup the eating tent. At 5:00 P.M., the food arrived and all of the volunteers, guides, and re-enactors ate. The food was very good. Barbara and Tommy sat toward the rear of the tent. They watched the re-enactors as they laughed and joked with one another. Ray Jr. was dressed as Captain English, one of the earliest settlers of the city. Frequently Ray Jr. would stand and yell at the other re-enactors, "Follow me! We must attack the Indians before they attack us!"

The re-enactors would laugh. Barbara and Tommy sat quietly. When they had finished eating, they walked to the gates of the pauper section. The entire cemetery had been decorated with white paper bags. Inside, a candle was lit. Barbara and Tommy decorated the graves of the pauper section. They stood at the gates watching.

The re-enactors walked to their places as the front gates were opened. The crowd waiting was small. From the gates, Barbara and Tommy could see the parking lot. It wasn't full. The guides waited at the front gates to lead the visitors. The guides waited until ten people were ready for the tour. Then, they led the people to the first stop.

No one came to the pauper's section. The last stop was near the main entrance. Barbara and Tommy stood watching. The people completed the tour then they walked toward the parking lot. The crowds were small.

6:19 P.M. – December 23, 2007

Barbara and Tommy stood by the gates at the entrance to the poor section of the cemetery. When the sun had set, the guides lit their lanterns. They watched the lantern lights of the tour guides wind around the graves. As they were watching, Barbara heard a noise toward the rear of the pauper's cemetery. She turned and looked toward the stone wall. A young man was looking over the top motioning for her to come to the wall. "Miss. can you help us?" he whispered.

Barbara looked toward the young man and she walked to the stone wall. She spoke to him for a few minutes then she turned and walked quickly to Tommy. "Tommy, come quickly! There are some people at the back of the cemetery in the alley. They need your help!" she said quietly.

Tommy and Barbara walked to the back of the cemetery to the stone wall. Tommy looked over the top of the wall to see three men, one woman, and a dog standing in the alley. Two of the men were old. They looked about sixty years old. One man looked young. He was about twenty. The woman looked about fifty years old and the dog - looked old but well groomed. They were dressed in worker's overalls and they wore knit hats.

"Mister, can you help us?" the young man asked.

Tommy looked over the stone wall. "What do you need?" he asked.

The woman held several papers in her right hand. She pushed them toward Tommy. In her left hand, she held a small rock. "Will you place these papers on Mason's grave? Put this rock on top so the wind won't blow them," she answered.

One of the older men leaned toward the stone wall. "Mason's grave is near the front of the gate," he said. "It's twelve back from the gate. If you stand at the gate, walk twelve graves back and four to the left. The headstone says UNKNOWN MALE DIED 2005."

Tommy looked surprised! "Who's Mason?"

The young man leaned toward the stone wall. "He is our friend. Mason died March 12, 2005," he answered.

Tommy looked at Barbara. "What are the papers?" he asked.

One of the older men looked at Tommy. "They're letters," he said. "We wrote Mason some letters. Can you put them on his grave? Put the rock on top so they won't blow."

"Why can't you do it?" Barbara asked the old man.

"They won't let us in!" the woman answered. "They won't let us in unless we pay five dollars each."

Tommy's face filled with anger! "Wait here!" Tommy said quickly. He turned and ran toward the parking lot. He ran to the front entrance where a woman was sitting taking money for tickets. A policeman was standing beside her.

"Three men and a woman tried to come in!" he said angrily. "You wouldn't let them in unless they paid!"

"They're bums!" the woman answered. "Nobody gets in unless they pay five dollars."

The policeman looked at Tommy. "Are these people bothering you? I told them to leave," he said.

Tommy was livid. "These people didn't come here to hear some stupid sixteen year old boy tell lies about killing defenseless Indians! They came here to visit the grave of their dead friend!" he said.

The policeman's eyes widened.

The woman shrugged her shoulders. "The cemetery is closed! It is only open so people can take the tour and learn about the famous people buried here." She snarled her nose. "Ray Jr. is doing an excellent job portraying Captain English.

Nobody gets in unless they pay five dollars. If these people want in, tell them to come back tomorrow when the tours are over."

Tommy's eyes widened. "This cemetery is never closed to anyone that wants to visit a friend or relative," he said, angrily.

The woman shrugged her shoulders. "Everybody has to pay. No one gets in without paying. Only the volunteers get in free!" she snarled.

Tommy looked at the policeman. "They are volunteers! They arrived late!" he told the policeman.

The woman smirked. "Mrs. Barkley is in charge! She personally picked all the volunteers from the families of the City Council. I know everyone of them." She looked at the policeman. "My daughter is leading one of the groups. These people are not volunteers! They are not on the list." She was sitting in a chair and a table was in front of her. She pounded her fist on the table. "If they want in, they pay! If they can't pay, they can come tomorrow."

"They're my volunteers!" Tommy said softly. "I picked them! They're late!" He looked toward the policeman. "I'm bringing them in."

"You can't pick volunteers!" the woman snapped at Tommy. "Mrs. Barkley picked all of the volunteers. If they want in, they have to pay five dollars each!"

"Take it up with the council!" Tommy snapped at the woman. He looked at the policeman. "They're my volunteers! I'm bringing them in."

The policeman smiled and he walked quickly toward the eating tent.

Tommy hurried toward the rear of the cemetery where the three men, one woman, and the dog were waiting in the alley. He smiled. "It's OK! Come in!" he said, "I need some volunteers to help me decorate some graves."

The people smiled and the man with the dog leaned downward. He took a length of rope and began to tie the dog to a small bush near the wall.

"What are you doing?" Tommy asked.

The older man looked upward as he was tying the dog. "They won't let Lucky in. She will have to wait for us," he answered.

"Bring her!" Tommy said smiling. "She can come in!"

The older man untied the rope from the bush. He held to the rope and the people followed Tommy to the front entrance where Barbara was waiting. The policeman was standing beside Barbara. "Mr. Davidson," the policeman said.

"They're volunteers!" Tommy said. "They are going to help me decorate some of the graves."

The policeman smiled. "Mr. Davidson, my name is Terry Clark," he continued. "All volunteers get to eat free. Most of the others have already eaten but there is plenty of barbecue left." He looked at the people. "My wife Sally is one of the servers. She has prepared plates for them. There is plenty." He looked at the dog. "She prepared a plate for the dog also."

Tommy grinned.

The four people followed Terry, Tommy, and Barbara to a tent that had been setup to feed the volunteers. When they entered, a section of table had been setup with four barbecue plates. "Hello!" an older woman said, as she greeted them. "My name is Sally and I will be serving you! We have coffee, hot chocolate, hot cider, and soft drinks. What would you like to drink?" she asked smiling.

"Coffee will be fine," one of the three men said. The woman nodded.

Sally led them to the table. "Is water OK for your dog?" she asked the man holding the rope.

"Yes ma'am," the older man replied. "I only give her water."

Sally nodded and walked to her husband. "Thanks honey!" he said, as he kissed her on the cheek.

Terry looked at Tommy. "If there is anything you need Mr. Davidson, just ask." He looked at the people. "Enjoy your meal," he said, with a grin on his face. He turned and left the tent.

Sally brought four coffees and a bowl of water. She had a small bowl of barbecue for the dog. When she placed the coffee on the table, the four people lowered their heads and prayed. Then, they began to eat quickly.

Tommy and Barbara sat beside them. They watched them eat.

"My name is Tommy and this is Barbara," Tommy said.

The woman was eating and she looked upward. "My name is Carolyn," she said. She looked to her left toward the older man with the dog. "That is Gerald and his dog Lucky." She looked to her right. "The youngster is Mark. Sitting beside him is Burris."

Tommy smiled as he looked at Gerald. The dog was sitting beside him eating. The dog was a collie mix and small. She was well fed. The hair color was a reddish blonde with many white hairs on her snout. Lucky was old, perhaps seven of our years. Her hair was brushed. On her neck was a collar. Tommy could see the rabies tag and read the date. It was current. "Why did you name your dog Lucky?" he asked Gerald.

Gerald was eating. He looked upward and drank some coffee. "I found her in an alley downtown," he answered, "She was a puppy and somebody dumped her." He reached downward and petted Lucky. "She was pretty starved and scared. I named her Lucky because it was luck that brought us together. I don't go anywhere without her."

Barbara smiled. "How did Mason die?" she asked.

Mark looked upward. "I found him!" he said quietly. "It was that cold snap we had in March. He got sick and I guess the cold got him."

Tommy's eyes narrowed. "Where did he die?" he asked Mark.

Mark was eating and he looked upward. "The river, we all live by the river," Mark answered. "Mason was sick and we were going to take him to the clinic. He must have died during the night. He looked OK that night but he had a cough." Mark lowered his head. "He died before we could take him to the clinic. We didn't know how sick he was."

Barbara's eyes began to water.

"Thank you for helping us," Carolyn said.

Tommy smiled. "Do you come here often?" he asked.

Burris was eating and he looked upward at Tommy. "Once a week," he answered. "We try to come every week depending on the weather." He looked toward the cemetery. "We have to come before the sun sets. They lock the gate about sunset. We used to come late at night but they fixed the stone wall." He turned and took a bite of baked beans. "We came today but there were a lot of people. We tried to get in but they wouldn't let us in. We waited in the alley. We were going to wait until everybody left but the weather is changing. It will be cold tonight. Thank you for helping us."

Barbara's eyes began to tear. She sniffled. "You come every week to visit your friend Mason's grave?" she asked.

"No ma'am," Burris answered. "We have a lot of friends here we visit. There's Dottie, Sharon, Alex, and Chad. Mason died two years ago."

Barbara sniffled. "How long have you been coming?" she asked Burris.

Mark shrugged his shoulders. "About three years," he answered. "I have been here three years and we come together. We come every week to visit our friends."

"Just because were poor don't mean we don't have feelings," Carolyn interrupted. "We are all one family! We come every week. Mason was closest to us. We wrote him some letters and we came to place them on his grave."

Barbara quickly stood. There were tears on her cheeks. "Excuse me," she said softly. She covered her face with a paper napkin and walked quickly toward the tent entrance. As she left the tent, she was sobbing.

Tommy smiled politely.

"What was Mason like?" Tommy asked.

Gerald looked upward. "He came about three years ago from up north," he answered. "He came south because it's not as cold. We met him at the rescue mission. Mason has a problem with alcohol. Once he started, he couldn't stop."

Mark smiled. "He was in Korea. When he came back, nothing was the same. The war messed him up pretty bad." He looked toward Gerald. "He and Gerald liked to play checkers," he said, with a snicker.

Carolyn leaned forward and grinned. "He always beat Gerald at checkers," she added.

"That's not so," Gerald said smiling. "I beat Mason many times."

"When?" Mark asked Gerald. "I never saw you win. You came close a few times but Mason always beat you."

Gerald laughed.

Carolyn looked at Tommy. "We are close. We don't have anything but each other," she said. She looked toward Gerald and Mark. "When one of us dies, it's pretty rough. Just because your dead don't mean we forget you." She smiled at Tommy. "We were real close to Mason so I guess we miss him the most."

"We can add his name to the marker. Do you know Mason's full name?" Tommy asked.

Burris nodded. "I don't think that was his real name. We don't know his last name," he answered. He looked at Mark. "My real name isn't Burris. I made it up. I have family and I don't want them to know where I am."

Carolyn smiled. "What is a name? Is a rose still a rose if the name is different?" she asked laughing.

Tommy looked at Carolyn and smiled.

Gerald reached downward and petted Lucky. "My name is Gerald. Gerald Winston," he said. "I was born in St. Louis. I got into some trouble and spent time in jail. When I got out, nobody would have anything to do with me. I couldn't get a job and my parents wouldn't let me live with them."

He looked upward at Tommy. "I drifted south and came here. It's a good place and I have lots of friends." He looked at Mark and Burris. "They don't care about my past."

"Excuse me," Tommy said. "I want to check on Barbara. Will you be OK?"

Carolyn nodded and Tommy stood. He walked out of the tent and looked for Barbara. She was standing by the gates of the poor section. He walked to her. "Are you OK?" he asked.

Barbara sniffled, "I'm OK. It's so sad." She sobbed softly, "Those people."

Tommy smiled. "They're OK. They live in a world that they feel they belong in. They have each other and they care for each other," he said. Tommy looked toward the main section of the cemetery. He could see a small group of people following one of the tour guides. The tour guide was a young girl. She was dressed in a 19th century dress and carried a lit lantern. The people followed her to a grave where a woman was standing. The grave was the grave of Merideth Norton. She was the wife of a physician that lived in the city. Straw bales had been placed around the grave. The guide led the people to the grave and they sat on the straw bales. When they sat down, the woman began telling the story of Merideth Norton.

Tommy looked at Barbara. "They have more than a lot of people. Did you notice they were the only ones that prayed before eating?" he asked, as he lowered his head. "I forgot to pray."

Barbara smiled. "I forgot to pray also," she said. "I guess they were more thankful than I was."

"Come back in. They're waiting," Tommy said softly.

"No. I will wait here for them. I'm OK," Barbara answered.

Tommy turned and he walked back to the tent. When he entered, Carolyn and Mark were standing and waiting. Burris and Gerald were eating. "Can we visit Mason's grave?" Mark asked.

Burris and Gerald stood quickly and nodded their heads. "Can we visit Mason's grave?" Gerald asked.

Tommy nodded and they walked to the poor section. When they entered the gates, Barbara smiled as they walked past her. They walked twelve graves forward and four to the left. Carolyn bent downward beside the grave and placed the letters on top. She placed the rock on top of the letters. "Hello Mason! We miss you," she said.

"I miss you a lot!" Gerald said, as he kneeled near the grave. Gerald held the rope tied to Lucky. When Gerald kneeled, Lucky lay on the grass beside the grave. "Mark is learning how to play checkers but he's not a big challenge." He looked toward Mark and smiled. "He'll learn."

"I almost got a job," Mark said, as he kneeled near the grave. "It was a good job that paid five dollars and fifty cents an hour. It was near the railroad tracks doing clean up. Mr. Carson from the First Baptist Church got it for me. I went for the interview but I was told it was filled."

Burris kneeled beside the grave. "The river rose about one foot a couple of days ago," he said. "We moved our camp further up." He looked upward. "It's going to be cold tonight but we're OK."

"We brought you something to read when you're not busy," Carolyn said smiling. "I know you're OK. You're probably playing checkers with some of the angels and beating them. When you take a break read them."

"We'll see you next week," Mark said, as he stood.

They stood and walked to several graves and kneeled beside them. Tommy watched them visit the graves. When they were finished speaking, they walked to Mason's grave. As they walked past the grave, they each said, "Good Night!"

Mason was watching the checkerboard intently. He had Gerald cornered! There was no way he was going to win. Mason attempted to smile but his mouth wouldn't move. He was waiting for Gerald to move a checker.

He looked beside Gerald where Lucky was laying. She was asleep. To the side, Carolyn and Dottie were talking. He could see the river. It was summer and the trees were full of leaves.

The sky was clear and he could see the stars. The light from the fire was enough to play checkers by. It wasn't cold. They lit the fire to play checkers.

In the river was the dinner boat. It usually left the dock at 9:00 P.M. and carried the people up river. It took two hours to make the trip. The boat was in the middle of the river headed north. It just left the dock. He could see the lights on the dinner boat and the lights from the city. Mason looked at the boat. 'Something must be wrong," he thought. The boat hadn't moved since Gerald made his last move.

During the summer, a nice cool breeze came from the river. The river had a good smell and the breeze felt good. Mason attempted to smell the river. He couldn't. He couldn't smell anything. He attempted to feel the cool breeze. He felt nothing.

Mason looked at Dottie. She was smiling. He wondered what she was saying. Her mouth was opened but he couldn't hear what she was saying. Mason attempted to listen to what she was saying. He couldn't hear anything.

He watched the checkerboard. Gerald was trapped! He waited for Gerald to make his move. As he waited, he planned his next move.

They walked to the front entrance of the City Cemetery. Barbara followed them. "Can I give you a ride home?" Tommy asked, as they stood at the front entrance to the cemetery.

"No. We'll walk," Carolyn answered. "It is a nice evening. We'll get home before its cold. We like to walk and talk. We'll talk about Mason."

Sally came walking toward them. In her hand, she held a large, white bag. "I'm glad you hadn't left yet," she said smiling. "I made some extra plates of barbecue and several cups of coffee."

Mark smiled, as he took the bag. "We have some friends that would like it. The barbecue beans were real good," he said.

Terry walked toward them. In his hand, he held a key. "I'm sorry about the misunderstanding," he said, as he handed the key to Carolyn. "It is a key to the lock on the gates. Come anytime."

"What if we lose it?" Gerald asked.

Terry smiled. "This is my beat. I come by at least twice a day. I'll stop tomorrow and place a key there," he said as he pointed toward the sign that read City Cemetery. "I'll put a spare behind the sign."

Gerald nodded.

Tommy, Barbara, Sally, and Terry watched them walk away. As they walked, they laughed. "Do you remember when it rained three years ago and Mason dropped that checker down the drain?" Gerald asked.

"Oh man!" Mark answered. "I thought he was going to die! He was so angry."

Burris laughed, "I thought he was going to tear the whole street up to get that checker."

Carolyn laughed. "Do you remember the time that Mason brought us that old ham?" she asked Gerald.

Gerald laughed, as he punched Mark. "You ate it!"

Mark laughed. "It was good!" he giggled.

They laughed as they walked on the sidewalk toward the river. The river was less than three miles from the City Cemetery. The street ended near the Arkansas Bridge. As they walked toward the river, they talked and laughed. They were telling stories about Mason.

Terry turned to look at Tommy. "Mr. Davidson, I'm sorry about the misunderstanding," Terry said. "I was told they attempted to enter without paying. I didn't know they came to visit the grave of a friend. I'll let the other officers know what happened. They'll look out for them."

Tommy nodded. "I hope you don't get into any trouble with Mrs. Barkley."

Terry laughed. "The chief will understand. It's all over. The show is over. It's a bust!"

Barbara looked puzzled. "What do you mean?" she asked.

"Less than six hundred people came," Terry said as he looked toward the main section of the cemetery. "Mrs. Barkley has decided to cancel next year. She believed more than two thousand people would show up. The re-enactors are complaining of the cold."

"It's not cold!" Barbara said.

Terry laughed. "These people don't know what cold is! They expected two thousand people." He looked toward Tommy and Barbara. "That stupid kid kept forgetting his lines. He began telling the people all kinds of garbage," he said, with a laugh.

Sally smiled and looked at Barbara. "We lost money!" she said. "They didn't make enough to cover the barbecue."

Terry placed his arm around his wife's waist. "Mr. Davidson, it looks like next year everything will be back the way it was." He hugged Sally. "Sally and I volunteer to help next year," he said.

Barbara smiled. "Thank you! Are you sure it's over?" she asked.

Terry smiled. "Mrs. Barkley has already telephoned the Mayor," he answered. "She refuses to have anything more to do with it. The weather is too cold and very few people came." He looked toward the main section of the cemetery. "The re-enactors refuse to come next year. The people that came said it was boring."

Tommy saw Mrs. Barkley walking toward him. Her husband, Ray Sr. was walking behind her. As they walked toward the front gate, Mr. Barkley turned and he walked toward the parking lot. Mrs. Barkley turned toward the front gate and she walked to where Tommy and Barbara were standing. "We're shutting everything down!" she said, as she waved her hands and looked at the parking lot. The lot wasn't full. "I don't understand it. Last year was magnificent! There were people everywhere. We should have made more than ten thousand dollars. We don't have enough money to pay the re-enactors."

Tommy looked startled. "You're paying the re-enactors?" he asked.

"Of course!" she snapped at Tommy. "You don't think these people are doing this for free! Look at this weather. It's cold! They spent hours preparing for their roles." She looked toward the main section of the cemetery. "The costume for Ray Jr. cost three hundred dollars. These people didn't come here for free!"

She looked at Tommy. "It's all yours!" she said. "Do what you like! I wash my hands of the whole affair. The people of this city don't understand the sacrifices these people made. They don't care enough to come and pay five dollars to see and hear history." She turned and began to walk away when Barbara stopped her.

"Mrs. Barkley," Barbara said. "I noticed your perfume. Where did you get it?" she asked.

Mrs. Barkley stopped walking and smiled. "It belonged to my great-grandmother," she answered. She smiled and pointed at her dress. "This was hers. I altered it so it would fit. The perfume has been in my family for many years. It was hers. It is named Midnight Dew."

Barbara smiled slowly. "I had smelled it and I recognized the scent. Is it available? Do you know where I may purchase a bottle?" Barbara asked.

"No. I don't think it is available," Mrs. Barkley answered. "I wore it tonight so I would look and smell the part of Mrs. Harrison."

Barbara lowered her head.

"Take it!" Mrs. Barkley said, as she opened a small, beaded purse. "There is almost a whole bottle and I won't need it." She reached into the purse and removed a small bottle. She handed the bottle to Barbara.

"Are you sure?" Barbara asked puzzled, as she took the bottle.

"I'm sure," Mrs. Barkley answered. "I don't like it! When I wear it, it gives me strange, terrible dreams." Mrs. Barkley made a frown, as she pointed toward the bottle. "When I began preparing for my role, I wore the perfume. I began to have terrible dreams. I don't like it!"

Barbara's eyes widened. "What type of dreams?" she asked quickly.

Mrs. Barkley's eyes narrowed and she lowered her head. "Pain, much pain!" she said softly. She placed her hands on her stomach. "I feel ill. Help me to sit."

Terry reached for a chair and he helped her to sit down. She sat in the chair and moaned softly. Mrs. Barkley looked upward toward Barbara. "The dreams are very strange," she said. "There is a man and his wife. She is pregnant and he brings her several presents." She pointed toward the perfume bottle in Barbara's hand. "He brings her the perfume and this dress and purse."

Mrs. Barkley frowned. "They have many arguments over the money he spent. They are poor and he spent money to purchase these things."

Mrs. Barkley stood slowly. "I feel better," she said. "The pain is gone." She turned toward Terry. "The delivery is very difficult. The baby is breeched. During the delivery, the man refuses to leave the room. The doctor pushes him out of the room."

Mrs. Barkley placed her hands to her stomach. "The pain is horrible! It feels like I am actually giving birth."

Barbara stepped closer to Mrs. Barkley. "When did the dreams start?" she asked softly.

Mrs. Barkley smiled. "They began many years ago," she answered. "They started when I was a young girl. I smelled great-grandmother's perfume and I had the dreams. They began again this week when I smelled it. Each time I smell the perfume, I begin to feel ill. I feel like I am in labor."

She smiled. "Tonight, I will have the dreams again. In my dreams, I am in labor," she added.

"How do the dreams end?" Barbara asked softly.

Mrs. Barkley turned her head. She spoke softly, "The man is pushed out of the room. The doctor tells the woman that the baby is breeched. The woman is in much pain. The man is beating on the door attempting to get in. The dream ends just before the baby is delivered."

"They sound terrible," Sally said.

Mrs. Barkley smiled softly. "No," she answered. "The entire dream is not terrible. There are many beautiful parts. The man in the dream is named Silas. The woman is named Stitch."

Barbara and Tommy looked at each other. They raised their eyebrows.

Mrs. Barkley sat in the chair. "The woman's name is not really Stitch," she said. "That is what Silas calls her. Silas worked in a clothing factory and Stitch was one of the workers. They fell in love and married. There are many beautiful parts. They are poor but they love each other very much." Mrs. Barkley lowered her head. "The only bad part of the dream is the labor. It is very painful! I feel like I am actually in labor."

Barbara leaned closer to Mrs. Barkley. "Is there anyone in your family named Silas?" Barbara asked.

Mrs. Barkley raised her head. Her eyes were beginning to water. "Yes," she said slowly. "My great-grandfather was named Silas. My great-grandmother was named Margaret. She died in labor when she was nineteen. My grandfather, Jonathan, was a breech baby. She died delivering him."

Barbara's eyes widened. She looked at the bottle of perfume in her hand.

Mrs. Barkley lowered her head. "My great-grandfather died when Jonathan was eight," she said sadly. "There was a fire at the clothing factory and he died in the fire. There was no one to care for Jonathan and he was placed at an orphanage." Mrs. Barkley looked upward at Barbara. "Silas never remarried."

Mrs. Barkley slowly turned her head. "Jonathan stayed at the orphanage until he was eighteen. When he left, he started a small clothing business," she said as she lowered her head.

Mrs. Barkley raised her head and laughed, "Jonathan had a lot of nerve!" She looked at Tommy. "When World War I started, he took a train to Washington. He placed a bid with the War Department for uniforms for the soldiers. He won the bid!"

Barbara and Tommy looked at each other. They had never seen Mrs. Barkley laugh.

Mrs. Barkley stood and laughed. "He came home to Memphis," she said smiling. "Jonathan didn't have any workers or sewing machines. In his hand, he held an order for ten thousand uniforms. He went to the poorest section of Memphis for workers. Jonathan made them a deal. If they helped him, he would double their pay when he was paid."

"He borrowed money to purchase sewing machines and he placed them in the worker's homes. He delivered the cloth and he taught them how to sew. When the uniforms were delivered, Jonathan received an order for twenty thousand more. He paid the workers triple their pay."

Mrs. Barkley sat in the chair. "That is where the family fortune started," she said softly. "Jonathan made uniforms for the soldiers. He received contracts for World War I and World War II."

"He met my grandmother, Elizabeth, at one of his factories." Mrs. Barkley lowered her head. "She was poor but he loved her. Jonathan never forgot that he was raised in an orphanage and his parents were poor. Jonathan never forgot the poor. He gave them jobs and he paid them well," she added.

Mrs. Barkley looked upward. There were tears in her eyes.

Barbara smiled. "Mrs. Barkley do you know what your great-grandmother looked like?" she asked.

"No," Mrs. Barkley answered. "Silas and Margaret were not wealthy. There are no photographs of either one. My grandfather obtained his mother's dress, purse and perfume. They have been in my family for many years."

Mrs. Barkley stood slowly. "My father inherited Jonathan's business and he sold everything," she said sadly. "He placed the money in stocks. He was not interested in defense contracts."

Barbara smiled. "Mrs. Barkley, I can't accept this perfume. It is a reminder of your great-grandmother."

Mrs. Barkley reached for Barbara's hand. She smiled, as she held to Barbara's hand. "Silas loved me very much and I loved him," she said. "It was a mistake to yell at him for purchasing the perfume. When I was giving birth, he was yelling to come into the room."

Barbara's eyes widened. "Mrs. Barkley!" she said surprised.

Tommy, Terry, and Sally stared at Mrs. Barkley. She looked like she was in a trance.

Mrs. Barkley smiled. "You keep the perfume. It reminds me of the argument we had. I was wearing it when I was in labor. You keep it!" she said, as she patted Barbara's hand. "I have my memories of Silas."

Barbara slowly pulled her hand from Mrs. Barkley. Mrs. Barkley smiled as she placed her hands on her stomach. "The dreams will come tonight," she said softly. "They are wonderful dreams! They end just before the baby is born."

Mrs. Barkley smiled. "Mr. Davidson, I owe you an apology," she said softly. "I owe them an apology," she said, as she pointed toward the pauper's section of the cemetery. "I had forgotten what it is like to be poor. I had forgotten how much love people can have if they only have each other."

Mrs. Barkley smiled curtly, turned, and walked quickly away.

"That was strange," Terry said, as he placed his arm around his wife's waist.

Tommy smiled at Barbara. "What are you going to do with the perfume?" he asked. "Is it a scent Brad will like?"

"It's not for Brad, it's for me," Barbara said smiling as she placed the small bottle in her purse.

"You got visitors," Sally said, as she pointed toward the pauper's section.

Terry hugged his wife. "Showtime!" he said smiling.

Tommy and Barbara looked to the poor section. There was a man and a woman walking through the gates. They left Terry and Sally and walked quickly to the gates.

"Thank you for coming," Tommy smiled, as he stopped the man and woman.

The man and woman stopped walking and looked at Tommy and Barbara.

"This was the original City Cemetery," Barbara said, smiling. "It was built in the year 1822." She pointed toward the iron gates. "The gates were made in New York and placed here when it was built. The stone walls were carefully crafted by artisans of Irish descent."

Tommy smiled. "An epidemic of cholera occurred in 1823 and the epidemic mainly affected the poor. As the poor were buried here, the wealthy refused to be buried here." He pointed toward the rear of the cemetery. "Several wealthy families had been buried here but their remains were exhumed and buried there," he said, as he pointed toward the main section of the cemetery.

As Tommy and Barbara were speaking, several people walked toward the gates to listen. Others in the cemetery saw the crowd at the gates and walked to join them. Tommy smiled as more than thirty people came to the gates to listen.

"This section of the cemetery is known as Potter's Field," Barbara said. "It was named after the field purchased by the thirty pieces of silver Judas returned to the Pharisees. It is also called the Field of Blood as the money used to purchase the field was the blood money of an innocent man."

Tommy smiled. "Judas returned the thirty pieces of silver because he did not know what he had done. The Pharisees refused to touch it. The money was used to purchase land to bury dead Gentiles and people who were unknown," he said. "The land purchased had been used by the potters. They dug the clay to make pottery. The land purchased was named the Potter's Field. It was a place for the unknown and forgotten and those considered of no value."

Barbara pointed toward the main section of the cemetery. "When the poor and the unknown began to be buried here, the wealthy families expanded the cemetery," she said. "They refused to be buried near the poor." She pointed toward the gates and the stone wall. "Everything remained."

"Follow me," Tommy said, as he turned. "There are graves near the back where it is believed several soldiers from World War I are buried. The bodies were exhumed from graves in France and returned." He turned and looked at the crowd. The number of people had increased. There were more than fifty people standing and listening. Tommy stopped and walked to stand beside Barbara. "They were buried here because the bodies were so decomposed they could not be identified. No one knew who they were," he continued.

Tommy looked toward the main section of the cemetery. Many people were walking toward the parking lot when they noticed the crowd at the pauper's section. They stopped and began walking toward the crowd. Tommy waited until the people came to the gates. He quickly counted about seventy people.

"Not everyone buried here was poor," Barbara said. She pointed toward her left. "Near the wall a family of five is buried. They were believed to be wealthy."

One of the men in the crowd raised his hand. "Are these the people the Indians killed?" he asked. "The young boy portraying Captain English said there was an Indian attack."

Barbara smiled. "No," she answered. "This family died many years after the alleged Indian attack. They were murdered in 1862. They died by being shot."

The man raised his hand again. "How do you know they weren't poor and murdered by Indians?" he asked.

Barbara answered, "All we know is that they were headed south. They were found near their wagon. They had been shot and everything of value was taken."

The man raised his hand again. "How do you know they were not poor if everything was taken?" he asked with a grin.

Barbara smiled as she leaned toward the people in the crowd. "Everything was taken but one thing! Whoever murdered them left one thing," she answered. She looked at the man who asked the question. "The family had a piano in the wagon. It was busted up. Whoever murdered them attempted to take the piano. Poor people didn't own large wagons or own a piano. Indians weren't in this area in 1862. It is believed the family was from Ohio. They came south to escape the war."

The man nodded his head.

A woman raised her hand. "How come these people are unknown?" she asked.

Tommy smiled. "The records of this section of the cemetery were well kept until the main section was built. Then, the people in charge didn't bother to record the information," he answered. "If a person wasn't known, they were buried here. No attempt was made to discover who they were. Many of the old records don't even record if the person buried was a man, woman, or child. The year they were buried is not recorded." Tommy pointed toward the wall where the family of five was buried. "The record shows a man and woman and three children. The man's age was listed as thirty and the woman's age was listed at thirty. There was a young boy age ten and a young girl age eight. An infant child is also listed as age one. The infant child was female. The record shows they were buried in 1862."

Tommy looked at the crowd. It had increased in size. Many people in the cemetery had seen the crowd and walked to the gates to listen.

Barbara smiled and she spoke loudly, "The most famous person buried here was Blackjack Calhoun! He was a riverboat gambler caught cheating. He was shot in the head as he was picking up his winnings." Barbara pointed toward the rear of the cemetery. "The people in the city didn't want him buried with the good folks. He was buried here in the poor section."

Tommy smiled. "When his friends heard about him being buried here, they came at night and exhumed him." Tommy pointed toward the main section of the cemetery. "They exchanged bodies! Blackjack Calhoun is buried somewhere in the main section and whoever he replaced was buried here."

Several of the people began looking at their maps. "That's not on the tour!" one man remarked.

A man in the crowd laughed, "That's the best damn story I have heard all night!"

"How do you know this?" one woman asked.

Barbara laughed. "His friends waited two years before telling anyone what they did. Blackjack's grave was dug up. It wasn't him," she answered.

Tommy laughed. "Blackjack was buried in his gambling best. The local newspaper covered the story and described how he was put away. A deck of cards was placed on his chest. A newspaper reporter witnessed the burial. The story was intended as a lesson to anyone that gambled," he said.

Barbara laughed. "When they exhumed Blackjack's body, there were no cards on his chest. Blackjack was buried in a plain pine box. The casket in the grave was made of metal." Barbara started laughing. "Inside the metal casket was a woman!" she said, laughing.

The people in the crowd began laughing.

"What did they do?" one man asked.

Tommy smiled. "They refused to dig up any of the women in the main section and they refused to allow a woman of quality and breeding to remain here. She was moved to the main section and buried toward the rear. There is a monument that reads - *A WOMAN OF NOBLE CHARACTER IS BURIED HERE*," he answered.

The people laughed.

"Did they ever discover who the woman was?" a man asked.

"No," Barbara said, "there are several theories." She smiled as she pointed toward Tommy.

Tommy laughed. "One theory is that Blackjack Calhoun is buried beside Mayor James Harrison. The woman buried in his place was the Mayor's wife Caroline Brown Harrison," he said.

The people laughed.

"Did they ever discover where Blackjack was buried?" a woman asked.

"No. No one knows," Barbara answered. "His friends didn't tell. All we know is that Blackjack was buried here. When his body was exhumed, it wasn't there. A woman was buried in his place."

"What happened to Blackjack's grave? Where is it?" a man asked, as he looked at his map.

Tommy had a serious look on his face. "It remained empty until 1922. There was an influenza epidemic in the city and many people died," he said sadly. "The poor were buried here. They used the empty grave of Blackjack."

Many people moaned.

Barbara looked at the crowd. It had increased. It looked like about one hundred people.

"Anybody else buried here that was famous?" a woman asked.

Barbara laughed as she turned to look at Tommy. "Should I tell them?" she asked Tommy.

"Yes!" Tommy answered. "There is a story that one of the most famous people in history is buried here." Tommy turned and pointed toward the cemetery. "It's only a rumor and most people don't believe it."

"Who is it?" a man asked.

Barbara laughed. "It's only a rumor and most people don't believe it. No one has been able to prove it," she said. Barbara pointed toward the back of the cemetery. "There are several graves that were unmarked. At one time, there was a marker on one of the graves."

Tommy smiled. "A drifter came into town and he got killed in a saloon fight. The story is that the man shot six men before someone shot him in the back," he said, as he turned toward Barbara.

Barbara smiled. "No one knew who he was and he was buried here. A few days after he was buried, a man came into town looking for him. The man he was looking for fit the description of the man killed in the saloon fight." Barbara smiled and looked at Tommy. "Should we finish the story?" she asked. "It's only a rumor."

"Finish it!" a young boy standing near the front shouted.

The people in the crowd began to laugh.

Tommy shrugged his shoulders and he looked at the crowd. "It's only a rumor," he said.

"Finish it!" several people in the crowd, shouted.

"Who is it?" one man asked.

Barbara smiled. "OK," she said. "It's only a rumor and there is no basis of fact. The man who was killed had a stone placed on his grave. The year was 1827. His friend placed the stone. When people saw the name, rumors began to fly."

Barbara laughed. "People came from all over the state to visit the grave. They came from as far away as Kentucky and Ohio," she added.

Tommy laughed. "The townspeople got tired of the questions so they removed the stone. We don't know where he is actually buried. There were several unmarked graves and his was one of them," Tommy said laughing.

Barbara smiled. "Are you ready for the name?" she asked the crowd. "It's only a rumor! There is no basis in fact!"

"Who is it?" the young boy near the front shouted.

The people in the crowd laughed.

"Are you ready?" Tommy asked the crowd.

The people in the crowd laughed.

Tommy turned toward the back of the cemetery and pointed. "In 1827 there was a tombstone in this cemetery that read," he said as he turned and pointed at Barbara.

"Are you ready for the name?" Barbara shouted.

"Were ready!" several people in the crowd shouted.

Barbara smiled. "It's only a rumor!" she yelled.

The people in the crowd were very quiet.

Barbara closed her eyes. "Daniel Boone!" she shouted.

"Daniel Boone!" the young boy in the front shouted. "He's buried here?"

Tommy laughed. "It's only a rumor!" he yelled.

"Daniel Boone is buried here!" several people in the crowd said.

One man looked at his map. "This isn't on the list of stops!" he said angrily.

Tommy laughed. "Do you want to hear the rest of the story about Daniel Boone?" Tommy asked.

"There's more?" a woman asked.

"Much more," Barbara said smiling, "and it concerns the Mayor's wife Caroline Brown Harrison."

"What about her?" a man in the crowd yelled. "Tell us!"

Tommy smiled. He looked at the crowd. It had increased in size. He could see people in the main section of the cemetery walking toward the large crowd. They had heard the laughter and they were walking toward the gates. Tommy waved his hands toward the people. "Hurry up or you'll miss the story!" he yelled. The people walking toward the crowd began to walk quickly. Tommy waited for them to join the large crowd of people at the gates of the pauper's section.

"This is good!" one of the men in the crowd told the people that joined them.

"After the first Mayor died," Tommy continued, "it was discovered that the cousin of one of the wealthiest families in town had been buried here by accident. Mrs. Caroline Brown Harrison was furious! She ordered that the poor section of the cemetery be purged of anyone of wealth, fine breeding, and importance."

"The cemetery was checked for any possibility of a mistake," he added.

"Several graves were moved," Barbara said. "But there was a problem."

Tommy pointed toward the rear of the cemetery. "There were four graves that they were not certain about," he said. "Mrs. Caroline Brown Harrison had a problem. She didn't want to bury poor people in the main section but she didn't want a person of wealth, fine breeding, or importance buried beside the poor."

Barbara smiled. "It took her several days to make her decision. She decided it was more important to bury four poor people among the wealthy, well bred, and important than to have one good person buried beside many of the poor. The four graves were moved to the main cemetery," she said.

"Was Daniel Boone one of the four?" a young boy asked.

"No," Tommy answered.

"What?" a man asked.

Barbara reached into her coat pocket. She smiled, as she removed a newspaper from her pocket. "Mrs. Caroline Brown Harrison was asked about moving the grave of Daniel Boone. She was interviewed by a reporter for the local newspaper *The Republic*. This was her answer," Barbara said. She looked at the paper. "And I quote from the newspaper." 'Question - Mrs. Harrison do you plan to exhume the body of Daniel Boone and move it to the main section. Answer – The main section of the cemetery is for those people of wealth, fine breeding, and importance. It is unfortunate that Mr. Boone did not have those qualities. Mr. Boone is where he belongs! His remains will not be moved.'

Many people in the crowd moaned.

Barbara smiled. "There's more!" she said, excitedly.

Tommy looked at the crowd. It had increased in size as more people came to listen. "The story gets very involved at this point. It involves the Mayor, the death of two policemen, and the most sensational trial in the cities history," he said.

Barbara smiled. "It also involves Mrs. Caroline Brown Harrison," she added.

"What did the witch do?" a man in the crowd yelled.

The people in the crowd began to laugh.

Barbara and Tommy laughed.

Tommy smiled. "To hide the mistake of the cousin of one of the wealthiest families being buried here, she ordered the destruction of all records of the poor cemetery. Mr. George Nelson, the county clerk, heard about her plan and he made a duplicate set of records," he said.

Tommy pointed toward Barbara.

"Mrs. Caroline Brown Harrison ordered the Chief of Police to confiscate and destroy the records," Barbara said. "In case you haven't guessed it, Mrs. Caroline Brown Harrison was very wealthy. She controlled the police department."

Barbara pointed toward Tommy.

"Several policemen confiscated the records. However, they confiscated the duplicate set. Mr. Nelson hid the original records," Tommy said smiling. "He took them to the current Mayor as the first Mayor had died."

Barbara smiled. "Mrs. Caroline Brown Harrison ordered the police to take the records from the Mayor and destroy them. Several policemen went to the Mayor's home," she said.

Barbara leaned forward toward the crowd as her eyes widened. "The Mayor greeted the police at his front door with a double-barreled shotgun," she said, as she waved her hands.

The people in the crowd made an awe sound.

"The Mayor refused to give the police the records. When they attempted to storm his home, he killed two of them on the front porch of his house," Barbara added.

Many people in the crowd gasped.

Barbara leaned forward toward the crowd. "Mrs. Caroline Brown Harrison ordered the Governor to send the militia to burn the home of the Mayor and arrest him for murder," she said.

The people in the crowd gasped.

Tommy leaned forward. "The Governor sent the militia to the Mayor's home," he said.

Barbara leaned forward toward the crowd and she placed her hands on her hips. "In case you haven't guessed it, Mrs. Caroline Brown Harrison controlled the Governor," she said.

Many people in the crowd gasped.

Tommy continued, "The Governor sent the militia to the home of the Mayor and he was arrested for murder."

Barbara stood straight and smiled. "Then, began the most sensational murder trial in the history of the city," she said. "The newspapers ran many headlines concerning the case."

"One headline read – *Police killed as corruption discovered in the Mayor's office*," Tommy said smiling.

"One headline read – *Mayor prevents two policemen from fulfilling their duty*," Barbara said smiling.

"One headline read – *Mayor murders two policemen in cold blood*," Tommy said frowning.

Barbara placed her hands on her hips and she leaned toward the crowd. "In case you haven't guessed it, Mrs. Caroline Brown Harrison controlled the local newspapers," Barbara said laughing.

The people in the crowd made an awing sound.

Tommy waved his hands in the air. "The murder trial was sensational!" he yelled. "The widows of the two policemen were called to the stand. The children of the two policemen were called to the stand. The trial lasted three weeks and people made claims of corruption in the Mayor's office and told stories of how they witnessed the Mayor kill the two policemen in cold blood."

"The jury was handpicked by Mrs. Caroline Brown Harrison and was composed of some of the wealthiest and most influential people in the city."

"For three weeks, the prosecution and the defense presented their cases," Tommy added.

Barbara smiled. "The jury left the courtroom to consider all of the facts in the case. They walked to the jury room, entered, and then closed the door," she said.

Barbara pointed toward Tommy.

Tommy smiled. He spoke softly, "Then the door opened and the jury walked out. In their hands, they held their verdict, Guilty of All Charges!"

Barbara leaned forward toward the crowd and placed her hands on her hips. "In case you haven't guessed it, Mrs.

Caroline Brown Harrison controlled the judge and the jury!" she said loudly.

The people in the crowd made an awe sound.

Tommy laughed. "Then, the biggest surprise happened! Something happened that no one expected!" he shouted.

A woman standing in the crowd pushed her way forward toward Tommy. "What happened?" she asked Tommy excitedly.

The people in the crowd laughed.

Barbara leaned forward toward the woman. "Everyday of the trial, a man came to the courtroom. He sat behind the Mayor. He sat exactly behind the Mayor. It was hot but he wore a long coat," she whispered.

Tommy leaned forward toward the woman. "He arrived before the court began and he left after everyone had left," he whispered. "He sat behind the Mayor. He sat exactly behind the Mayor. It was hot but he wore a long coat. He came to court everyday of the three weeks. He sat exactly behind the Mayor."

Barbara leaned upward toward the crowd. "He was waiting for the verdict!" she whispered. "He came to court everyday and he sat behind the Mayor. He sat exactly behind the Mayor. It was hot but he wore a long coat. He came before the court began and he left after everyone had left."

Tommy turned quickly and he walked to a cardboard box that was sitting on the ground. He quickly pulled several items out of the box and he returned to stand beside Barbara. He was wearing a long, dark coat.

"Did the coat look like this one?" Tommy asked, as he looked at Barbara.

The people in the crowd laughed.

"Yes!" Barbara answered, laughing. "He also wore a big hat. He wore it to the courtroom and he removed it and placed it on his lap."

"Like this one?" Tommy asked. He had placed a big hat on his head.

The people in the crowd laughed.

"Yes!" Barbara answered. "He came every day to the court. He arrived before everyone came and he left after everyone had left. It was hot but he wore a long coat. He wore a big black hat and he removed it and placed it on his lap."

Tommy stood straight. "When the verdict was read, the man that sat exactly behind the Mayor reached into the pocket of his long coat and he pulled something out of the long inside pocket of his coat," he said.

"Who was it? What did he do?" the woman, near the front, asked.

The people in the crowd laughed.

Barbara leaned forward toward the crowd and she spoke softly, "He came everyday to the court. He was waiting for the verdict! He sat exactly behind the Mayor. It was hot but he wore a long coat. He sat exactly behind the Mayor and he placed his hat on his lap. He came before court started and he didn't leave until everyone left. He was waiting for the verdict."

Many people in the crowd leaned forward to listen.

Tommy smiled. "When the jury returned a guilty verdict, the judge approved it and sentenced the Mayor to death by hanging for the cold-blooded murder of two policemen whom he killed as they attempted to uncover corruption in the Mayor's office," he said, with a grin on his face. "When the man heard the verdict, he reached into the inside pocket of his coat and he removed..." Tommy stopped speaking.

The people in the crowd were quiet.

"What was in the pocket?" the woman, near the front asked.

The people in the crowd laughed.

"He removed a long sheet of paper and wrote on it," Tommy answered. "Then he stood and he addressed the court."

Tommy removed a long piece of paper from the inside of his coat. He acted like he wrote something on it, then he held the long paper upward and he read from the paper, "I am saddened by the recent events that resulted in the deaths of two police officers. I am saddened that these two police officers leave widows and children. I am further saddened that Mayor

Brian James has been found guilty of their deaths and sentenced to death. I am appreciative of the efforts the jury made to reach a sound and honest verdict. However, I am also saddened that I believe a miscarriage of justice has occurred. After reviewing all evidence in this case, I am convinced that Mayor Brian James is not guilty for the crimes he was charged and convicted of."

"As Governor of the state and by the power vested in me by the Constitution of the United States of America and the Constitution of this state, I officially pardon Mayor Brian James of the murder of these two men and any other crimes he may be charged with in this incident."

The people in the crowd began to yell and cheer. Many in the crowd clapped their hands.

Tommy laughed. "The man in the courtroom was sent by the Governor! In his pocket was the pardon! He was waiting for the verdict to be given," he yelled.

Barbara laughed. "The story is that the Governor signed the pardon before the trial began. The only thing missing was the date! The man was waiting for the verdict so he could write the date," she said. She laughed very hard and then pointed toward Tommy.

The people in the crowd cheered.

Tommy smiled. "He also had these under the long coat." Tommy pushed the sides of the long coat backward to reveal twin holsters and guns. He reached for the guns and quickly pulled them from their holsters. Tommy held the two guns upward and spun them in his hands. "Colt forty-four double-action revolvers!" Tommy yelled loudly.

The people in the crowd gasped and moved backward. Then, the people in the crowd cheered.

"The man in the courtroom was Robert Galloway!" Barbara shouted. "He was the roughest, toughest lawman to ever walk the streets of the city." Barbara leaned toward the crowd. "Robert Galloway was a Texas Ranger! The Governor of Texas sent Robert Galloway to Memphis at the request of the

Governor. The Governor gave him four orders." She held her right hand upward and raised one finger. "Order number one!" she shouted.

Tommy spun the two guns in his hands. "Protect the Mayor at all cost!" he yelled.

Barbara held two fingers upward. "Order number two!" she shouted.

Tommy spun the two guns in his hands. "Shoot first and ask questions later!" he yelled.

Barbara held three fingers upward. "Order number three!" she shouted.

Tommy spun the two guns in his hands. "Reload as many times as you have to!" he yelled.

The people in the crowd laughed.

Barbara began laughing. She laughed very hard. Then, she raised four fingers in the air. "Order number four!" she shouted, as she laughed very hard.

Tommy stopped spinning the two guns. "Get the Mayor and leave very quickly!" he yelled.

"Wait one minute!" Barbara shouted. "Are you sure those were the Governor's exact words?" she asked Tommy, laughing.

The people in the crowd laughed.

"Close enough!" Tommy answered, as he spun the two guns in his hands. "I think everybody gets the idea," he laughed.

The people in the crowd laughed.

Tommy spun the two guns and replaced them in their holsters. He reached for his hat and he removed it. "Everyday Robert Galloway came to the courtroom. He arrived before anyone else and he removed his hat and he placed it on his lap. Under his hat he held this," Tommy said, as he removed a third pistol from the hat. "He held a third Colt forty-four double-action revolver. It was cocked and Robert Galloway kept his finger on the trigger."

The people in the crowd took a deep breath.

Tommy smiled as he cocked the pistol. "The Governor ordered Robert Galloway to protect the Mayor at all cost," he said. "When the verdict was read, he was to sign the date on the pardon and present the pardon to the court. Then, he was to make sure the Mayor was safely returned to his home. His orders were to shoot to kill anyone that may attempt to harm the Mayor or stop them from leaving."

Many people in the crowd yelled and clapped.

"Did he kill anybody?" the young boy near the front of the crowd asked.

The people in the crowd laughed.

Barbara raised her hands to quiet the crowd. "As Robert Galloway and the Mayor were leaving the courthouse, four policemen were standing at the bottom of the steps waiting for them. As the policemen pulled their guns, Robert Galloway fired both guns. He killed all four of them on the steps of the courthouse. One policeman was shot four times in his heart. When the policeman's body was examined, there was only one bullet hole in his heart," she answered.

Many people in the crowd gasped.

"He missed?" the young boy in the crowd asked. "A Texas Ranger missed?"

"Hell No!" a man in the crowd yelled. "All four bullets went into the same hole!"

"Wow!" the young boy yelled.

The people in the crowd laughed and cheered.

"Robert Galloway didn't kill four policemen!" the man in the crowd yelled.

The people in the crowd stopped cheering. They turned to the man who had yelled twice. The man was elderly. He was wearing a khaki colored cloth flop hat and a matching khaki colored jacket. The man had a short white beard and he held a cane in his left hand. "Robert Galloway didn't kill four policemen, he killed six!" the man yelled.

The people in the crowd looked at the man.

"Robert Galloway killed four policemen on the steps of the courthouse as the policemen attempted to murder Brian James," the elderly man told the people in the crowd. "Robert Galloway led Brian away from the courthouse to where a carriage was waiting."

The elderly man looked at the young boy near the front. "Two policemen followed them," he said. "As they were getting into the carriage, the two policemen drew their guns. Robert Galloway shot both of them before they could raise their guns." The elderly man placed his right index finger to his forehead. "He shot both of them between their eyes!"

The young boy's eyes widened. "Wow!" he yelled.

Tommy waved his hands at the elderly man. "We have a rare treat," Tommy yelled to the people in the crowd. "The man that just spoke is Mr. Herbert Redkin. Mr. Redkin is a local historian. He knows more about the city than anyone."

The people in the crowd clapped and Mr. Redkin bowed to the crowd. "I am sorry I arrived late," Mr. Redkin said. "I just arrived as you began telling the story of Robert Galloway." He looked at the people in the crowd. "Everything they said is true!" Mr. Redkin yelled. "Everything is verifiable at the archives of the city. I can personally vouch for the story on Jonathan Harding and his wife Elizabeth."

"Who are they?" a woman in the crowd asked.

Mr. Redkin looked toward Tommy and Barbara. "You didn't tell them the secret of the cemetery?" he asked surprised.

"What secret?" a man asked.

A man looked at his map. "Jonathan and Elizabeth Harding are buried in the main section of the cemetery," he said.

"No they are not!" Mr. Redkin said. He pointed toward the rear of the cemetery. "They are buried here!"

Tommy blushed. He lowered his head slightly as he looked at Mr. Redkin. "That is only a rumor," Tommy said. "We did not tell them the story because it is a rumor."

"It is not a rumor!" Mr. Redkin answered. "It is fact!" He turned and looked at the people in the crowd. "Do you want me to tell you the story of Jonathan Harding? It is the best kept secret of the cemetery."

"Yes!" many people in the crowd answered.

Barbara motioned for Mr. Redkin to come forward. He walked through the people in the crowd to stand beside Barbara and Tommy. Mr. Redkin looked at the people in the crowd. "Jonathan Harding was the richest man to ever live in the city," he said. "By today's standards, he was worth an estimated billion dollars."

The people in the crowd gasped.

"Jonathan Harding was raised in an orphanage. At the age of eighteen he started a small clothing business. He obtained orders from the Department of Defense to make uniforms for the soldiers," he said grinning.

The people in the crowd moved closer to listen.

Mr. Redkin grinned. "Jonathan placed a bid with the War Department when World War I began. He won the bid. Jonathan had no workers or equipment to make the uniforms," he said. Mr. Redkin leaned toward the people in the crowd. "He went to the poorest section of Memphis for workers. He made them a deal!"

The people in the crowd listened intently.

Mr. Redkin continued, "If they would help him, he would double their pay when he was paid. Jonathan borrowed money to purchase cloth and sewing machines. He placed the sewing machines in the homes of the workers and he taught them how to sew. It took several months to complete the order. When Jonathan delivered the ten thousand uniforms, he had missed the deadline for delivery."

Many people in the crowd made an awe sound.

Mr. Redkin looked at Tommy and Barbara. "Representatives of the Defense Department were so impressed by the quality of the uniforms; they altered the delivery date on the contract. Jonathan was awarded a contract for an additional twenty thousand uniforms," he said grinning.

The people in the crowd cheered.

"Jonathan broke his deal with his workers," he added.

"What?" a man in the crowd asked.

Mr. Redkin raised his hands. "He gave them triple their pay and awarded the workers stock in his company," he yelled.

The people in the crowd cheered.

Mr. Redkin motioned for the people in the crowd to quiet down. The people in the crowd stopped cheering and listened intently.

"Jonathan met Elizabeth at one of his factories. She was poor but he loved her very much," he said. "Jonathan never forgot that he was raised in an orphanage. He never forgot the poor. He gave them jobs and he paid them very well. Jonathan provided healthcare for them. He provided a pension for the elderly."

Many people in the crowd made an awe sound.

"Jonathan gave his wealth to his workers as compensation for their hard work," he said, smiling. "The more he gave them, the more he received."

Mr. Redkin lowered his head and he looked upward toward the crowd. "Jonathan and Elizabeth were shunned by the wealthy in the city. The wealthy would have nothing to do with them."

"Jonathan and Elizabeth's wealth was equal to Firestone and Ford. He could buy and sell every one of them!" he yelled. "But they would have nothing to do with them. Jonathan and Elizabeth could build the largest, grandiose home in Memphis instead; they chose to live in a two bedroom house on Baker Street."

Mr. Redkin snickered to himself, "A multi-millionaire, and a billionaire living in a two bedroom house on Baker Street."

He smiled to the people in the crowd. The people in the crowd were silent. They listened to every word he was saying.

"Jonathan and Elizabeth's dinner guests were not the wealthy of the city," he said. "Jonathan and Elizabeth's dinner guests included Martha, who made button holes and Agnes, who cut the cloth for the pants."

Mr. Redkin suddenly laughed. He laughed very hard. "Agnes Farnsworth!" he shouted.

The people in the crowd looked intently at Mr. Redkin.

"Agnes Farnsworth smiled when Jonathan and Elizabeth presented her with the annual Christmas bonus. She received cash, a large ham, and a brown envelope. The brown envelope contained documents that listed the number of shares of stock Jonathan and Elizabeth had given her."

Mr. Redkin grinned. "Jonathan and Elizabeth were very generous. Agnes Farnsworth received a very nice Christmas bonus. She received ten dollars in cash, a ham, and stock that had a value of two million dollars."

"What?" a man in the crowd yelled. "Jonathan gave Agnes two million dollars? Did he give all of his employees the same?" he asked.

"Yes," Mr. Redkin answered. "Jonathan and Elizabeth treated all of their employees the same. They rewarded their hard work and dedication." He chuckled. "The grandson of Jessie Burgess was surprised to learn that his grandfather had stock. Jessie had been dead many years before the business was sold. Jessie swept the floors. Jessie picked up the shards of cloth and he cleaned the sewing machines. Jessie's stock was worth two million dollars."

"Lies! Lies! Damn Lies!" a woman shouted from the crowd.

The people in the crowd turned to look at a woman standing near the light post at the gates. The people in the crowd could see her clearly from the light. She was middle-aged wearing a mink coat with a matching mink hat. She was glaring at Mr. Redkin.

"Charlene!" Mr. Redkin said excitedly. "I didn't know you were here! You look wonderful! New coat? New hat? How was Paris? Can you make lunch next Wednesday?" he asked grinning.

Charlene began to push her way toward Mr. Redkin. Her eyes were glaring at him as she pushed her way through the people in the crowd toward him.

A man near Barbara leaned toward her. "Is this a part of the show?" he whispered.

Barbara's eyes were widely opened. Tommy heard the man's question and he leaned toward the man. "Mr. Redkin comes every year and tells stories. I have never seen this woman. I don't know who she is," he answered quietly.

"I do!" the man answered. "That's Charlene Cannon. She and her husband are developing land west of the State Line Road. She is one of the wealthiest people in the city. Her money is old money!"

Tommy and Barbara looked at each other. Their eyes were widely opened as Charlene pushed her way toward them.

"Lies all lies!" Charlene yelled as she approached Mr. Redkin. She glared at him and then turned toward the crowd. "Jessie Burgess never worked for Jonathan and Elizabeth! He made his money selling cars! Jessie had one of the first Ford dealerships in town," she yelled to the people in the crowd.

Mr. Redkin smiled at Charlene.

"His picture is on the wall of the dealership," she yelled. "I buy a new Ford every year from Scott Burgess. Scott is an honest man! If you want a good deal, see Scott. My new Ford came equipped with leather seats and stereo speakers. Scott gave me the cruise control because I buy from him every year."

"Charlene, you sound like a commercial," Mr. Redkin said laughing.

Many people in the crowd laughed nervously. They didn't know what was going on.

Charlene looked at Mr. Redkin. Her eyes were filled with anger.

She turned toward the crowd. "Jessie's picture is on the wall of the dealership!" Charlene yelled. "If you don't believe me, visit the dealership. Ask for Scott. He will show you the picture."

Mr. Redkin smiled. "Ah yes," he said, "The famous picture with Jessie standing beside a 1924 Ford. In his hands, he is holding a piece of paper."

Charlene turned and looked at Mr. Redkin.

Mr. Redkin laughed. "Charlene, there are several photographs of people standing beside the same car," he said. "The car belonged to General Paul Hatton."

The people in the crowd whispered to each other.

"Folks! Folks!" Mr. Redkin yelled, as he held up his hands. "The car belonged to General Paul Hatton. He came to visit Jonathan's factory and present certificates of appreciation to the workers from the Department of the Army."

"It was a holiday!" he added. "Jonathan closed the factory and ordered food for a picnic. Many of the workers had never seen a new car and Elizabeth arranged for a photographer to take their picture standing beside the car. In their hands they are holding the certificate of appreciation."

"It is not!" Charlene yelled.

Mr. Redkin laughed. "When did the owner of a car dealership come to work wearing overalls?" he asked Charlene.

The people in the crowd laughed.

Charlene turned to look at the people in the crowd. She glared at them. When the people in the crowd saw her eyes, they quit laughing. "He was wearing the overalls because he was proud of the car," she answered. "It was the first delivery! He was washing it!"

Mr. Redkin laughed very hard. He slapped his hand against his pants leg. "Charlene, my dear!" he said laughing. "When did Ford Motor Company deliver new cars with U.S. Army printed on the side?"

Charlene became angry. "I'm warning you Herbert!" she yelled as she shook her hand toward Mr. Redkin.

The people in the crowd moved backward.

Mr. Redkin laughed, "Charlene, I haven't said anything about your great-grandmother. If I remember correctly, she worked for Jonathan and Elizabeth more than ten years. She made lapels!"

Many people in the crowd made an awing sound.

"What was her stock worth?" Mr. Redkin asked. "Five, ten million?"

The people in the crowd made an awe sound.

Charlene turned quickly toward the crowd. She pushed her way through the people in the crowd toward the gates. As she neared the light post, Mr. Redkin yelled, "Lunch Wednesday! I'll have my people call your people!"

Charlene turned quickly toward Mr. Redkin when she heard his comment. By the light of the light post, the people in the crowd could see her face. She was very angry. She raised her right hand and pointed her middle finger toward Mr. Redkin.

Mr. Redkin laughed, as Charlene stormed her way toward the parking lot. "She is really a very nice person once you get to know her," Mr. Redkin remarked.

The people in the crowd were quiet.

"Where was I?" Mr. Redkin asked himself. He placed his right hand to his chin and he shrugged his shoulders. "Jonathan's friends were the poor," he said to the people in the crowd.

The people in the crowd were very quiet. They weren't sure what they had seen and heard. Everyone knew Scott Burgess! He owned the Ford dealership. The dealership had been passed down from father to son. Scott made silly television commercials to sell cars. Many of the people looked at each other. It was part of the show.

The man that asked Barbara the question was Hamilton Andrews. Hamilton stood beside Barbara listening to Mr. Redkin. He met Mrs. Cannon several times as they worked on a land development deal. Mrs. Cannon was always prim and proper. No one, he knew, called her Charlene. Everyone called her Mrs. Cannon. Mr. Redkin seemed to know her very well as Mrs. Cannon called him Herbert. He shrugged his shoulders. 'Part of the show," he thought.

Tommy looked thoughtful. He recognized the name, Agnes Farnsworth. Tommy remembered the name from one of the markers. He lightly tapped Barbara on her shoulder. "I'm going to check on something. I will only be gone a few minutes," he whispered.

Barbara nodded her head as Tommy removed a flashlight from his coat pocket. He turned and walked slowly toward the north wall.

He walked toward the wall, pointing the light toward the markers. Most of the markers read UNKNOWN. Tommy found the marker he was looking for. It was newer than most. The marker was made of white marble. He pointed the flashlight beam on the marker. AGNES MARION FARNSWORTH BORN 1877 DIED 1945, it read.

Tommy looked thoughtful. He had never heard of Agnes before. Mr. Redkin never mentioned her. He turned the flashlight off and he looked toward the crowd. Mr. Redkin was speaking. The people in the crowd were silent.

"Have you seen my goat? The farmer asked the young boy. The goat is chained to a log!" Jonathan said laughing.

Agnes laughed. "That is a terrible joke, Jonathan," she said.

"He only knows six jokes," Elizabeth said. Elizabeth laughed and then she turned toward the sewing machine. The sewing machine made a whirring sound as she pressed the foot pedal.

"I can't fix it here," Jessie said, as he looked at Jonathan. "The bar on the ballast is bent. I will need to machine a new part." Jessie turned to look at Agnes. "It may take a few days but I can fix it."

Agnes sipped her hot apple cider. "This one you brought me looks and sounds good. Take as much time as you need," she answered.

"You should reconsider," Jonathan said to Agnes. "Your pension is more than enough to live on."

Agnes nodded her head. "There will be enough time to rest when it is all over," she answered. She sipped her hot cider and smiled. "Jonathan, tell me again?"

Jonathan smiled. "The battle began December 16 and the fighting has been intense. We are slowly winning the Battle of the Bulge. The German Army is being pushed back!" he said, as he leaned toward Agnes.

Elizabeth smiled. "We wanted you to be the first to know! We are visiting everyone to tell them the good news," she said, as she continued to sew.

Agnes slowly stood. She took the basket from the floor and placed it on the small table. She removed the ham and the brown envelope. Agnes smiled as she placed the brown envelope on the bookcase. She turned to Jonathan and smiled. "This is the best day of my life!" she sighed. "I don't know how long it has been since I have enjoyed such good company." She looked at Elizabeth. "We all thought the last war would end the problems. Perhaps this one will settle much. I couldn't think of a better Christmas present than the good news. Perhaps, it will soon be over."

Agnes walked to her chair and she sat. She sipped the hot cider and laughed and joked with Jonathan, Elizabeth, Jessie, and her son, James. They talked for several hours. It was daylight as Elizabeth completed the sewing.

Agnes walked to the stack of flight jackets. "Excellent!" she said, as she looked at the linings of the pockets. "Double stitched!"

Elizabeth smiled as she hugged Agnes. Jonathan hugged Agnes as he put on his coat. "Merry Christmas!" Jonathan said, as he helped Elizabeth with her coat. "We have others to see."

"This has been a good day!" Agnes said, as she opened the door. She looked outside. The snow had fallen and the ground was a brilliant white. "It will soon be over," she said, as she hugged Elizabeth one last time.

"This has been the best day of my life!" Agnes said, as she waved goodbye to Jonathan and Elizabeth. She slowly closed the door as the flashes of white appeared before her. The flashes were bright and intense.

"Have you seen my goat? The farmer asked the young boy. The goat is chained to a log!" Jonathan said laughing.

Agnes laughed. "That is a terrible joke, Jonathan," she said.

"He only knows six jokes," Elizabeth said. Elizabeth laughed and then she turned toward the sewing machine. The sewing machine made a whirring sound as she pressed the foot pedal.

"I can't fix it here," Jessie said, as he looked at Jonathan. "The bar on the ballast is bent. I will need to machine a new part." Jessie turned to look at Agnes. "It may take a few days but I can fix it."

Agnes sipped her hot apple cider. "This one you brought me looks and sounds good. Take as much time as you need," she answered.

"You should reconsider," Jonathan said to Agnes. "Your pension is more than enough to live on."

Agnes nodded her head. "There will be enough time to rest when it is all over," she answered. She sipped her hot cider and smiled. "Jonathan, tell me again?"

Jonathan smiled. "The battle began December 16 and the fighting has been intense. We are slowly winning the Battle of the Bulge. The German Army is being pushed back!" he said, as he leaned toward Agnes.

Elizabeth smiled. "We wanted you to be the first to know! We are visiting everyone to tell them the good news," she said, as she continued to sew.

Agnes slowly stood. She took the basket from the floor and placed it on the small table. She removed the ham and the brown envelope. Agnes smiled as she placed the brown envelope on the bookcase. She turned to Jonathan and smiled. "This is the best day of my life!" she sighed. "I don't know how long it has been since I have enjoyed such good company." She looked at Elizabeth. "We all thought the last war would end the problems. Perhaps this one will settle much. I couldn't think of a better Christmas present than the good news. Perhaps, it will soon be over."

Agnes walked to her chair and she sat. She sipped the hot cider and laughed and joked with Jonathan, Elizabeth, Jessie, and her son, James. They talked for several hours. It was daylight as Elizabeth completed the sewing.

Agnes walked to the stack of flight jackets. "Excellent!" she said, as she looked at the linings of the pockets. "Double stitched!"

Elizabeth smiled as she hugged Agnes. Jonathan hugged Agnes as he put on his coat. "Merry Christmas!" Jonathan said, as he helped Elizabeth with her coat. "We have others to see."

"This has been a good day!" Agnes said, as she opened the door. She looked outside. The snow had fallen and the ground was a brilliant white. "It will soon be over," she said, as she hugged Elizabeth one last time.

"This has been the best day of my life!" Agnes said, as she waved goodbye to Jonathan and Elizabeth. She slowly closed the door as the flashes of white appeared before her. The flashes were bright and intense.

Tommy stood thinking. He turned his flashlight on and pointed the beam to markers near Agnes' marker. The markers read, UNKNOWN. He pointed the beam to Agnes' marker. AGNES MARION FARNSWORTH BORN 1877 DIED 1945, the marker read.

Agnes walked to the stack of flight jackets. "Excellent!" she said, as she looked at the linings of the pockets. "Double stitched!"

Elizabeth smiled as she hugged Agnes. Jonathan hugged Agnes as he put on his coat. "Merry Christmas!" Jonathan said, as he helped Elizabeth with her coat. "We have others to see."

"This has been a good day!" Agnes said, as she opened the door. She looked outside. The snow had fallen and the ground

was a brilliant white. "It will soon be over," she said, as she hugged Elizabeth one last time.

"This has been the best day of my life!" Agnes said, as she waved goodbye to Jonathan and Elizabeth. She slowly closed the door as the flashes of white appeared before her. The flashes were bright and intense.

"Have you seen my goat? The farmer asked the young boy. The goat is chained to a log!" Jonathan said laughing.

Agnes laughed. "That is a terrible joke, Jonathan," she said.

Tommy turned the flashlight off. He had been told a story that Jonathan and Elizabeth Harding were exhumed from the main section of the cemetery and buried near the graves of several of their workers, in the pauper's section. He didn't believe the story as it made no sense. "Why would a person of wealth be buried among the poor?" he asked himself. The grave of Agnes Farnsworth was the only grave, in this section, with a name and date. The marker was newer than the others; it appeared to have been placed about twenty years ago. Before the City Council approved the markers, only three graves in this section had markers. There were two markers that read, UNKNOWN, and the marker for Agnes Farnsworth. He remembered her marker because it was the only one with a name.

Tommy turned the flashlight on and he pointed the beam to the left of Agnes' marker. There were two graves that were empty. 'A mystery!" he thought to himself. The two empty graves were purchased about twenty years ago. The names of the two people, which are planned for burial, are being kept a secret. No one knows who will be buried here. Tommy shrugged his shoulders, turned the flashlight off, and he walked quickly to where Barbara and Mr. Redkin were standing. The people in the crowd were quiet as they listened to him speak.

Mr. Redkin laughed. "One Christmas, it snowed! Jonathan and Elizabeth visited every home in the poor section. He brought the children toys and he delivered food to the families."

"Jonathan made the poor wealthy. He rewarded their hard work and dedication," he added.

Mr. Redkin smiled at the crowd. "Jonathan and Elizabeth had character and morals," he yelled to the crowd. "One day, before World War II began, he received a large package from Germany. In the package was a contract for thirty thousand uniforms and sample uniforms. The contract was double the usual cost and it was approved by Adolph Hitler."

"What?" a man in the crowd asked.

The people in the crowd made an awe sound.

"Jonathan was angry," Mr. Redkin continued. "He tore up the contract and he burned the sample uniforms. Several months later, Jonathan learned that several representatives of Germany were coming to visit him. They wanted to tour his factory and learn how he made such excellent uniforms."

"Jonathan closed the factory! He paid his workers for the days the factory was closed. He had the windows painted black and large chains were placed on the doors. Jonathan was afraid! He was afraid the representatives would learn his secret. He was afraid the representatives would see his secret on the wall of the factory or speak to one of his workers. He was afraid one of his workers would inadvertently reveal his secret."

Barbara became very excited. She placed her hand on Mr. Redkin's shoulder. "I have never heard this part," she said excited. "What was on the wall of the factory? What was Jonathan's secret?" she asked.

Tommy was excited. "I haven't heard this part either. What was it?" he asked.

Mr. Redkin smiled softly. "The plant was closed for two weeks," he answered. "During those two weeks, Jonathan paid his workers. The representatives from Germany came every day to find the plant closed. They attempted to locate Jonathan but no one knew where he lived. After two weeks, the representatives returned to Germany. Jonathan reopened the plant." Mr. Redkin shrugged his shoulders. "The black paint was scraped from the windows and work continued. On the wall of the plant was a sign. It was Jonathan's secret of making the best uniforms in the world. It was the same sign he placed in the homes of his workers when he received his first order. Jonathan's workers looked at the sign as they made the uniforms."

Mr. Redkin smiled at Tommy and Barbara. "Jonathan's secret was a simple one," he said. He looked at the crowd. The people in the crowd were listening very intently. "The sign was only two sentences. The sign read WE DON'T MAKE UNIFORMS FOR SOLDIERS. WE MAKE UNIFORMS FOR HEROES!"

"Jonathan's secret was not in the cloth or the machines. It was in the patriotism of his workers," he said softly.

The people in the crowd were silent. Then, they began to clap very softly.

Mr. Redkin looked at Tommy and Barbara. "The representatives from Germany couldn't locate Jonathan because he lived in a very modest home. When he died he was buried in the main section of the cemetery. When Elizabeth died, she was buried beside him. Several months after Elizabeth was buried, their bodies were exhumed and buried here," he said as he pointed toward the rear of the pauper's cemetery.

"Why?" a woman in the crowd asked.

Mr. Redkin smiled softly. "Jonathan and Elizabeth wanted to rest beside the people they loved. They were buried in the rear. There is a simple headstone that reads, UNKNOWN," he answered.

Tommy raised his hands in the air. "It is only a rumor!" he shouted.

"It is not a rumor," Mr. Redkin answered. "My grandfather helped to move Jonathan and Elizabeth. He showed me the graves. I know where they are buried."

A man looked at his map. "This isn't on the list of stops," he said. He looked at Mr. Redkin. "Are you saying the graves of Jonathan and Elizabeth Harding are empty?"

"Yes!" Mr. Redkin answered. He pointed toward the rear of the cemetery. "They are buried in graves with a simple headstone that reads, UNKNOWN."

A woman leaned forward toward Mr. Redkin. "Why did they do this? Were they eccentric?" she asked.

"No," Mr. Redkin answered. "Jonathan and Elizabeth were not eccentric. They were good people who remembered where their wealth came from. They wanted to be buried among the people they cared for and loved."

Several of the women in the crowd began to weep softly.

"Why do the headstones read UNKNOWN?" a man in the crowd asked.

Mr. Redkin smiled. "Jonathan and Elizabeth were very religious. Jonathan had no desire to be buried under a large monument. God knows where he and Elizabeth are resting. God knows their names," he said softly.

"Why have we never heard of them?" a woman in the crowd asked.

Mr. Redkin smiled softly. "Jonathan's son inherited the business and he sold everything," he said. "The bulk of Jonathan's fortune went to the workers as Jonathan had given them stock. The poor suddenly became very wealthy." He raised his hands in the air and waved them. "The rich today were the poor of yesterday. The wealthy don't talk about him because it reminds them that they were very poor. Jonathan shared his wealth with the unfortunate. The rich today refuse to share what their grandparents and great-grandparents earned."

The people in the crowd were silent.

"How do you know this?" a woman in the crowd asked.

Mr. Redkin smiled softly. "My great-grandparents and my grandfather worked for Jonathan and Elizabeth," he answered. "Jessie Burgess did more than sweep the floor. He and my great-grandfather visited the factories of Jonathan twice a week. They oiled the sewing machines and repaired them." Mr. Redkin lowered his head. "They slept at the factory."

The people in the crowd were silent.

Mr. Redkin raised his head and smiled. "Only fifty people worked at the main factory!" he yelled. "Agnes Farnsworth worked in her home. She lived in a two-room shack. She was sixty-two years old and she worked twelve to fourteen hours a day seven days a week."

Mr. Redkin raised his cane in the air. "America was at War!" he screamed. "While the wealthy of the city were having their parties and their dances, the poor of the city were making uniforms for heroes!" he yelled. "Jessie Burgess delivered cloth to the homes! He repaired the sewing machines and he kept them running!"

The people in the crowd were silent.

Mr. Redkin lowered his head. He looked at the crowd and smiled softly. "You don't need to ask Scott to see his great-grandfather's picture. You can see it yourself," he said, as he raised his eyebrows. "The next time you have your tires rotated and balanced, walk to the service area. The picture isn't difficult to see! It is at the back near the grease pit where they lubricate the wheel bearings. It is taped to the wall beside the calendar of the semi-naked woman. It is above the water fountain that doesn't work."

He smiled. "The picture is faded as it is not in a frame. Jessie is smiling proudly. In his hands, he holds a certificate of appreciation. The certificate was presented to him by General Hatton," he said slowly.

The people in the crowd were silent.

"Agnes Farnsworth!" Mr. Redkin yelled. "She couldn't read! None of Jonathan's workers could read or write. They couldn't read the sign on the plant wall or the sign in their homes. They knew what the sign read but they couldn't read it. When Jonathan visited her home to deliver her Christmas bonus, she couldn't read the information in the brown envelope." Mr. Redkin waved his hand in the air. "Agnes placed it with the others. When World War II started, Agnes continued to work. She was older and she had health problems but she worked as best she could."

Mr. Redkin raised his cane in the air. "When the American soldiers stormed Normandy Beach many were wearing uniforms made by Agnes!" he yelled.

"When the sailors battled at Coral Sea many were wearing uniforms made by Agnes, Sharon, Robert, John, and seventy others!" he shouted.

The people in the crowd were silent.

"December 24, 1944!" Mr. Redkin yelled. "At 11:00 P.M., the wealthy of the city were having their annual Christmas dance and dinner. Jessie Burgess was at the home of Agnes Farnsworth. The pedal on the sewing machine was damaged! He couldn't repair it! Jessie and my great-grandfather had to return to the plant to replace it!"

"Mr. Redkin lowered his head. "It snowed that day," he said as he raised his head. He looked at the people in the crowd. "The snow wasn't deep but it took Jessie more than two hours to make the trip. When he returned to Agnes' home, Jonathan and Elizabeth were with him."

The people in the crowd were silent.

Mr. Redkin adjusted his cane. He moved it from his left hand to his right hand. "Jonathan and Elizabeth believed Agnes was working too hard. While Jonathan and Jessie sat and talked to Agnes, Elizabeth continued her work. Elizabeth laughed and joked with Agnes as she prepared the linings for the pockets," Mr. Redkin said softly. "Every one of Jonathan's workers was cross-trained. Agnes was sewing the lining of the pockets on the flight jackets. The flight jackets would keep the heroes warm as they flew in the bombers."

He laughed. "Imagine a multi-millionaire, a billionaire spending Christmas morning in a two-room dump!" he said. "While the wealthy of the city were returning to their homes in the wee morning hours, the wife of a billionaire was sitting in front of a sewing machine sewing pocket linings."

The people in the crowd were silent.

"Agnes Farnsworth!" Mr. Redkin yelled. "Jonathan paid her well for her work! She made enough money to move from the two-room dump she lived in but she didn't! She didn't spend it on herself. She used the money to purchase cloth and thread! She worked many hours she did not report!"

The people in the crowd were silent.

Mr. Redkin smiled at the crowd. "Jonathan's workers were illiterate. They never had anything. They made enough money to move but they didn't! They used their pay to purchase cloth and thread. They worked hours they did not report!"

The people in the crowd were silent.

"Agnes Farnsworth!" Mr. Redkin yelled. "When she died, no one noticed the large stack of brown envelopes she had placed on her bookcase. There was only one book on her bookcase, the Bible! Agnes couldn't read but she owned a Bible."

The people in the crowd were silent.

"Agnes Farnsworth!" Mr. Redkin shouted. "When she died, her total assets were three dollars!" He pointed toward the cemetery. "She was buried here!"

The people in the crowd made an awe sound.

"Her brown envelopes were worthless!" Mr. Redkin shouted. "Her brown envelopes were nothing more than a reward for loyalty and devotion!"

"Jonathan and Elizabeth only had one child, their son Franklin. Franklin spent most of his youth at a private school in Mississippi. The school was for children of wealthy parents. He became arrogant at the school. Franklin was embarrassed that his parents did not have a large home with servants. He was ashamed of the old car his father drove and the two-bedroom home on Baker Street."

"Franklin had no interest in the business. He disliked the workers. Many were elderly and every one of them was poor. When Jonathan died, he returned briefly to Memphis for the funeral." Mr. Redkin lowered his head. "Elizabeth died several months after Jonathan died. Franklin quit school and returned to Memphis. The war was over and the work had stopped. The plant was idle."

Mr. Redkin raised his head. "Franklin refused to visit the plant!" he yelled. "It was dirty and many of the workers were elderly. When news of Jonathan and Elizabeth's death reached the major clothing manufacturers in the United States, representatives of the manufacturers descended upon Memphis like vultures. They bid for the remainder of Jonathan's defense contracts. All of the contracts had a clause that allowed a renewal."

"Franklin knew nothing of the business. He decided to sell everything. It was a sad day when the workers were informed of the sale. Franklin requested that the workers come to the main plant. They arrived early. Franklin expected trouble!"

Mr. Redkin looked at the people in the crowd. He removed his hat and wiped his brow. He replaced his hat and continued, "Franklin expected trouble. There were many police present in case of a riot. Two senior partners of the law firm, Clark and Higgins, were present to explain how Franklin could, legally, stop the pensions. A representative of the United States Department of Defense was present to explain how the contracts had been sold to other companies. Franklin was prepared for anything! He expected a riot and possible legal challenges." Mr. Redkin leaned toward the crowd. "He was prepared for anything except sixteen year-old Teresa Barnes," he said smiling.

The people in the crowd began to whisper to each other.

"Franklin was not kind to the workers," Mr. Redkin said. "He criticized their work and quality. He told them it was necessary to sell everything. He told them there was nothing they could do. As owner of the company, he had the legal right to sell everything and he had already signed the papers of sale. Their services were no longer needed. He held a shirt upward toward the workers and he blasted plant number sixteen. He told the workers the quality was below standard and that plant number sixteen had missed production schedules for more than one year."

Mr. Redkin glared angrily at the people in the crowd. "Franklin told the workers there was no severance pay! He told them the pensions would stop immediately!" he yelled. "Franklin told the workers that plant sixteen would receive no pay for the last months work. He would demand that the pay be returned."

The people in the crowd were silent.

Mr. Redkin removed his hat and wiped his brow. He paused to catch his breath. He was very angry.

"One of the senior partners of the law firm Clark and Higgins held upward a piece of paper," Mr. Redkin said softly. "The law firm had filed a legal suit against plant number sixteen for the return of monies paid. If the money was not repaid in ninety days, legal proceedings would begin to recover any and all assets of the workers."

Mr. Redkin grinned. His face lit up in excitement. "It was then that sixteen year-old Teresa Barnes and her twelve year-old brother James stepped forward," he said smiling. "She walked to the partner of the law firm and accepted the legal suit. She then walked to the representative of the United States Department of Defense and, with tears in her eyes, apologized for the poor quality of her work."

Mr. Redkin lowered his head.

"It appears that Teresa's mother had been dead for several years and her father had died the previous year. She and her brother James continued their work. They did the best they could," he said sadly.

The people in the crowd were silent.

Mr. Redkin raised his head. "It was at this time; Teresa opened a cloth purse she was carrying. Inside the purse was a large stack of brown envelopes that had been given to her mother and father. Teresa's mother and father had been told by Elizabeth Harding, in the event the company was sold, they were to locate a representative of the United States Army and present the envelopes."

The people in the crowd began to whisper to each other.

He looked at the people in the crowd and laughed. "The brown envelopes were worth nothing unless the company was sold!" he said laughing with a gleam in his eye. "Jonathan didn't give his workers stock! He made them partners!" he yelled as he held his hands in the air.

The people in the crowd gasped.

"Franklin was surprised to learn that the factories Jonathan owned were not factories, they were the homes of his workers. Jonathan had assigned each home a number. The home of Agnes Farnsworth was plant number six. The home of Teresa Barnes' mother, Eileen Barnes, was plant number sixteen. Jonathan had contracts with the United States, Great Britain, Canada, the Philippines, Australia, and the Netherlands. Franklin believed the factories of Jonathan were located in various countries. He was wrong! The factories were located in the poor section of Memphis. Jonathan didn't own seventy-two factories; they were the homes of his workers!"

Mr. Redkin laughed. He laughed very hard and he slapped his hand against his pants. "Franklin inherited his father's business. He believed the business was worth more than one hundred million dollars!"

"He was Right!" Mr. Redkin shouted, as he held his hands in the air. "Jonathan had contracts with all the allies of World War I and World War II!"

The people in the crowd gasped as they moved backward. They were shocked! They looked at each other and they whispered to each other, then, they clapped very loudly.

Mr. Redkin laughed very hard. "The founder of the law firm Clark and Higgins was Nathan Clark. Nathan Clark had personally prepared the documents and signed every one of them," he laughed. "The documents in the brown envelopes stated that in the event the company was sold, in addition to the partners sharing equally in the sale of the company's contracts, all cash assets would be divided equally among Jonathan's partners. If the partner was deceased, their share would go to their heirs. Only the partners, living and deceased would share the cash assets. The owner would not be included."

Mr. Redkin stopped laughing. He looked at the people in the crowd with a serious look on his face. "Franklin didn't care," he said, as he shrugged his shoulders. "There was more than enough money to go around. The company had no cash to speak of! When Elizabeth died, Franklin searched for any cash his parents had. Franklin located less than twenty-five thousand dollars in cash. Jonathan's company had less than ten thousand dollars in the bank. The bulk of the cash was discovered in a safe located in Jonathan's office at the main plant. He discovered a lock box in his parent's home. The lock box contained more than thirty thousand dollars in cash. The money in the lock box was his parent's savings."

Mr. Redkin nodded his head and looked upward. "The money was in the contracts Franklin had sold and the value of the plant and property," he said slowly. "Franklin had already signed the papers for sale when he realized he would receive less than ten percent of the sale price. The tax for sale and inheritance came from his share!"

"The legal suit against plant number sixteen was quickly and quietly dismissed. The law firm of Clark and Higgins represented the partners. Their fee was high but it came from Franklin's share."

The people in the crowd were quiet.

Mr. Redkin shrugged his shoulders. "Franklin was in a hurry to get his money! He did not care that the workers would divide the twenty-five thousand dollars. It was chicken feed! Franklin's share of the sold contracts and the plant and property was worth millions! He was in a hurry to get everything over with."

"The law firm of Clark and Higgins was also in a hurry to get everything over with. Senior partners argued before the court that the documents prepared by Nathan Clark were exact! The word cash meant cash! Franklin was in the process of selling the plant and the property. As the owner, Franklin had the legal right to sell and the partners would receive no share of the property. The documents only mentioned the contracts and cash assets related to the company. The cash Franklin found in his parent's home was not to be included. Only the partners living would receive an equal share of the sale of the contracts. The documents specifically mentioned the living and deceased partners as sharing equally in all cash assets."

Mr. Redkin leaned toward the people in the crowd and grinned. His eyes were widely opened and he chuckled, "The court agreed with the law firm! Only the living partners would share in the sale of the contracts. The sale of the plant and property were not included as cash assets."

Mr. Redkin smiled. "Cash was defined as cash. The cash found in the home of Jonathan and Elizabeth was their money and not the property of the company. Jonathan's safe contained two hundred dollars in war bonds that had matured. The senior partners argued that the matured bonds were not a cash asset. The bonds were an investment. Jonathan had purchased each dollar bond for fifty cents. The bonds were an investment! They were not cash assets!"

"The court disagreed! Negotiable stocks and bonds are a cash asset because they hold a cash value and could be liquidated within a twenty-four hour period. The two hundred dollars in matured war bonds would be divided equally among the partners and the heirs of the deceased partners."

The people in the crowd moaned.

"What a screw job!" a man in the crowd yelled. "The lawyers attempted to take the two hundred dollars."

The people in the crowd looked at the man that yelled and nodded their heads.

"I am an investment banker!" a man in the crowd yelled. "Bonds are considered a cash asset because they have a cash value. It doesn't matter if they have matured or not."

The people in the crowd turned to look at the man that yelled.

"There was a famous case in Memphis in the late 1940's where people inherited matured war bonds," the man yelled to the crowd. "A lower court ruled the matured bonds were a cash asset. The plaintiff argued that the matured bonds were an investment. The court's ruling was appealed! The case went to the State Supreme Court and the lower court's ruling was upheld. The case was Harding versus …" The man stopped speaking. His eyes were widely opened as he looked at Mr. Redkin. Mr. Redkin nodded and grinned at the man.

The man grinned and he laughed. "Sorry for interrupting," the man said. He grinned and moved closer toward Mr. Redkin to listen.

The people in the crowd smiled and turned to look at Mr. Redkin.

Mr. Redkin smiled softly. He lowered his head slightly and looked at the crowd. "The senior partners wanted the court to handle the disbursements of cash assets. As a law firm, their fee to the partners and the heirs of the deceased partners, would take most of the company's cash. It was the duty of the court to account for and equally divide all cash assets."

Mr. Redkin spoke softly, "The court quickly agreed."

The people in the crowd began to whisper among themselves. A woman leaned toward Mr. Redkin. "Something is not right!" she yelled. "They screwed those poor people over!"

Many people in the crowd began to get angry. "Damn lawyers and judges!" one man yelled.

"They twisted the words on the documents!" a lady yelled. She turned and looked at the people in the crowd. "Any damn fool can see they twisted the words!"

The people in the crowd nodded their heads in agreement. The people in the crowd were angry.

Mr. Redkin held his hands upward to calm the crowd. The people in the crowd began to calm down.

"Judge Randolph Jackson was appointed by the court to oversee the disbursement of any and all cash assets," Mr.

Redkin said sadly. “Judge Jackson was called the Hanging Judge,” he laughed. “The story is if Judge Jackson believed you were guilty he would hang you. If he didn’t think you were dead enough, he would have you shot and hang you again. Everyone was afraid of Judge Randolph Jackson! Judge Jackson issued a court order for Franklin and all of Jonathan’s partners to bring to his court, any cash that was the property of the company. The cash would be counted and divided equally. He arranged for a special court hearing to formally count all cash and divide the cash equally among the partners.“

Mr. Redkin laughed softly to himself.

He looked upward, and smiled, as he searched his memory. Mr. Redkin began to speak softly and slowly. The people in the crowd moved closer to listen. He began to describe things, strange things. “It rained Tuesday,” he said softly. “It was summer and the rain was warm. The rain fell softly as it cleaned the dust from the road and the trees. It stopped near midnight, as the workers of Jonathan and Elizabeth gathered at the home of Robert Sanders.” Mr. Redkin paused and he looked upward. “They began the eight mile walk to the courthouse at 2:30 A.M. The rain softened the dirt, in the road, just enough to feel good on bare feet. Small puddles were to the sides and it felt good to wade through them. As they neared the home of Mr. Hollis Taylor, they could smell the honeysuckle. A large row of wild honeysuckle grew beside his fence. The rain made everything smell fresh and clean. The honeysuckle smell gave sweetness to the fresh air.”

Mr. Redkin talked strangely! He described things so vividly and exactly that the people in the crowd could visualize, in their minds, what he was saying. Not only could they visualize what Mr. Redkin was saying, they were there! They were there as the events unfolded! They relaxed and listened as the words and phrases of Mr. Redkin carried them backward, in time, to a place and an event.

3:12 A.M. – April 23, 1947

Mr. Hollis Taylor didn't walk too well. He waited at his house for the workers of Mr. Jonathan to come get him. Mr. Burns brought his mule and wagon. They used the wagon to carry the women and the very elderly. Mr. Thomas and Mr. Bruce helped Mr. Hollis in the wagon and they continued to walk to town. They walked more than seven miles before they had to stop and leave the wagon; it wasn't allowed in the town. Mr. Jacob's son, Sam, watched the wagon. He would wait until they returned.

The town was quiet as they walked the remaining one mile to the courthouse. At 5:00 A.M., the streets of the city were deserted. The rain had washed the streets and the buildings clean. There was a smell of bread from a bakery located near Booker Street. As they approached Adams Street, they could see the courthouse. Many of Jonathan's workers had never seen the courthouse. They gasped as they looked at the huge building with the six statues. The statues were twelve feet tall and cut from white marble. They adorned the facade facing Adams Street.

To the eyes of the young, they were taller than twelve feet, the statues appeared as giants!

The rain had washed them clean and in the early morning, the rising sun caused the six statues to appear lifelike. One statue was Wisdom, with the head bowed. Justice was of a woman, who held a bowl in each hand and a sword was to her side. A blindfold covered her eyes. Authority appeared gigantic with large muscles. Two statues held harps in their hands, Liberty and Peace. Prosperity had water and fruit flowing from within.

As the workers of Jonathan Harding walked up the steps to the courthouse doors, they marveled at the six statues and the immense building before them. The rain had washed the stone walls and steps clean! Jonathan's workers walked up the steps looking at the statues. When they approached the doors, they were locked. They waited until 7:00 A.M. for the doors to open, then, they walked up three flights of stairs to the courtroom of Judge Randolph Jackson. The hallway was very long with many windows facing the statues. Along the walls were many wooden benches. One section of the hallway had been recently painted. The smell of paint was in the hallway.

Jonathan's son, Franklin, arrived in the long hallway close to 8:00 A.M. Jonathan's workers attempted to speak to him but he refused to talk to them. Robert Sanders attempted to speak to Franklin several times but Franklin would not speak. He walked quickly into the courtroom, slamming the door as he closed it.

The special hearing began promptly at 8:00 A.M. The court clerk watched the clock on the wall as the second hand slowly moved to the 12. The time was 8:00 A.M. The court clerk stood and faced the people in the courtroom. "Hear Ye! Hear Ye! Please rise for the Honorable Judge Randolph Jackson. All those having business before the court and interested persons rise!" he yelled.

The people in the courtroom stood as the door to the judge's chambers quickly opened and Judge Jackson walked quickly into the courtroom. He was impressive! Judge Jackson was more than six feet tall and weighed two hundred pounds. His head was balding with a small amount of hair to the sides of his head. His face was clean shaven except for a long handlebar moustache that he kept waxed with pointed ends. Judge Jackson walked quickly to his bench and sat in his chair.

The people in the courtroom sat down.

The court clerk approached the bench and placed a packet of papers in front of the judge. "This is docket 198256, disbursement of cash assets from the liquidation of the company Harding and Associates," he said quietly.

Judge Jackson leaned backward in his chair. He reached into his robe and removed a small knife and a long twist of tobacco. He used the knife to cut the tobacco and he placed a large piece in his mouth. "Swear them in!"

The clerk asked everyone to stand and raise their right hand. The people in the courtroom were sworn in and then asked to sit.

Judge Jackson opened the packet and he began reading the contents. He looked at several forms and reached for a large mug on his bench. He spit into the mug and looked upward. The courtroom was filled with many people. Most of the people were elderly and poorly dressed. He looked at the table in front of him where Franklin Harding was sitting; he was dressed very nicely. As Judge Jackson looked at the people in the courtroom, he noticed an elderly lady sitting in the back row. He quickly stood and walked to the elderly lady.

As he approached the elderly lady he smiled. "Mrs. Mayo, how are you?" he asked with a grin on his face.

Mrs. Mayo started to stand.

Judge Jackson leaned toward her and raised his hands. "Don't stand! You just sit and rest. There is no need for you to stand in my court!" he said. "Is there anything I can get you? Would you like some water, coffee, or lemonade?"

"I'm fine," Mrs. Mayo answered, as she slowly sat on the bench.

"How is your son Eugene?" Judge Jackson asked.

"Fine," Mrs. Mayo answered. "He's a good boy. He hasn't been in any trouble since that night. That night was a mistake."

Judge Jackson stood upward. "Eugene is a good boy and a fine man! That night was a mistake but he learned from it. I noticed on the list that he still worked for Mr. Jonathan Harding. Has he found work?" Judge Jackson asked.

Mrs. Mayo lowered her head. "No," she answered softly. She looked at the people in the courtroom. "Were all looking but we have not found anything."

Judge Jackson nodded his head. "I'll ask around. Eugene is a fine man. If there is something available, I'll send word," he said.

Mrs. Mayo nodded her head. Judge Jackson turned and walked toward his bench. As he neared the bench, Mrs. Mayo spoke, "Randolph!"

The court clerk was sitting in a chair near the bench when he heard Mrs. Mayo call the Judge, 'Randolph." He quickly stood and pointed toward Mrs. Mayo and he started to speak. Judge Jackson saw him stand and motioned for him to sit. The court clerk quickly sat in his chair.

Judge Jackson turned slowly and walked to Mrs. Mayo. He leaned toward her. "Mrs. Mayo, do you have a question?" he asked.

Mrs. Mayo looked upward. "Randolph, are they going to take our pensions?" she asked. "If they do, we have no money to live on. The plant is closed and there is no work."

Judge Jackson leaned upward and he looked at the people in the courtroom. "That question is still being decided," he answered. "The law is specific in many cases but there are situations where many things must be considered. Judge Lawrence Brown has the question under advisement. Whatever he decides, we must accept." He looked at Mrs. Mayo. "The money you will receive today will help." He turned slowly and walked to his bench and sat down. Judge Jackson spit in the mug and nodded to the court clerk.

The court clerk stood and motioned for Franklin to stand. Franklin stood and handed documents to the clerk. "Judge," he said. "These documents were prepared by the law firm of Clark and Higgins."

Judge Jackson quickly interrupted Franklin. "My name is not Judge," he said. He leaned forward and spit in the mug. "Mr. Harding, you will respect this court and this court's proceedings. You will address me as Judge Jackson or Your Honor."

Franklin looked at the court clerk and the court clerk nodded. Franklin looked downward then he looked backward toward Mrs. Mayo.

Judge Jackson looked at Franklin as he looked toward Mrs. Mayo. "Mr. Harding is there a problem?" he asked, as he spit in the mug.

Franklin turned toward Judge Jackson. "No Your Honor," he answered, quietly.

Judge Jackson leaned forward and waved his hand toward Franklin. "Continue," he said.

Franklin looked at the documents in the clerk's hand. "Your Honor the law firm of Clark and Higgins prepared these documents. I concede that the documents are accurate and valid. I concede that the cash assets of my father's company are to be divided equally among his partners. I concede that only the partners living," he turned and looked at Mrs. Mayo, "and working at the time the company was sold, will share in the profits of the sale of the defense contracts."

He looked at the court clerk and he handed him an additional sheet of paper. "The law firm and I disagree that the matured war bonds are a cash asset. They are investments," he added, smiling.

Judge Jackson leaned forward. "Another court has ruled that the war bonds, in question, are not investments," he answered. "The documents clearly refer to cash assets. Bonds hold a cash value and they can be liquidated within a twenty-four hour period."

Franklin shrugged his shoulders, "Your Honor, we respectfully disagree," he said grinning.

Judge Jackson leaned forward and spit in the mug. "Mr. Harding, do you know what cash is?" he asked, as he reached into his pants pocket. He removed a one-dollar bill and held it upward toward Franklin. "I can take this piece of paper to any bank and get any combination of coins." He pointed toward a table in the courtroom that held the contents of the safe in Jonathan's plant and the cash from the company's liquidated bank account. "I can take those matured war bonds to any bank and get any combination of coins." He placed the one-dollar bill on his bench and spit into the mug.

Franklin shrugged his shoulders. "Your Honor, we respectfully disagree," he said grinning.

Judge Jackson leaned forward and he held his hand outward toward Franklin. "Mr. Harding, hand me the appeal," he said.

Franklin looked toward the clerk and he narrowed his eyes. "Your Honor, there is no appeal," he answered.

Judge Jackson placed the one-dollar bill in his pocket and spit in the mug. "Mr. Harding you have the constitutional right to disagree with a court's ruling and the legal right to appeal that ruling," he said, as he leaned backward in his chair. "If there is no appeal, the court will continue with the proceedings at hand. The company of Harding and Associates has been liquidated! Everyone is in agreement to the terms of the liquidation. The purpose of this court hearing is to account for the cash assets of the company and those cash assets will be divided equally among the people who worked for the company. If the person is deceased, their share will be given to their heirs."

Franklin sat down in his chair.

Judge Jackson looked toward the courtroom. "Are the workers and their heirs or a representative of the workers or the heirs present?" he asked the court clerk.

The court clerk nodded his head. "There is someone here for each person listed as workers," he answered.

Judge Jackson looked toward the courtroom. "Where are they?" he asked. "There are only a few people here."

The court clerk held upward a list. "The courtroom is too small to hold all of them," he answered. He looked toward the doors of the courtroom. "They are in the hallway. I have their names. When they are called to receive their share, they will come into the courtroom."

Judge Jackson nodded his head. He reached into his mouth and removed the tobacco and dropped it into the waste basket beside his chair. He then reached for the knife on the bench and cut a piece of the twist of tobacco. "Continue," he said, as he placed the cut of tobacco in his mouth.

The court clerk looked at two men sitting beside the table that held the combined cash and the war bonds. One of the two men stood. "Your Honor, I represent the accounting firm of Nichols, Chambers, and Locke," he said. He held upward a sheet of paper. "We have accounted the cash from the bank account of Harding and Associates and the contents of the safe located in the main plant." He walked toward the judge's bench and handed the list to Judge Jackson.

Judge Jackson looked at the list. "Mr. Harding is this all the cash assets of the company?" he asked Franklin.

Franklin stood. "Your honor, there was cash in my parent's home but the court has ruled that it was their money," he answered.

Judge Jackson was reading the list and he looked upward toward Franklin. "Mr. Harding I am aware of Judge Brown's ruling concerning the cash located in your parent's home," he said irritated. "I just asked if this was all of the cash assets of the company."

Franklin looked at the two accountants. "Your Honor, they have accounted for everything I found," he said, as he shrugged his shoulders. "The documents prepared by the law firm of Clark and Higgins, verifies what was found and turned over to the court."

Judge Jackson leaned backward in his chair. He looked at Franklin and the table where Franklin sat. Franklin was the only person sitting at the table. "Where are the representatives of the law firm?" he asked.

Franklin smiled and shrugged his shoulders. "Your Honor, they are busy," he answered smiling.

Judge Jackson leaned forward and spit into the mug. "Busy?" he asked. "Busy doing what?"

Franklin grinned. "Your Honor, they are completing the sale of the plant and property," he answered with a grin on his face. "This is a simple hearing. Everyone has agreed to the terms."

Judge Jackson looked at the table that held the contents of Jonathan's safe. He could see a stack of paper bills, various silver and copper coins, gold coins, and a small stack of war bonds. Beside the money he could see several pencils, a paper weight, envelopes, and various small items. "What are those things?" Judge Jackson asked as he pointed toward the table.

"Your Honor, I was ordered by the court to bring all cash assets to court today," Franklin answered. "I was in a hurry! So I put everything from my father's company safe in a box. There are pencils, envelopes, and some junk."

Judge Jackson narrowed his eyes as he looked upward. He swiveled his chair to the left and right, then, he turned his chair a complete circle so his back was toward Franklin. "Mr. Harding," Judge Jackson said in an elevated voice, "as the sole heir to your father's company, you have the legal right to sell everything. You have the legal right to sell the plant and property and the defense contracts. I am curious as to why you were in such a hurry you simply dumped the contents of your father's safe in a box and brought it here."

The courtroom was silent.

"Answer the question," the court clerk said.

"Your Honor, if you will look at me, I will answer the question," Franklin answered.

The people in the courtroom whispered.

Judge Jackson slowly turned his chair toward Franklin. He leaned forward in his chair and folded his arms on the bench. "Mr. Harding is this better?" he asked.

"Your Honor, when I was before Judge Brown he always looked at me when he asked a question," Franklin said, as he looked at Judge Jackson with his eyes narrowed. "I am a very wealthy man! I am in the process of selling the plant and property and negotiating the final terms of the sale of the defense contracts. I am very busy!"

Judge Jackson unfolded his arms and leaned backward in his chair. "What was so important that you were so busy you didn't have time to properly and respectfully remove the contents of your father's safe?" he asked.

Franklin stepped from behind the table to walk toward the bench. "Your Honor," he said frowning. "As I told Judge Brown, I didn't make the deal with these people! It was my father's company and he could do as he pleased while he owned it! It's mine now! I decided to sell everything!" He turned and looked at the people in the courtroom. "I don't know them and I don't owe them!" He turned toward Judge Jackson. "I had an appointment to have some suits made. I complied with the court order! I put the contents of the safe in a box and I brought it here."

Judge Jackson narrowed his eyes and he leaned forward. "Mr. Harding are you going to stay for the remainder of the court proceedings or are you too busy to stay?" he asked.

Franklin smiled. "Your Honor, I have fulfilled my obligations to the court," he answered. "In a few days, I will be a very wealthy and important man! I would like to leave because I have an appointment to purchase a new car!"

Judge Jackson spit in the mug. "Mr. Harding everything appears to be in order," he said, as he looked at the documents on his bench. "You have complied with the court order and I am convinced that you have turned over to the court all cash assets of your father's company." He leaned forward and spit in the mug. "Mr. Harding you may leave!"

Franklin nodded and picked up a stack of papers on the table. He smiled at the court clerk and turned to walk toward the doors. As he turned, he spoke softly, "Trash!" He walked quickly toward the closed doors. As he approached the doors, a loud voice boomed out, "Mr. Harding, I didn't hear your last comment!"

Franklin turned quickly to look toward Judge Jackson's bench. Judge Jackson was standing! The bench was raised above the floor almost two feet and Judge Jackson was more than six feet tall. His head almost touched the ceiling. Dressed in his black robe, he looked like a huge park statue. Judge Jackson leaned to his right and he spit into the trash basket beside his chair. "Mr. Harding, I didn't hear your last comment! Would you please repeat it?" he asked in a raised voice.

Franklin's eyes widened. "I didn't say anything," he answered quietly.

Judge Jackson leaned to his right and spit into the trash basket beside his chair. He looked toward the court clerk. "Did Mr. Harding say what I thought I heard him say?" he asked the clerk.

The clerk looked at Judge Jackson. "Trash!" he answered.

Judge Jackson reached into his mouth and he removed the tobacco. He looked to his right and dropped the tobacco into the trash basket. "Mr. Harding is that what you think about your father's workers?" he asked.

Franklin looked at Judge Jackson with a defiant look in his eyes. "Your Honor," he answered arrogantly. "Does it matter what I think? My father didn't care about these people! If he did, he would have left them more than two hundred dollars each." He snickered. "He would have used a better lawyer than Nathan Clark to specify what he left them!"

Judge Jackson narrowed his eyes and cocked his head. "Mr. Harding, Nathan Clark was a fine lawyer and a fine man. He argued before the Supreme Court twice," he answered.

Franklin snickered. "Your Honor, will all due respect, the senior partners of his law firm disagree! The documents were poorly written! He specifically specified that all partners, living and deceased would share equally in all cash assets. He made a mistake! He should have used the same wording on the sale of the defense contracts and the plant and property but he didn't! He is the laughing stock of his company!"

Franklin looked at Jonathan's workers in the courtroom. "They get two hundred dollars and I get millions!" he added.

Judge Jackson leaned forward toward his bench. "Mr. Harding," he said loudly. "Nathan Clark was a brilliant lawyer!" He picked up one of the worker's contracts from his bench and he held it upward toward Franklin. "Nathan Clark was very specific! His use of the word assets was designed to specifically address the war bonds!"

Franklin shrugged his shoulders. "Your Honor, that is debatable," he answered with a defiant look in his eyes. "There are only two hundred dollars in war bonds! Everybody knows an asset includes bonds! Judge Brown was tricked!"

Judge Jackson leaned forward with a puzzled look on his face. "Tricked?" he asked.

Franklin laughed. "Your Honor, the senior law partners tricked Judge Brown into ruling on the validity of the war bonds found in my father's safe. The ruling only covers the bonds found in my father's safe at his plant! The ruling only covers any bonds found on company property! I found lots of bonds in my father's home!" he said laughing.

Judge Jackson was angered.

Franklin laughed. "Your Honor," he giggled, "Judge Brown ruled that what was found in my parent's home was personal property! Anything found on the property of my father's company was to be divided equally among the partners! My father didn't care about these people! If he did, he would have left them the money in his home!"

Judge Jackson was angered. "Mr. Harding your father and mother were very caring and loving," he said quickly.

Franklin laughed. "Your Honor, how do you know? Did you ever meet them?" he asked with a snicker.

Judge Jackson lowered his head. "Mr. Harding you know nothing of your father and mother. I met them only once! I met them here in my courtroom," he said softly.

Franklin quit laughing. "When?" he asked.

Judge Jackson sat in his chair. He took his knife and cut a piece of tobacco from the twist. He placed it in his mouth and leaned forward. "It was two weeks after the invasion of Normandy," he said softly. "Mrs. Mayo's fifteen year-old son, Eugene, worked for Jonathan Harding. He and two of his friends celebrated. They got drunk and rowdy. When they were arrested, Jonathan Harding paid their bail. They were brought before me."

Judge Jackson spit in his mug. "When the three boys were brought before me, Jonathan and Elizabeth Harding were with them. The three boy's mothers were also here. Jonathan Harding asked to speak in their behalf. I allowed it!" Judge Jackson leaned forward and spit in his mug. "Jonathan Harding spoke for almost one hour. Elizabeth Harding spoke for two. They talked about the boy's character and how he worked long hours at their plant."

Judge Jackson leaned forward. "Jonathan and Elizabeth Harding were busy people. The plant ran twenty-four hours a day seven days a week. They weren't too busy to come here. The three boy's fathers were not here, they were busy! One was in North Africa with General Patton. One was in the Philippines with McArthur. One was in the Normandy invasion."

Judge Jackson stood. He spit in his mug. "I let them go! I let all of them go!"

Franklin shrugged his shoulders. "Touching story, Your Honor," Franklin said grinning. "My father and mother never had time for me. When I came home from school they were always working. They attempted to get me interested in the business but the plant was noisy and smelly. The workers were either very old or very young."

Judge Jackson stood looking at Franklin. "Mr. Harding it appears that you are unaware we have just come through a war. Your father's plant ran twenty-four hours a day seven days a week. There were only the elderly and the young because all able-bodied men were at war."

Franklin shrugged his shoulders.

Judge Jackson leaned to his right and spit in the waste basket beside his chair. "Mr. Harding you are a very busy man, you may leave," he said as he sat in his chair.

Franklin turned quickly and walked through the doors into the hallway. The hallway was filled with his father's workers and members of their family. One man approached Franklin as he came through the doors. "Mr. Harding," he said, "I need to speak to you about Mr. Jonathan's deal he made with us."

Franklin stopped and looked at the man. He was elderly and dressed in a white shirt and overalls. The white shirt was starched and pressed. Franklin smiled softly. "I am afraid everything is being taken care of by Judge Randolph Jackson," he said, as he looked toward the closed courtroom doors. "I no longer have anything to do with my father's company." Franklin turned to look at the man. "Judge Jackson will answer any question you have."

The man smiled and held his hand toward Franklin. "It was a pleasure to work with Mr. Jonathan and Miss. Elizabeth," the man said. He held his hand outward to shake Franklin's hand but Franklin did not extend his hand. Franklin looked at the people in the hallway. "I no longer have anything to do with my father and mother's company! Judge Jackson will answer any questions you have," Franklin said. "Judge Jackson is very tall and his head looks like an egg. He is easy to spot as he chews tobacco." Franklin giggled. "Everybody calls Judge Jackson, The Hanging Judge! When you speak to him, call him Hanging Judge." He laughed as he walked down the hallway to the stairway.

Judge Jackson sat quietly in his chair. He looked at the people in the courtroom. They sat quietly with smiles on their faces. They didn't understand what was going on. Franklin was pushing to stop all pensions and it appears, he found money in his parent's home he didn't report. Judge Jackson had already approved the cash assets and Franklin had complied with his court order. He frowned.

"Your Honor," one of the accountants said. "I am ready to read the list of items brought to the court by Franklin Harding."

Judge Jackson looked at the accountant and nodded his head. He looked at the contract Nathan Clark had prepared as the accountant began listing the items. Judge Jackson was concerned. It appears the law firm of Clark and Higgins may have tricked Judge Brown. They placed a smoke screen around the two hundred dollars in matured war bonds to keep from revealing the bonds discovered in Jonathan Harding's home. There was an issue of the worker's pensions and their funding.

He lowered his head as the accountant was completing his list.

"Six pencils, one eraser, seventy-two keys, four paper binders," the accountant said.

Judge Jackson quickly raised his head and looked at the accountant. "Repeat that last item!" he said.

The accountant looked at his list. "Your Honor it is only junk we found in a small box. We listed the items because Mr. Harding brought them. They have no cash value."

"Repeat them," Judge Jackson said.

The accountant shrugged his shoulders. "Four screws, two wooden toothpicks," he said as he read the list, "six pencils, one eraser, seventy-two keys, four paper binders..."

"That's it!" Judge Jackson interrupted, "Keys! Seventy-two keys!" He looked at the accountant. "Where are the keys?"

"They are here, Your Honor," the accountant answered. He reached into a small cardboard box, removed a ring of keys and held the ring upward toward the judge. "They are all numbered from one to seventy-two. The number is stamped into the head of the key."

Judge Jackson was puzzled. He looked at the ring of keys. "What are they for? What do they unlock?" he asked the accountant.

"I don't know," the accountant answered as he shrugged his shoulders.

A young girl sitting in the courtroom stood. In her hand, she held a key. "One of the keys matches this one!" she answered.

Judge Jackson looked at the girl. "What is your name?" he asked.

The young girl smiled. "Your Honor, my name is Teresa Barnes," she answered. "The key with the number sixteen matches this one." She held the key in her hand toward the bench.

The accountant, sitting in the chair, quickly stood. "What does it unlock?" he asked quickly.

Teresa pointed to a large box sitting on the floor pushed under the bench.

The accountant walked quickly to Teresa. He pulled the box from under the bench and held it upward toward the judge. The trunk was made of wood! The dimensions were two feet wide and three feet long. The height was two feet. A large brass lock kept the lid closed. On the top of the lid was painted the number sixteen.

Teresa handed the accountant the key. He walked quickly to the table as the other accountant removed items from the table. He started to place the key in the lock when Judge Jackson stopped him. "Don't open it!" Judge Jackson yelled. He looked at Teresa. "Where did you get this box?"

Teresa looked frightened! She lowered her head.

Judge Jackson stood. "Don't be afraid to answer. Where did you get this box?" he asked again.

Teresa raised her head slowly. Her brother, James, was sitting beside her. He quickly stood and placed his arm around her waist. "Mr. Judge," he said slowly. "It is my mother's box. It came from our house."

The court clerk quickly stood. He started to speak but Judge Jackson motioned for him to sit. The clerk quickly sat in his chair. "If it is your mother's box why did you bring it here?" Judge Jackson asked.

Teresa looked frightened. "Mr. Judge," she answered. "We were told to bring our parent's box to court today."

Judge Jackson looked confused. "Who told you that?" he asked.

"You did," Teresa answered quietly.

Judge Jackson smiled softly. "Miss. Barnes, I didn't tell you to bring your mother's money here," he said.

James looked at Judge Jackson and he pointed toward the table. "Yes you did," he answered. "Mr. Franklin brought his money and we brought ours."

Judge Jackson laughed. He removed the tobacco in his mouth and dropped it in the waste basket beside his chair. He removed a handkerchief from his pants pocket and wiped his mouth. "I must be getting old," he said laughing. He looked at Teresa and her brother James. "I didn't ask you to bring your mother's money here. I asked Mr. Harding to bring any money that belonged to Jonathan Harding's company here." He pointed toward the table. "Mr. Harding brought money that belonged to Harding and Associates. He didn't bring his own money."

Teresa shrugged her shoulders. "That is what we did!" she answered.

Judge Jackson laughed. He walked to the front of his bench and motioned for the accountant to return the box to Teresa. The accountant picked up the box then stopped. He sat the box on the table and he looked at Teresa. "Does one of the keys on the ring open this lock?" he asked.

Teresa and James nodded their heads.

Judge Jackson narrowed his eyes. He looked at the accountant and he looked at Teresa. He looked angry and he took a deep breath. "Why did Jonathan Harding have a key to your mother's box?" he asked calmly.

James pointed toward the accountant holding the box. "That is not our mother's box," he answered. "It belongs to Mr. Jonathan and Miss. Elizabeth."

Judge Jackson looked confused. He walked quickly to where Teresa and James were standing and he kneeled. His face lit up in a big smile as he leaned toward James. "If the box is your mother's, why did Jonathan Harding have a key to your mother's box?" he asked grinning.

James smiled and he pointed toward the table. "Mr. Jonathan and Miss. Elizabeth used one of those keys when they came to our house to put money in the box," he answered.

Judge Jackson's eyes widened and he became very angry. He stood quickly and pointed toward the court clerk. "Secure those doors!" he yelled, as he pointed toward the courtroom doors. "Don't let anyone in or out!"

The court clerk stood quickly and ran to the doors. He removed a key from his pants pocket and quickly locked the doors.

Judge Jackson glared at the people in the courtroom. "You will not repeat anything these two children have said!" he yelled. "That's an order!" He looked to a woman near his bench who was recording what was being said. "Stop!" he yelled. "Tear up those last pages and get Judge Brown!"

The woman quit writing. She stood very quickly and walked to the courtroom doors. The clerk unlocked the doors to allow her to leave then he quickly locked the doors.

Judge Jackson was livid! He was angry, very angry! He breathed heavily to calm down. He looked downward and sighed. Slowly, he raised his head and kneeled before Teresa and James and he smiled brightly. "Is your mother or father here?" he asked Teresa.

Teresa lowered her head. "They are both dead," she answered. "Mother died two years ago and father died last year."

Judge Jackson's face flared with anger. He turned his head away from Teresa so she could not see his face. He was angry! He breathed heavily to calm himself. He slowly turned toward Teresa. "Mr. Harding and his wife brought that box to your house after your parents died?" he asked calmly.

"No," James answered. "He brought it to our house when my mother started working for him. I wasn't born when he brought the box."

"I wasn't born either," Teresa added.

Judge Jackson cocked his head slightly. "When did Mr. Harding bring the box to your mother and father's house?" he asked calmly.

James smiled. "When the first war started," he answered.

Judge Jackson stood quickly. "1917?" he asked, with a surprised look on his face.

"I don't know the year," Teresa answered. "Mr. Jonathan wasn't married. When my mother started working for him he brought a sewing machine to our house and he put that box in our house."

Judge Jackson leaned downward toward Teresa. He had a puzzled look on his face. "Why did Mr. Harding do this?" he asked with a polite smile.

Teresa smiled. "He used the money to pay for cloth, zippers, buttons, and thread," she answered.

Judge Jackson stood quickly. He had a very puzzled look on his face. He walked quickly to his bench and sat down. He took the knife and cut a piece of the tobacco twist. He began to place it in his mouth when he stopped. He looked at Teresa and her brother James. "Did your mother and father know what was in the box?" he asked as he placed the cut of tobacco in his mouth.

"Yes Sir!" Teresa answered quickly. She pointed toward the accountant. "Sometimes Mr. Jonathan and Miss. Elizabeth were real busy and they couldn't come to our house. Mr. Jonathan gave my mother a key so she could pay for anything she needed to work."

Judge Jackson leaned backward in his chair and he motioned for Teresa and her brother James to sit down. They sat down. Judge Jackson leaned forward and spit in the mug. He looked at the accountant. "Open it!" he said. "Don't use her key, use the key on the ring."

The accountant placed Teresa's key on the table and he picked up the ring of keys. He looked for the key marked sixteen and placed the key in the lock and turned it.

Click!

The accountant removed the lock and slowly raised the lid. "Whew!" he whistled as he looked inside. He turned toward Judge Jackson as the other accountant walked quickly toward the table to look in the box. "Whew!" the second accountant whistled.

Judge Jackson rose quickly from his bench and walked to the table. He looked inside the box. "Lock it!" he ordered.

The accountant lowered the lid and replaced the lock. He pushed the lock together.

Judge Jackson looked at the people in the courtroom. His eyes widened as he raised his arms upward toward his side. "Did anybody else know about this box?" he asked with a surprised look on his face.

The people in the courtroom nodded their heads.

The door to the judge's chambers opened slowly as Judge Brown walked into the courtroom. He stopped and looked at Judge Jackson. "What's wrong?" he asked.

Judge Jackson looked at the accountants. "Show him!" he said.

The accountant motioned for Judge Brown to come to the table. When Judge Brown approached the table, the accountant used key numbered sixteen from the ring of keys to open the lock. He raised the lid as Judge Brown looked inside.

Judge Brown looked upward with a surprised look on his face. "Where did this come from?" he asked quickly.

Judge Jackson smiled. "It's the strangest thing I have ever seen! Mr. Jonathan Harding placed that box in the home of one of his workers more than twenty years ago." He turned and looked at Judge Brown. "These people knew about it!" he said, as he placed his hands on his hips. "They knew about it!"

Judge Brown walked quickly toward Judge Jackson to stand beside him. Together, they appeared very comical. Judge Jackson was tall and Judge Brown was short. "I am Judge Lawrence Brown!" Judge Brown yelled. "I am considering the issue of your pensions. Answer me honestly! Does Mr. Franklin Harding know about this box?"

The people in the courtroom nodded their heads, no. Teresa and her brother James both nodded their heads, no. An elderly man stood. "When Miss. Elizabeth died, we tried to tell him but he wouldn't talk to us." The man turned to look at a woman sitting beside him. "You can ask Martha! I tried to tell him more than three times but he wouldn't talk to me."

"I tried to tell Mr. Franklin but he wouldn't talk to me either!" an elderly woman said. She nodded her head. "I tried to tell him this morning but he wouldn't talk to me."

"Who are you?" Judge Brown asked the woman.

She quickly stood. "My name is Nell Eckerd," she answered. "I am on the list to get my two hundred dollars."

Judge Jackson motioned for the woman and man to sit and they sat down on the bench.

Judge Jackson and Judge Brown laughed. Judge Jackson bent over in laughter. "Miss. Barnes thought I ordered her to bring the company's money to the courtroom like Mr. Franklin Harding!" he laughed, as he placed his arm around Judge Brown's shoulder. "She brought Mr. Jonathan Harding's money!" he giggled.

Judge Brown laughed. "Mr. Franklin Harding couldn't find any money because his father hid it in a worker's home!" he giggled.

Judge Brown quit laughing. "It will take a few weeks to sort things out but I think this money will help in my decision concerning your pensions," Judge Brown laughed.

"That's not pension money!" an elderly man said as he stood. "That's company money!"

Judge Jackson stopped laughing. "What are you talking about? That box of money belongs to Mr. Jonathan Harding," he said.

"No it doesn't!" the elderly man answered. "That's company money! Eileen Barnes used it to purchase cloth and thread."

Judge Jackson looked at the elderly man. "Mr. Jonathan Harding hid that money! That money is his! It doesn't belong to the company!" he answered in a gruff tone.

"Mr. Judge!" an elderly woman said, as she stood. "The money in the box was used to purchase cloth and thread and anything else we needed. I had to use some of the money to pay a truck driver to deliver uniforms to Mississippi."

Judge Jackson narrowed his eyes. "You have a key to the box in Miss. Barnes' home?" he asked with a puzzled look.

"No Sir!" the elderly woman answered. "I have my own box! I brought it like you ordered me. It is here under the bench. I'll need some help to put it on the table."

The eyes of Judge Jackson and Judge Brown widened. The two accountants ran quickly to where the elderly woman was standing and they looked under the bench. Under the bench was a box like the box Teresa Barnes brought to the court. They looked under the benches where the people were sitting. They quickly counted eight boxes.

One of the accountants quickly stood. "There are eight boxes here!" he said excitedly.

"Did Mr. Jonathan Harding and his wife put money in all those boxes?" Judge Jackson asked with a surprised look on his face.

"No Sir!" the elderly woman answered. "Sometimes Jessie Burgess put money in the boxes. He would come to my house to check the sewing machine." She pointed toward the table. "He would use one of those keys to open the box and he put money in it."

"Who is Jessie Burgess?" Judge Jackson asked.

"He is one of us," the elderly woman answered. "Jessie Burgess worked for Jonathan to repair the sewing machines." She lowered her head. "Jessie died two years ago."

Judge Jackson and Judge Brown turned and walked slowly toward the bench. They whispered to each other as they walked. When they neared the bench, Judge Brown turned toward the people and he raised his hands. "I'm afraid I may have spoken too soon concerning your pensions," he said softly. "I thought the money in the box was Mr. Jonathan Harding's personal money. We are not sure who the legal owner is. It appears the matter of the pensions is still under advisement."

The people in the courtroom nodded their heads and frowned.

Judge Jackson raised his hands in the air. "These boxes create a problem!" he yelled. "I will need to decide who the legal owner is. Until I make my decision, the accountants will list the contents." He pointed toward the two accountants. "Bring the boxes here and list their contents. Use the keys on the ring of keys to open them." He turned toward Judge Brown. They began to speak softly to each other as the accountants carried the boxes toward the table. They sat them on the floor and opened each one with a key from the ring of keys. Each box was numbered and a key, with the matching number, opened the lock. Inside the boxes was money! Lots of money!

Judge Jackson and Judge Brown looked at the contents of the boxes. "Lock them for now!" Judge Jackson said. The accountants closed the lids and replaced the locks.

"Open the doors!" an elderly man yelled.

"No one is allowed in or out!" the court clerk yelled.

The two judges turned quickly to see one of the people in the courtroom attempting to open the doors and leave the courtroom.

"This courtroom is sealed by my order!" Judge Jackson yelled. "You have to stay until the contents of the boxes are listed."

The elderly man turned and looked at Judge Jackson. "How are the others going to get in?" he asked.

"They can't get in until I change my order!" Judge Jackson yelled. "They have to stay outside."

The elderly man shrugged his shoulders. "How are you going to check the boxes if they are outside?" he asked.

Judge Jackson walked toward the elderly man. "What boxes?" he asked.

"Their boxes," the elderly man answered, with a frown on his face.

Judge Brown walked toward Judge Jackson. "What boxes?" he asked the elderly man with a puzzled look on his face.

The elderly man pointed toward the table. "Each key on that ring fits the lock on a company box," he answered. He raised his hands in the air. "There wasn't enough room for everyone to come inside and I had to leave my box outside in the hallway. The other boxes are outside!"

Judge Jackson's eyes widened. He ran toward the doors of the courtroom as the court clerk unlocked them. Judge Jackson ran into the hallway to see many people sitting and standing. Lying under the benches were many boxes, like the ones inside his courtroom, sitting on the floor. He stopped and paused as Judge Brown ran from the courtroom to stand beside him. Their eyes were widely opened.

An elderly man approached Judge Brown. "Are you Judge Jackson?" he asked Judge Brown.

Judge Jackson frowned as he looked at the elderly man. "I'm Judge Jackson. That is Judge Brown," he said gruffly.

The elderly man's eyes widened. "Judge Brown I need to speak to you about the pension money!"

Judge Brown frowned. "I haven't made my decision," he answered.

"Have they stopped?" the elderly man asked.

"No," Judge Brown answered.

The elderly man looked at Judge Jackson. "Mr. Franklin told me I am to ask you any question. Do you want me to pay the pensions this month?" he asked.

Judge Jackson's eyes narrowed. "Mr. Franklin Harding told you to ask me any question? When did he say that?" he asked gruffly.

"When he left the courtroom," the elderly man answered. "I stopped him because he is the owner and I wanted to know if he wanted me to pay the pensions and the utilities. He told me he wasn't the owner anymore. He told me that you would answer any questions we had." The elderly man was carrying a small briefcase and he lifted it upward. "The pension envelopes are ready and I have the utility bills ready. Is it OK for me to pay them?" he asked.

Judge Brown leaned toward the elderly man. "Who are you?" he asked.

"I'm Robert Sanders," he answered. "Jessie Burgess paid the pensions and the utilities until he died two years ago. Mr. Jonathan gave me the job. I prepare the pension envelopes and give them out. I also pay the utilities. They are a month late but the people know me and they know that they will get paid."

"How do you pay the pensions?" Judge Brown asked.

"Jessie Burgess kept the pension fund until he died. I keep it now," Robert answered.

Judge Brown looked at Judge Jackson and then he looked at Robert. "I was under the impression that the pensions were paid from the company's money and that there was no money left," he said.

Robert laughed. "Who told you that? We got plenty of money! Do you want me to pay the pensions?" he asked.

Judge Brown narrowed his eyes as he looked at Robert. "Where are the pension funds?" he asked.

"My house," Robert answered. "They were kept at Jessie's house until he died. Mr. Jonathan asked me if I wanted the job and when I accepted, he brought the boxes from Jessie's house to my house. The pension boxes are at my house."

Judge Jackson narrowed his eyes. He looked at the hallway and all the boxes sitting on the floor. "Why aren't they here?" he asked.

"Pension money is different from company money," Robert answered. "Only pensions are paid from the boxes. Mr. Nathan was very strict." He turned and pointed toward a box sitting on the floor. "That is my box! The pension fund boxes are at my house."

"Who is Mr. Nathan?" Judge Jackson asked.

"Nathan Clark. He's a lawyer," Robert answered. He lowered his head. "He's dead now."

Judge Jackson's eyes widened as he looked at Judge Brown. "Did you know Nathan Clark?" he asked Robert with a puzzled look on his face.

Robert raised his head. "Yes Sir!" he answered, "he came to our houses about once a year and he told us what we could and could not do."

Judge Jackson looked at Judge Brown. "Excuse me," he said. "I'll be back in a few minutes." He looked at the hallway where a section of bench was empty and he pointed toward the bench. "Sit," he said quietly.

Judge Brown and Robert sat at the empty section of bench. Judge Jackson walked quickly into his courtroom. Within one minute, he had returned. There was an armed court guard with him. In his hands, Judge Jackson held the waste basket that sat beside his chair and his mug. "This is Mr. Wilkins," he said. "He will take you to your house. It is necessary that you bring the pension fund to Judge Brown's courtroom.

Judge Brown nodded his head. "Bring everything with you that you use to prepare the pension envelopes," he said smiling.

Judge Jackson sat beside Robert. He placed the waste basket and mug on the floor. "Before you go," he said as he reached into his robe to remove a twist of tobacco and his knife, "I have a few questions on the utility bills and how you pay them."

Robert nodded his head.

Judge Jackson cut a section of tobacco and placed it in his mouth. He folded the knife and placed it beside him on the bench. "Who pays the utility bills?" he asked as he spit in the mug.

"The company," Robert answered. "The company pays the electric bill and water bill."

Judge Jackson leaned backward on the bench. "When did this start?" he asked as he spit in the mug.

Robert leaned toward Judge Jackson. "It started when Mr. Jonathan got his first order. He came to our house and he made us a deal," he answered. "If we would help him, he would double our pay when he was paid. We agreed! Mr. Jonathan brought sewing machines into our homes. When he was paid, he paid us triple what we had agreed on. Mr. Jonathan brought Mr. Nathan to our homes one day and he made us another deal."

"What kind of deal?" Judge Jackson asked.

"He wanted to lease our homes," he answered. "If we agreed, he would fix them up some. Not fancy but fix them so they weren't so cold in the winter and hot in the summer. When the wires and pipes came to our area, he put in electricity and running water. He gave our house numbers. Mine is thirty-two. The company pays the water and electric bills."

Judge Brown leaned toward Robert. "Is there a lease?" he asked.

"Yes Sir!" Robert answered. "Mr. Nathan wrote it up and we all signed it. The lease is good for ninety-nine years."

Judge Jackson removed the tobacco from his mouth and dropped it into the waste basket. He pulled his handkerchief from his pocket and wiped his mouth. "I think I have heard enough," he said to Judge Brown as he slowly stood. Judge Brown nodded his head and stood.

Judge Jackson removed his pocket watch and looked at the time. "Are they in place?" he asked Mr. Wilkins.

"Yes Your Honor," Mr. Wilkins answered. "There should be an armed guard at every entrance and exit of the courthouse."

"Seal it!" Judge Jackson ordered, "No one gets in or out!"

Mr. Wilkins nodded his head. He looked at Robert. "I will be back in a few minutes. Do you mind waiting?" he asked.

Robert nodded his head.

Judge Brown reached into his pocket and removed his car keys. "Take my car," he said, as he handed the keys to Mr. Wilkins."

Mr. Wilkins took the car keys. "I will only be gone a few minutes," he said to Robert as he turned and walked away.

"Pretty airtight," Judge Brown said as he smiled at Judge Jackson. "The workers signed a lease and the company pays the utility bills."

Judge Jackson nodded his head. "Yes," he said smiling. "It appears that Mr. Jonathan Harding had lots of company cash assets. He kept them on company property protected by company employees."

Judge Brown looked at Robert and he sat down beside him. "Why did Nathan Clark insist that the pension fund be kept separate from the other funds?" he asked.

Robert smiled. "Mr. Nathan said the pension was a benefit to the company employees," he answered. "It has to have enough money to last. It can't be mixed with the other money because it has to have a minimum balance at all times. If the company is sold or goes broke, the pension fund can't be touched! It has to have enough money to fulfill the obligation the company has made to the employee."

Judge Jackson looked at Judge Brown with a smile on his face. "Company benefit and company obligation," he said.

Judge Brown smiled. "Interesting use of words," he said as he stood. Judge Jackson smiled as they walked toward Judge Brown's courtroom.

When they neared the door to Judge Brown's court, Judge Brown stopped and looked at Judge Jackson. "Randolph, there are times I really hate my job," he said as he turned and looked at the people sitting and waiting in the hallway. "I delayed as long as I could on the pensions. I was going to rule today." He turned and looked at Judge Jackson. "Did you know what it would be?"

Judge Jackson frowned. "Yes," he answered. "Considering the information you had there was only one logical and legal answer." He looked at the people sitting and waiting in the hallway. "I understand how you feel! There are times I hate my job too! We have to obey the law and apply it equally to everyone." He pointed toward the window. From where they stood, they could see the statue of *Justice*. The statue was of a woman holding a bowl in each hand. A sword was to her side. A blindfold covered her eyes. "*Lady Justice* is a symbol of the fair and equal administration of law. The law must be administered without corruption, greed, prejudice, or favor. I understand what you almost had to do today. You had to administer the law despite what you feel. My job was much simpler."

"So is mine now," Judge Brown answered. "I am glad I delayed. The discovery of the pension funds makes my decision pretty clear. The pension plan of Harding and Associates was a benefit to the employee. The company has an obligation to fund it adequately and fulfill its obligation. Jonathan Harding provided adequate funding and he kept the money for the employee benefit separate from the day to day operational funding. It doesn't matter if the company is sold. If the funding is there, the company must fulfill its obligation."

"I couldn't have said it better myself," Judge Jackson said smiling. "Is that your ruling?"

"Pretty much," Judge Brown answered. "I'll need to see the actual funding and verify amounts but I think there is enough there. I'll pretty the wording up a little and use some fifty cent words to impress the senior partners of Clark and Higgins."

Judge Brown laughed. "How much money do you think they will get?" he asked.

Judge Jackson smiled. "I have no idea," he laughed. "Did you see the stack of war bonds in one of the boxes?"

"Yes!" Judge Brown answered, "The stack I saw was a lot thicker than two hundred dollars."

"Lawrence I have an idea but I will need your help in case there are legal questions or a possible appeal," Judge Jackson said as he turned toward Judge Brown. "These people are going to get a lot of money! When word of this leaks out, everyone is going to attempt to take advantage of them and attempt to take what they rightfully earned. To protect them, I can have the court records sealed. However, to make the ruling valid, I will need something from you concerning the pension fund."

"What do you need?" Judge Brown asked.

"The company of Harding and Associates has been liquidated," Judge Jackson said. "Mr. Franklin Harding has fulfilled his obligation to my court to turn over any and all cash assets of the company. I believe he has done this and I have released him. He doesn't know about the boxes in the worker's homes or that there was a separate fund for the pensions."

Judge Brown laughed, "I see! Mr. Franklin Harding believed the funding for the pensions came from the cash he found in his father's bank account and safe. There was less than twenty-five thousand dollars and he believed once that money was spent, he was liable for any remainder. The law firm is fighting the pensions because they believe the company must pay for the pensions from any personal money Mr. Jonathan Harding had or from the sale of the plant and property."

Judge Jackson nodded.

"Makes sense," Judge Brown said as he nodded his head. "If they agreed to continue to fund the pensions Mr. Franklin Harding would have to report the dollar value of the war bonds he found in his father's home."

"You know about the bonds Mr. Franklin Harding found in his father's home?" Judge Jackson asked surprised.

"Yes!" Judge Brown answered. "We have been judges for a long time and we have seen good attorneys and poor ones. There are only two ways you can argue the law, what the law says and the intent of the law. When the senior partners of the law firm of Clark and Higgins appeared in my court and began arguing about the character of Mr. Franklin Harding, I knew something was up."

"Every time the money found in Mr. Jonathan Harding's home was mentioned, they quickly changed the subject to the two hundred dollars in war bonds."

Judge Jackson frowned. "Mr. Franklin Harding bragged in my court today that he tricked you," he said, as he narrowed his eyes.

Judge Brown laughed and he held his two hands upward. "They kept my attention on the left hand hoping I would not notice the right hand," he said giggling. "Everyone knows that a good magician uses both hands! Just because I watched their left hand doesn't mean I ignored their right hand. Sometimes a trick works best if both parties are aware of the trick and its purpose. A good participant doesn't reveal the trick."

"Considering the type of work Mr. Harding's company did, and the number of years his company has been operating, two hundred dollars in matured war bonds made no sense! There had to be more war bonds and if they were found in his home, they were personal assets. He did not have a personal bank account that I could find. The amount of money reported in his home was a reasonable amount, eighty-five thousand dollars. I guessed that there was even more in war bonds. However, it was fun listening to their arguments."

Judge Jackson laughed. "Sometimes tricks backfire and they don't work like they were planned," he said with a grin on his face.

Judge Brown paused and placed his hand to his chin. "There is no one to administer the pension fund since the company has been dissolved," he said thoughtfully. "Mr. Franklin Harding can't administer it because of a possible conflict with his former workers. I can place the fund in a government account and have the pensions dispensed accordingly." He looked at Judge Jackson. "Since the life of the employee has a limited number of years and there are a limited number of members, there will come a time when there are no more members. At that point, any remaining funds would revert to the company. Since the company has been dissolved, the remaining funds become a cash asset. All cash assets are to be divided equally among all workers. If the worker is deceased, their share goes to their heir."

Judge Brown's eyes lit up! "Randolph, if you seal the court records related to anything having to do with the cash assets and their disbursements, since a portion of the pension fund will one day revert to a cash asset, it will be necessary for me to seal all records on the pension fund."

Judge Jackson laughed, "Mr. Franklin Harding would have no idea of the total amount of cash assets." He paused. "However, he may attempt to have the court order, to seal the records, reversed when the last worker has died."

"That's possible," Judge Brown answered. "Anything is possible but he would have to have a valid reason to have the records unsealed. Off hand, I can't think of one. It will be twenty to thirty years before he could attempt it. In that time period, his hands are tied!"

Judge Jackson and Judge Brown nodded at each other.

Judge Jackson looked out the window toward the statue of *Justice* and he pointed toward the statue. "*Justice* is blind because she wears a covering over her eyes. The reason she wears the covering is to judge the cases and the people on the merits of law and truthful facts in the case." He turned and looked at the people sitting in the hallway and then he turned to look at the statue. "It must have been a pitiful sight this morning when those people came to court with their boxes. They didn't know what was going on." He turned and looked at Judge Brown. "I have had strange things happen in my court where it appears the bad guy is going to win but something happens and the good guy comes out ahead. Sometimes I think *Justice* gets involved in a case. I think as those people came up the steps with their boxes, *Justice* peeked! *Lady Justice* placed one of the bowls on the ground and lifted her blindfold. She took a good look at the people coming before her court and then she replaced the blindfold and picked up the bowl."

"Damn Randolph! You should have been a poet!" Judge Brown said laughing. "Are you ready?"

Judge Jackson nodded his head. They turned from the window to see a young boy standing in front of them. The young boy looked to be seven to ten years old and small. He was wearing overalls, without a shirt, and his feet were bare and muddy. Judge Jackson and Judge Brown had puzzled looks on their faces. "Where did you come from?" Judge Brown asked.

The young boy pointed toward the window. Judge Jackson turned and looked at the window then he turned and looked at the young boy. "I didn't see you standing at the window," he said with a surprised look on his face.

The young boy pointed toward Judge Brown. "I wasn't standing by the window, I was standing behind him," he answered. "My father told me not to stand in front of people when they are talking." The young boy paused and he took a deep breath. "Mr. Hanging Judge, are you through talking?"

Judge Jackson frowned as Judge Brown smiled. "My name is Judge Jackson," Judge Jackson said as he leaned toward the young boy. "Who told you my name was Hanging Judge?"

"Mr. Franklin," the young boy answered.

Judge Jackson was angered. "When did he tell you that?" he asked in a gruff voice.

The young boy pointed down the hallway toward Judge Jackson's court. "When he came out of your court, we had a lot of questions to ask him," he answered. "He told us he had nothing to do with Mr. Jonathan's company." The young boy turned and looked at Judge Jackson. "He told us if we had any questions we were to ask you. He told us you were tall and your head looked like an egg and you chewed tobacco. He told us your name was Hanging Judge and we were to call you Hanging Judge."

Judge Jackson's eyes blazed with anger.

Judge Brown leaned toward Judge Jackson. "Mr. Franklin Harding just hung himself," he giggled. "*Lady Justice* must have peeked when he came up the steps."

"I didn't see her!" the young boy said.

"See who?" Judge Jackson asked.

The young boy pointed toward the window. "That woman statue with the bowls and blindfold," he answered. "You said she put her bowls on the ground and raised her blindfold when we came up the steps with our boxes. I looked at her but I didn't see her do anything."

Judge Brown and Judge Jackson looked at each other. Judge Brown kneeled on the floor and looked at the young boy. "How long have you been standing behind us?" he asked softly.

The young boy smiled. "I was waiting by the door when you came out. I was standing beside Mr. Robert when you talked to him. My father told me not to speak if someone is talking, so I didn't say anything. I followed you when you walked here."

Judge Jackson kneeled on the floor in front of the young boy. "I didn't see you," he said with a puzzled look on his face.

The young boy smiled. "My father told me not to stand in front of people when they talked," he said grinning. "I stood behind him. When he turned, I turned."

Judge Jackson and Judge Brown stood. Their eyes were widely opened. "What did you hear us say?" Judge Brown asked.

"Lots of things," the young boy answered.

Judge Jackson looked at the young boy. "What things?" he asked in a calm controlled voice.

The young boy shrugged his shoulders. "Mr. Franklin doesn't know about the boxes and the pension money," he answered. "You're going to give the pension to us but put it where Mr. Franklin can't find it. Mr. Franklin hid some money but you know about it. He is a magician and he tried to trick you but you tricked him because you watched his right hand. When everybody is dead you're going to give us money." He paused and thought. "You don't like your jobs. Mr. Franklin is a bad guy and he won't get any money because you're going to tie him up for thirty years."

Judge Jackson and Judge Brown's eyes widened as they looked at each other.

Judge Jackson leaned closer toward the young boy. "I am a judge and judges give orders," he said quietly. "Do you know what an order is?"

The young boy nodded his head.

Judge Jackson smiled as he looked at Judge Brown. "Judge Brown also gives orders. Do you know Mr. Robert Sanders?"

The young boy nodded his head.

Judge Jackson looked at the young boy. "If Judge Brown gives Mr. Robert Sanders an order, Mr. Sanders must obey that order," he said. "Mr. Sanders will be meeting with Judge Brown and if everything is OK, Judge Brown will order Mr. Sanders to give everyone their pension money and pay the electric and water bills. Mr. Sanders will have to obey Judge Brown's order."

The young boy nodded his head.

"Everyone must obey the order of a judge," Judge Jackson said quietly. "It is like a Captain in the Army, everyone must obey the Captain's orders."

The young boy nodded his head.

"So far so good," Judge Brown whispered.

Judge Jackson looked at Judge Brown with an irritated look on his face. He then looked at the young boy. "Do you understand what a judge's order is?" he asked quietly.

The young boy nodded his head.

"What you heard Judge Brown and me talking about is a legal discussion," Judge Jackson said quietly. "We were not talking to you. We were discussing legal matters. You did not hear everything we said. Do you understand?"

The young boy nodded his head.

Judge Jackson looked at Judge Brown. "So far so good," he said smiling. He looked at the young boy. "Mr. Franklin Harding told everyone in the hallway that he had nothing to do with Mr. Jonathan Harding's company. When he told them this, he spoke very loudly so everyone could hear what he said. When we were discussing the legal matters, we talked very low because we didn't want anyone to hear us. Do you know the difference?"

The young boy nodded his head.

Judge Jackson looked upward at Judge Brown and nodded his head. He then turned toward the young boy. "Judge Brown and I are going to give several orders today and everyone must obey them," he said quietly. "I am going to give you an order. You are not to tell anyone, not anyone, what you think you heard. Do you understand?"

The young boy nodded his head.

"Do you have any questions?" Judge Jackson asked quietly.

The young boy lowered his head and then raised it. "Did Mr. Franklin tell us the truth?" he asked.

Judge Jackson looked at the young boy. "Yes," he answered. "Mr. Franklin Harding has nothing to do with his father's company. I am very tall and my head looks like an egg. I chew tobacco and my name is Hanging Judge. You can ask me any question you want. I will try to answer it."

Judge Brown leaned close to Judge Jackson. "Randolph, do you know what you're doing? Because I don't know what you're doing," he whispered.

Judge Jackson stood upright and cleared his throat. "You said you had a question to ask. What is your question?" he asked in a gruff voice.

The young boy smiled. "It's not for me," he answered. "It's for a friend of mine! She is shy and I told her I would ask her question for her."

"Very noble, who is your friend?" Judge Jackson asked, in a gruff voice.

"I'll get her," the young boy said. He turned and ran down the hallway to a young girl sitting on the bench. They watched the young girl follow him as he ran toward Judge Jackson. "This is my friend Charlene," he said. "She wants to know if we can get ice cream."

Judge Jackson looked at the young girl. She was about five years old with blonde hair and blue eyes. She was wearing a blue print dress that was ironed and starched. Her feet were bare and muddy.

Judge Jackson looked at the young girl with a stern look in his eyes. "I am Hanging Judge. What flavor ice cream do you want?" he asked.

Charlene grinned. "Vanilla," she answered.

Judge Jackson looked at the young boy. "Everybody must obey a judge's order. I will order one of my staff to bring vanilla ice cream to my court," he said in a gruff voice.

Judge Brown cleared his throat. "I am Judge Brown," he said in a gruff voice. "I will order my staff to bring chocolate ice cream to my court. You can have two flavors. Now I order both of you to play and have fun."

The young boy and girl laughed as they ran down the hallway toward the people sitting on the benches.

"Close call," Judge Brown said.

Judge Jackson laughed. "Lawrence your learning but your voice needs to be deeper. Snort more!" he said. "That clinches the pensions."

Suddenly, he looked behind Judge Brown.

"No body there!" Judge Brown laughed. "I have already looked."

Judge Jackson laughed, "Mr. Franklin Harding told more than fifty people he had nothing to do with his father's company. Have everyone testify to what he said."

"Everything?" Judge Brown asked.

"Everything!" Judge Jackson answered. "I don't care that people know I am tall with a head that looks like an egg. Everybody knows I chew tobacco in court and the name, The Hanging Judge, just adds to my charisma and charm!"

They laughed as they walked down the hallway toward the people sitting on the benches. As they neared, Judge Brown held his hands upward. "Excuse me folks!" he said in a loud voice. "My name is Judge Brown."

The people sitting on the benches stopped talking and looked at Judge Brown and Judge Jackson.

"I have been speaking to Mr. Robert Sanders concerning your pension money for this month and the payment of the utility bills. I will be meeting with Mr. Sanders shortly to verify a few things. If everything is in order, I will authorize the payment of this month's pension. Mr. Sanders has already prepared the envelopes," he added.

The people nodded and grinned.

"I am Judge Jackson!" Judge Jackson said in a gruff voice. He looked toward Judge Brown and smiled. Then he turned toward the people. "I am called Judge Jackson, Your Honor, or as Mr. Franklin Harding told you, The Hanging Judge. You can refer to me by any of those three names. Mr. Franklin Harding has fulfilled his obligation to the court. However, there have been some new developments and before I can divide the cash assets of the company Harding and Associates, the contents of these boxes will need to be counted and verified. I also need to verify the lease you signed and the utility bills paid."

An elderly man raised his hand.

Judge Jackson looked at the elderly man. "Yes sir! You have a question?" he asked in a gruff voice.

"Mr. Hanging Judge," the elderly man said in a Southern drawl. "Which lease do you need to see?"

Judge Jackson's eyes narrowed as he looked at Judge Brown. "How many leases do you have?" he asked in a soft voice.

"Two," the elderly man answered. "Mr. Jonathan's lease is in that box and there is a list of the electric and water bills he paid. The other lease is in my box. Do you want me to go home and get my box?"

Judge Brown leaned toward the elderly man. "You have a box?" he asked.

"Yes Sir!" the elderly man answered. "That's the company box. My box is at my house."

"What is in your box?" Judge Brown asked.

"Mr. Nathan was very strict," the elderly man answered. "We each have a box in our house that belongs to us. We keep our lease in the box and a list of the electric and water bills Mr. Jonathan paid. Any repairs to our house are in our box. We have to keep everything together so Mr. Jonathan gave all of us a box."

Judge Brown's eyes widened. "Each one of these boxes contains the lease you signed and a listing of the utility bills paid?" he asked with a smile on his face.

"Yes Sir!" the elderly man answered.

Judge Brown leaned toward Judge Jackson. "Verify it! Count it! Divide it! Seal the records!" he whispered.

Judge Jackson smiled. "Is there anything else in your boxes?" he asked.

"Our savings," an elderly woman answered.

"Savings?" Judge Brown asked with a surprised look on his face.

"Yes Sir," the elderly woman answered. "Miss. Elizabeth paid us and she had us take most of our money and save it. We only used enough money to live on and get by. It really helped when the depression hit."

"Our war bonds are in the box," an elderly man added. "When Mr. Nathan came to our house to eat supper, he would bring us our war bonds."

Judge Jackson was startled. "Mr. Nathan Clark ate supper at your house? He brought you war bonds?" he asked.

"Yes Sir," the elderly man answered. "Mr. Nathan came to our house about once a year with Mr. Jonathan and Miss. Elizabeth. They ate supper with us and Mr. Nathan would tell us what we could and could not do. He would check our boxes and give us our war bonds that we paid for."

Judge Brown leaned backward with a surprised look on his face. "Did Nathan Clark come to your homes once a year for supper?" he asked the people sitting on the benches.

"Yes Sir," the elderly man answered. "Once a year, in the summertime, he came to our house and took us on a picnic. He would come in his car and take us to the river. Mr. Jonathan and Miss. Elizabeth were with him. We would go fishing."

Judge Jackson had a surprised look on his face. He walked slowly toward the elderly man. "I knew Nathan Clark for many years and he argued before my court on several occasions," he said smiling. "He never came to my house for supper and we never went fishing together. He must have thought a lot of you!" Judge Jackson extended his hand. "May I shake the hand of the man that broke bread with Nathan Clark and shared a can of worms?"

The elderly man smiled and shook Judge Jackson's hand. "Mr. Nathan once had lunch with President Woodrow Wilson," he said smiling, as they shook hands.

Judge Jackson's eyes narrowed. He smiled at the elderly man and walked to stand beside Judge Brown. They raised their eyebrows as they looked at each other.

"Mr. Hanging Judge," an elderly woman said as she stood. "Do we get our two hundred dollars today?" she asked.

The people sitting on the benches nodded their heads.

Judge Jackson narrowed his eyes. "The actual amount counted so far is two hundred fifty-seven dollars and forty-six cents. I don't know if we can get everything ready today. It may be tomorrow," he answered slowly.

The elderly lady nodded her head and sat on the bench.

"Mr. Hanging Judge," an elderly man said as he stood. "I have a question."

"I will answer it if I can," Judge Jackson answered in a soft voice.

"My name is James Farnsworth," the elderly man said. "My mother and father worked for Mr. Jonathan. Our names are on the list. My mother and father are dead. Do I get their two hundred fifty-seven dollars and forty-six cents?"

Judge Jackson looked at Judge Brown with a puzzled look on his face. "That is the amount counted so far," he answered in a quiet voice. "To answer your question, yes. If you are their legal heir, you will receive their share. That is the share of the cash assets Mr. Franklin Harding brought to the court."

James Farnsworth pointed to a young woman sitting beside him. "That is my daughter Betty," he said smiling. He pointed down the hallway where a young boy and a young girl were playing. "That boy is her son Herbert. He is playing with Charlene. Charlene is Mrs. Davidson's daughter." He turned and looked at Judge Jackson. "My mother would have wanted Betty to have her share of the money. She didn't leave anything in writing but I think she would have wanted her grand-daughter to have her share. Is it OK with the court if I give my mother's two hundred fifty-seven dollars and forty-six cents to Betty? Her husband is out of work and they could use the money."

Judge Jackson looked at Judge Brown. "Mr. Farnsworth, it's your money. You can do what you like with it," he answered softly. He placed his hands on his hips and looked at the people. "The purpose of today's hearing is to count the cash assets of the company of Harding and Associates and divide equally those cash assets among the workers of Jonathan and Elizabeth Harding. If the worker is deceased, their share goes to the legal heir. Do you understand?"

"Yes Sir," an elderly lady answered. "My grandfather worked for Mr. Jonathan and Miss. Elizabeth. He cut the cloth used to make pants and shirts. He is dead so I get his two hundred fifty-seven dollars and forty-six cents."

Judge Brown motioned for Judge Jackson to follow him. "Excuse me," Judge Jackson said as he turned to follow Judge Brown. They walked down the hallway to where the young boy and young girl were playing. When they approached, the two children ran past them toward the people sitting on the benches.

They stopped near the window and looked in all directions. "Randolph," Judge Brown said. "Those people don't know or understand that the money in those boxes is theirs."

Judge Jackson nodded his head.

"We can combine the two cases," Judge Brown said. "We will need to meet with each one of them and explain, in terms they understand, what has happened. It will probably take a few days. You can have the cash assets counted and divided and then seal the records on the amounts today. Tomorrow, we can formally meet with each one of them and explain their share."

Judge Jackson lowered his head and thought. "Yes, to combine the cases makes sense and it would be more efficient but it may be best, in the long run, to keep them separate," he said. "They are very honest people and they keep telling us things." He looked at Judge Brown. "If we keep the cases separate they may tell you something that they didn't tell me."

Judge Brown smiled. "I know. Mr. Farnsworth said something that I didn't know and what he said made me think," he said as he paused. "Did you know that Nathan Clark has a great-grandson that is an attorney? He was in my court several weeks ago arguing a property line dispute."

Judge Jackson's eyes narrowed. "He didn't say anything about Nathan Clark having a great-grandson," he said.

"No, not that," Judge Brown said. "He said Nathan Clark once had lunch with President Woodrow Wilson. Nathan Clark's great-grandson is named Woodrow Clark."

Judge Jackson narrowed his eyes. "Does he work for Clark and Higgins?" he asked.

"No," Judge Brown answered. "I asked him if he did but he doesn't. He works out of his home. I asked why he didn't work for his great-grandfather's company and he said something about starting on his own. He didn't really say anything but I got the feeling they didn't want him."

"Why?" Judge Jackson asked surprised.

Judge Brown shrugged his shoulders. "He's green and he has no fire or spirit," he answered. "The case he argued was basically dead! There were contracts related to the property boundaries. The owner argued over one section that referred to an oak tree as a boundary. Woodrow argued the case based on the intent of the original contract. He made a good case but it was basically dead."

"Everybody is green at first," Judge Jackson said. "It has to be more than that."

"It's his name, Woodrow Clark. It sounds old fashioned," Judge Brown said. "Would you want someone named Woodrow defending you? When Mr. Farnsworth said Nathan Clark had lunch with President Woodrow Wilson, the thought occurred to me that perhaps he was named after President Wilson. I had completely forgotten about him until I heard Mr. Farnsworth's comment."

"Perhaps he was named after President Wilson," Judge Jackson said thoughtfully. "I didn't know Nathan Clark had lunch with President Wilson or that he went fishing. All I knew was that he argued before the United States Supreme Court twice. We have learned a lot about Nathan Clark today. These people may know more things about him."

"I have an idea," Judge Brown said. "These cases have become more involved and these people need adequate representation. Since they knew Woodrow's great-grandfather, they may be interested in having him represent them."

"Yes," Judge Jackson said. "That is a good idea. There should be a legal representative. They all knew his great-grandfather. They knew him and respected him. The court will pay him. Do you think he has the time to adequately represent them?"

"I don't think he has any clients," Judge Brown answered. "He is pretty green and his name doesn't sound impressive."

"I disagree!" Judge Jackson said. "If I knew my attorney's great-grandfather argued before the United States Supreme Court twice and had lunch with a president, I would be impressed. I would be more impressed if I knew that the president was Woodrow Wilson and my attorney was named after him."

Judge Brown laughed as he looked out the window toward *Lady Justice*. "I shudder to think what could have happened," he said sadly. "If Mr. Franklin Harding hadn't been so arrogant, he would have talked to his father's workers. They are honest and they would have told him everything. He could have diverted the cash assets and pension fund, and then sold what was left."

Judge Brown looked at Judge Jackson. "Randolph, you are right!" he said smiling. "I think there are times *Lady Justice* does get involved in a case; but you are wrong!"

"I'm wrong about what?" Judge Jackson asked with a surprised look on his face.

Judge Brown smiled and pointed toward *Lady Justice*. "It was a pitiful sight when those people came up the steps with their boxes this morning," he said with a sad look on his face. "They believed they were bringing what rightfully belonged to Mr. Jonathan Harding. *Lady Justice* laid both of her bowls on the ground as they walked up the steps and lifted her blindfold. You're wrong! She didn't peek; she took the whole damn thing off!"

"Damn Lawrence! You should have been a poet!" Judge Jackson said laughing. "Are you ready?"

When they turned from the window, the young boy was standing in front of them. "Mr. Robert is here," the young boy said.

"How long have you been standing here?" Judge Brown asked.

The young boy smiled. "Mr. Robert is here," he said quickly as he turned and ran down the hallway.

They watched the young boy run down the hallway and Judge Jackson looked around where they stood. "Lawrence," he said in a gruff voice. "Your right but you're wrong!"

"Wrong! Wrong, about what?" Judge Brown asked with a surprised look on his face.

"*Lady Justice* does get involved in a case!" Judge Jackson answered. "It is rare but I believe it happens. Those people are honest. They brought to court what they believed was rightfully Mr. Franklin Harding's money. They attempted to tell him but he refused to even speak to him. If he was not so arrogant, he would have spoken to them and they would have told him the truth. Mr. Franklin Harding is a weasel! He would have diverted the money to other areas or placed it in his home and claimed he discovered it." He paused and looked toward the window. "It was a pitiful sight when those people came up the steps with the boxes. *Lady Justice* did lay her bowls on the ground and she did take her blindfold off to look at the people coming to her court for justice." He looked toward Judge Brown. "But Lawrence you're wrong! Mr. Franklin Harding is arrogant and his attitude stinks! When he came up the steps of the courthouse, *Lady Justice* didn't lay her bowls on the ground and lift her blindfold; she didn't need to! She could smell him!"

"Damn Randolph, we both should have been poets," Judge Brown said laughing.

Judge Brown and Judge Jackson laughed as they walked down the hallway to where the people were sitting and standing. "Folks," Judge Jackson said, as he raised his hands. "Judge Brown and I have been discussing some new developments in the pension fund and the disbursements of the cash assets of Harding and Associates. We both agree that you should have an attorney represent you. The court will pay the legal fees."

"The only lawyer I knew was Mr. Nathan and he's dead!" an elderly woman said.

"Where do you get one?" an elderly man asked.

"Do we have to have a lawyer?" an elderly man asked.

"No," Judge Brown answered. "However, we advise you to have someone represent you."

"Mr. Nathan Clark has a great-grandson that's a lawyer," Judge Jackson said in a gruff voice. "If you like, I'll send for him. If you like him, you can select him to represent you. If you don't like him, you don't have to use him."

"What's his name?" Mr. Farnsworth asked.

"His name is Woodrow Clark," Judge Brown answered.

"That's a good name! He was named after President Woodrow Wilson," Mr. Farnsworth replied, as he looked at the others. "Can Mr. Woodrow come and talk to us?"

The people sitting on the benches nodded.

Judge Brown smiled. "I'll send for him. If you don't like him, you select someone else," he said with a grin on his face.

"Why wouldn't we like him?" an elderly woman asked. "He's Mr. Nathan's great-grandson."

Judge Brown smiled. "I'll send for him," he said smiling.

The doors of Judge Brown's courtroom opened quickly as the two accountants walked into the hallway. They held many journal accounting books in their arms. They looked toward the end of the hallway where Judge Jackson and Judge Brown were standing. They walked quickly toward them.

"Your Honor!" one of the accountants yelled, as the two accountants walked quickly toward Judge Jackson. As the accountant approached Judge Jackson he held upward a list.

"Your Honor," he continued. "We found the accounting records of Harding and Associates in one of the boxes."

Judge Jackson smiled at Judge Brown. "Is there a problem?" he asked with a grin on his face.

"That depends, Your Honor," one of the accountants answered. He held upward a list of names. "The list of workers Mr. Robert Sanders gave the court matches exactly except there is a discrepancy in the accounting records."

"What discrepancy?" Judge Jackson asked as he narrowed his eyes.

One of the accountants held upward a journal book. "It is Mr. Harding's second order of twenty thousand uniforms," he answered. "There was a delivery date that had to be met. Mr. Harding hired several people to deliver uniforms. They only worked for two weeks. The six men were hired to deliver uniforms and the deliveries are well documented. They delivered uniforms to Washington D.C., Mississippi, and parts of Texas. Mr. Jonathan Harding was very meticulous in his accounting."

"Do you have their names?" Judge Brown asked.

"Yes Your Honor," one of the accountants answered. "Everything is here: their names, addresses, ages, and the delivery locations." The accountant looked at Judge Brown. "They were brothers! They were too young to enlist in World War I. The youngest brother was ten."

"Did Mr. Harding pay them?" Judge Jackson asked.

"Yes Your Honor," one of the accountants answered. "Everything is here! We have already certified these journal ledgers as the official accounting records for Harding and Associates. They were discovered in one of the boxes that contains the fund for the pensions."

Judge Jackson looked at Judge Brown. "If they worked for Harding and Associates and there is proof, they each get a share," he said as he nodded to Judge Brown.

"That was the agreement Mr. Harding made," Judge Brown said as he nodded his head.

"That was my understanding of Judge Brown's order," one of the accountants said. He motioned for Judge Brown and Judge Jackson to follow him. "We have additional problems."

Judge Brown and Judge Jackson nodded their heads. They followed the two accountants as they walked down the long hallway toward the end. They stopped and stood near the windows facing the six statues.

"Technically, Mr. Harding and his wife worked for the company," one of the accountants whispered. "They each received a modest salary. Their son Franklin also worked briefly for the company."

"When?" Judge Jackson asked surprised.

One of the accountants held upward a journal book. "When he was home from school," he answered. "He only worked one day. Mr. Harding fired him because he didn't work! Technically, Mr. Harding receives a share and the shares of his mother and father!"

"No he doesn't!" Judge Brown said quickly. "It was discussed at great length. The documents clearly state that the owner does not share in the cash disbursements! Mr. Franklin Harding gave away all rights to any shares when he took over the business as the owner. He is aware as it was discussed at great length by the law firm representing him. Mr. Franklin Harding gets nothing!"

"That was our understanding of the court order and the agreement," one of the accountants said smiling. He looked down the hallway to where the people were sitting and standing. The accountant pointed to an elderly woman sitting on the bench. "That is Mrs. Irene Davidson. The six men that worked briefly were her brothers." He turned and looked at Judge Jackson. "They are all dead! They enlisted in World War II and they all died in the war. She is the only heir."

Judge Jackson shrugged his shoulders. "She gets their share," he said in a gruff voice.

One of the accountants leaned toward Judge Jackson. "Your Honor, I don't think you understand," he whispered.

"Understand what?" Judge Jackson asked.

One of the accountants motioned for the two judges to come closer. Judge Jackson and Judge Brown leaned close to the accountant.

"We haven't counted all of the cash assets," the accountant whispered. He held upward a journal. "Mr. Jonathan Harding was very wealthy! Each box we have counted so far contained cash and matured war bonds. Each box is averaging three million dollars! We are only guessing, but each worker or their heir will receive a minimum of two million dollars. Mrs. Davidson's share, so far, is fourteen million dollars!"

Judge Brown and Judge Jackson's eyes widened. They looked at each other and then they looked toward the window. "*Lady Justice*!" they both said simultaneously. Then they began to laugh very hard. They laughed so loudly the people in the hallway looked toward them.

The two accountants laughed and smiled. "We are almost ready," one of the accountants said. "The accounting records list one additional worker that was not included on the list Mr. Sanders gave to the court. The person is deceased and there is only one heir. The heir lives in Memphis and he is not here. Do you want to wait until we can send for him before we proceed?"

"We should wait," Judge Jackson said. "Do you have an address?"

"Yes Your Honor," the accountant answered.

"Who is it?" Judge Brown asked.

The accountant held upward a journal book. "Mr. Harding had an attorney that he used," he answered. "The attorney received a modest salary but he performed many duties. The attorney arranged for the defense contracts and prepared the original documents. Mr. Nathan Clark is deceased and there is only one heir."

"Nathan Clark was on retainer," Judge Jackson said quickly.

"No he wasn't," one of the accountants answered. "Mr. Nathan Clark received a regular salary. He worked for Harding and Associates from 1926 until his death in 1943. Mr. Nathan Clark received the same modest salary as Mr. and Mrs. Harding."

Judge Brown leaned close to the accountant. "The law firm of Clark and Higgins represented Harding and Associates," he said abruptly.

"No they didn't," one of the accountants said as he held upward a journal. "Only Mr. Nathan Clark performed legal work. There was no charge for any of his legal services. Mr. Harding paid all expenses but Mr. Nathan Clark never charged. His title was Legal Counsel and he received a monthly salary."

"It's all here," the accountant added, as he held upward a journal. "Mr. Nathan Clark worked for Harding and Associates."

Judge Jackson and Judge Brown narrowed their eyes and looked at each other. "Why did Mr. Sanders leave the name out?" Judge Jackson asked in a gruff voice.

The two accountants looked at each other. "It wasn't intentional," one of the accountants answered softly. "I don't think it occurred to him. Mr. Nathan Clark was like a third owner."

"Then he gets a share," Judge Jackson said softly.

Judge Brown nodded his head. "Who is the heir?"

"The heir is Mr. Nathan Clark's great-grandson, Mr. Woodrow Clark," the accountant answered.

Judge Brown and Judge Jackson's eyes widened. They looked at each other and then they looked toward the window. "*Lady Justice*!" they both yelled simultaneously. Then, they began to laugh very hard.

"What else is in the journals?" Judge Jackson asked laughing.

The two accountants became very solemn. They looked at each other. "Many things," one of the accountants answered. "Parts of the journals are like a diary. Mr. Harding and his wife loved these people very much. They did a lot of things for them. They wrote many things in the journals."

"What things?" Judge Brown asked.

The accountants looked at each other then they lowered their heads. "They wrote a lot about their son," one of the accountants answered quietly. He slowly raised his head. "They were very disappointed in him. They had hoped he would continue the business but they knew he would not. They provided very well for him."

The other accountant raised his head. "I want to assure you that anything we have seen or discovered will remain a secret," he said. "We will not reveal any amounts or information we discovered in the journals."

"I know that," Judge Jackson said. "That is why I chose your company."

"There is one thing you should know," one of the accountants said. "I don't think it violates any confidence and I am sure anyone of Mr. Harding's workers will tell you if you asked." He looked toward the people sitting and standing in the hallway. Then he looked toward Judge Jackson. "Mrs. Elizabeth Harding was one of them. She lived in the poorest section of Memphis and she worked for Mr. Harding. She made uniforms. Mr. Harding fell in love with her and they married. It is all here."

"There is something else but I think it may betray a confidence," the accountant added. "It is not bad but something very good! You can read it if you like. It will explain much."

The accountant handed a journal to Judge Jackson. Judge Jackson did not extend his hand.

The accountant handed the journal to Judge Brown. Judge Brown did not extend his hand.

"When you have finished, place the journals in a container," Judge Jackson said. "I am going to seal all of the records. The journals will be sealed with the records."

Judge Brown smiled. "I am going to send for Mr. Woodrow Clark," he said. "When he arrives, Judge Jackson and I will meet with him and explain everything."

The two accountants smiled. They turned and walked toward Judge Brown's courtroom. As they approached the doors, one of the accountants turned. He opened one of the journals and removed a sheet of paper. "There is something else you should know," the accountant said as he held upward the sheet of paper. "Harding and Associates also made suits."

"Suits?" Judge Jackson asked with a surprised look on his face.

"They only made three but it is significant," the accountant said with a smile. He held the sheet of paper upward. "Mr. Nathan Clark traveled to England to negotiate a contract with the British government. While he was there, Mr. Winston Churchill ordered three suits. He specifically asked for Mrs. Eileen Barnes to make them."

The other accountant smiled as he held upward a journal. "Mr. Nathan Clark personally delivered them," he said grinning. "Mr. Churchill paid for them but Mr. Jonathan Harding donated the money to the British Red Cross."

The other accountant nodded his head and grinned. "Mr. Nathan Clark ate breakfast with Mr. Churchill and the Queen!" he blurted.

Judge Brown and Judge Jackson's eyes widened as they looked at each other.

"Is there proof?" Judge Jackson asked in a gruff voice.

The two accountant's eyes widened. "Yes Your Honor," one of the accountants answered.

Judge Jackson pointed his hand toward the journal books the two accountants were holding. "Is there proof that Mr. Nathan Clark had lunch with President Woodrow Wilson?" Judge Jackson asked in a gruff voice.

One of the accountants was startled at the question and he dropped the accounting books. He kneeled to the floor and picked up one of the books. "Yes Your Honor," he answered frightened, as he held the journal upward. "It is here! Dates and times."

Judge Jackson's face was angered. "You will not reveal this information! That is an order!" Judge Jackson said angrily.

The two accountant's eyes widened as they lowered their heads.

Judge Jackson laughed. He laughed very hard. "You will not reveal this information until I have had the opportunity to tell the senior partners of Clark and Higgins," he said laughing.

The two accountants raised their heads quickly.

"Good job!" Judge Jackson laughed. "Write everything down and certify it! Mr. Franklin Harding bragged in my court today that Mr. Nathan Clark was no good!"

Judge Brown laughed. "Good enough to break bread with a President, Prime Minister, and a Queen," he chuckled.

"I can't wait to tell Mr. Franklin Harding that one of his father's workers made suits for Winston Churchill," Judge Jackson giggled.

The two accountants quickly gathered the journal books. As they gathered the books, one accountant whispered to the other, "He already knows."

The other accountant nodded his head. They gathered the journals and walked quickly toward the doors of Judge Brown's courtroom.

Mr. Redkin's voice began to trail. The people in the crowd were laughing very hard at the story. He smiled and looked at Tommy and Barbara, they were laughing. The people in the crowd were laughing at the strange twist of events where Jonathan and Elizabeth Harding left their fortune to their workers, disguised as cash assets.

Mr. Redkin held his hands upward to quiet the people in the crowd. "Judge Jackson and Judge Brown had every proceeding of the court sealed!" he yelled. "Judge Jackson placed everyone that had knowledge of the proceeding under a gag order. Senior partners of the law firm Clark and Higgins immediately appealed the court's decision to seal the records. Mr. Woodrow represented the workers and their heirs; he defeated the law firm soundly in court!"

The people in the crowd yelled and cheered.

"I have heard of Mr. Woodrow!" a lady in the crowd yelled. "He represented the wealthiest people in Memphis! One of his clients had her dog picked up by animal control. Mr. Woodrow got a court order to have her dog released!"

Mr. Redkin smiled. "That was Mrs. Newsome's dog Brandy," he said with a large grin on his face.

The people in the crowd looked puzzled at Mr. Redkin's remark. Then they laughed loudly.

Hamilton Andrews stood beside Barbara listening to Mr. Redkin. He remembered the name Mr. Woodrow. He met him only once. It was the first land deal he was involved in with Mrs. Cannon. He was present at the meeting to finalize the deal. Mrs. Cannon arrived early and she refused to speak to anyone. When her attorney, Mr. Woodrow, arrived she began to laugh and joke with everyone. She grinned as she proudly introduced Mr. Woodrow. He asked several questions and advised her to agree. Mrs. Cannon quickly signed the documents. Mr. Redkin was correct! Mrs. Charlene Cannon is a very nice person but she seemed to change after Mr. Woodrow died. It seems she doesn't trust anyone! She trusted Mr. Woodrow.

"I didn't recognize the name!" the investment banker yelled.

The people in the crowd turned toward him.

"Franklin Harding appealed the court's ruling on the two hundred dollars in matured war bonds found in Jonathan's safe," the investment banker said. "He hired the best lawyers he could find. Franklin was the laughing stock of the investment community. People laughed at him because he was fighting for two hundred dollars. He told everyone that it was Principle! Franklin spent thousands of dollars in legal fees to get the lower court's ruling overturned."

"He lost the appeal!" the investment banker said smiling. "Franklin wasn't fighting for two hundred dollars. The rumor was that the actual amount was ten million dollars in matured war bonds. No one knows for sure. The court records were sealed! An attempt was made to have the court records unsealed about thirty years ago." The man looked at Mr. Redkin. "The records were misplaced!"

Mr. Redkin smiled slightly. "The sealed records in the case were discovered misplaced more than forty years ago," he said grinning. "They were discovered missing about three weeks after Charlene Davidson reached the legal age of twenty-one and inherited a portion of her great-grandmother's fortune."

The investment banker cocked his head slightly. He had a confused look on his face. "There was a question concerning the matured bonds. It was believed some of the bonds were forged and an attempt was made to unseal the court records to verify the serial numbers," he said.

The people in the crowd looked at the investment banker and then they looked at Mr. Redkin.

Mr. Redkin's face was solemn. "Judge Jackson had the IRS verifiy the serial numbers on all the war bonds," he said. "There were no forgeries. All of the bonds were purchased from the U.S. Department of War."

The investment banker was puzzled. He slowly shook his head. "If there were no forgeries, why did someone attempt to have the court proceedings unsealed?" he asked Mr. Redkin.

Mr. Redkin's face was solemn. There was no expression in his face. "A senior partner of the law firm Clark and Higgins believed if he could place doubt on the validity of the war bonds, he could get the original agreement prepared and signed by Nathan Clark nullified," he answered.

The people in the crowd looked at Mr. Redkin. Then they looked at the investment banker.

The investment banker shook his head. He had a puzzled look on his face. "I doubt that would happen," he said laughing.

"The documents sound airtight. The only thing that would happen is the partner would create a big stink!"

Mr. Redkin smiled. "The documents were sealed and no one knows the names of Jonathan's workers. Perhaps one or more heirs would prefer that information is not known," he said quietly. "Perhaps one or more heirs would pay handsomely for that information to remain secret."

The investment banker laughed. He laughed very hard. "A shake down!" he yelled, as he removed his cellular telephone from his coat pocket.

The people in the crowd were confused. They didn't know what the investment banker and Mr. Redkin were talking about.

The investment banker laughed. He smiled and he laughed. The people in the crowd began to giggle at him. The investment banker turned and walked through the people in the crowd toward the parking lot. As he walked, he opened his cellular telephone and dialed a number. He spoke softly in the receiver and then laughed very loud. Then, he dialed another number.

The people in the crowd laughed as they watched him walk toward the parking lot. He dialed a number, spoke softly, and laughed very loudly. He dialed more than ten telephone numbers before he reached the main gates of the cemetery. The people in the crowd laughed and cheered. They turned toward Mr. Redkin when they heard him weep.

Mr. Redkin had lowered his head and he was weeping. He sobbed very loudly. The people in the crowd were silent as they listened to his sobs. He slowly raised his head and sighed.

"April 24, 1947," Mr. Redkin said. "The workers of Jonathan and Elizabeth were present in the courtroom as the money was divided equally. Jonathan and Elizabeth only had forty-six partners left. Many had died. Only thirty-four partners were in the courtroom as Judge Jackson supervised the disbursement of the cash assets. Twelve of the partners were not present."

The people in the crowd made an awing sound.

A woman leaned toward Mr. Redkin. "Where were they?" she asked.

"Drunk!" a young man in the crowd laughed.

The people in the crowd turned toward the young man that had spoken. He was laughing. They glared at him.

"What?" the young man asked.

"Shut up!" a woman yelled.

The young man stopped laughing and lowered his head.

The people in the crowd turned to look toward Mr. Redkin.

Mr. Redkin looked upward. "The twelve partners met most of the day at the home of Ray Johnson," he sighed. "Ray lived in a four-room dump on Carrol Street. The twelve partners were all men. They met at the home of Ray Johnson to discuss what they would do later that night." Mr. Redkin sighed and he pointed toward the main section of the cemetery. The people in the crowd turned to look where he was pointing. "At 11:00 P.M., the twelve men met at the graves of Jonathan and Elizabeth Harding."

Mr. Redkin stopped speaking. He began to weep. He lowered his head and raised his head. Tears were streaming down his cheeks. "They exhumed the bodies of Jonathan and Elizabeth," he said sobbing. Mr. Redkin pointed toward the rear of the pauper's section of the cemetery. The people in the crowd turned to look where he was pointing. "They fullfilled Jonathan and Elizabeth's last wish. They were buried here! They were buried beside the people they loved and cared for. Their graves were marked with a simple marker that read, UNKNOWN. My grandfather was one of the twelve."

The people in the crowd were quiet.

Mr. Redkin breathed softly. He wiped his eyes with his handkerchief and blew his nose. "Jonathan's workers worked through two world wars. They each received certificates of appreciation. Jessie Burgess didn't receive one certificate of appreciation, he received two!" Mr. Redkin said quietly. "The first one was personally signed by President Woodrow Wilson.

The second one was personally signed by President Franklin D. Roosevelt before his untimely death on April 12, 1945."

The people in the crowd were quiet.

Mr. Redkin looked at the woman who asked him a question earlier. "You asked me how I know this, you asked?" he said softly. "I own Jessie Burgess' second certificate signed by President Franklin D. Roosevelt. I obtained it two years ago at a flea market. The price was high," he said, as he looked at her. "It cost fifty cents."

The woman that asked the question began to sob. She reached into her purse and she removed a handkerchief. She sobbed quietly as she held the handkerchief to her eyes.

He reached into his jacket and he removed the program each person received, as they began the tour. He held the program upward toward the people in the crowd. "Learn about History," he said. "Meet the people who shaped the destiny of our city and our country. Learn about the most important people that ever lived in Memphis!"

The people in the crowd looked at their programs. Mr. Redkin quoted the heading exactly.

"You're in the right spot!" Mr. Redkin said softly. "They are here! They are all here!" He turned and pointed toward the cemetery. "Jonathan, Elizabeth, Agnes, Jessie, Mark, Calib, Janice, Martha, Robert, Samuel, Eileen, John, Michelle, Charlie," he said.

"Charlie!" Mr. Redkin said, as he looked upward. "Charlie Glass!" he sighed.

He looked at the crowd. The people in the crowd were silent.

"Charlie Glass was born a mute!" Mr. Redkin said. "He lived near the bridge. Elizabeth met him one day as he begged for food. She brought him to the plant and Jonathan hired him. His job was a simple but important one. Charlie watched the spindles of thread. When the thread was low, he would motion for the technician."

Mr. Redkin smiled at the people in the crowd. "Jonathan treated him as the others. Each Christmas Charlie Glass received ten dollars in cash, a large ham, and a brown envelope."

He smiled softly. "When Franklin sold his father's company, Charlie had died. His younger brother received his share; more than two million dollars."

The people in the crowd gasped and moved backward.

"How do you know all this?" a woman asked as she wept into her handkerchief.

He looked at the woman who asked the question. She looked at him with tears in her eyes. "How do I know this?" he asked her. Mr. Redkin looked at the people in the crowd. "Tonight you met two of the people that were in the courtroom that day. You met the young boy who overheard the three conversations of Judge Jackson and Judge Brown and you met the young girl that asked for vanilla ice cream."

The people in the crowd had puzzled looks on their faces. Many of the people began to look at their maps of the list of stops.

"I was that young boy named Herbert. Charlene Davidson was that young girl. My great-grandmother's name is Agnes Farnsworth," he answered.

The people in the crowd gasped.

"I am very proud of her," Mr. Redkin said. "My great-grandmother didn't just work for Jonathan and Elizabeth, she worked for AMERICA!" he said proudly.

The people in the crowd were silent. Then, they began to clap their hands. They clapped louder and louder. Many in the crowd cheered and yelled.

Mr. Redkin held his hands upward to quiet the crowd. The people in the crowd stopped clapping and cheering.

"When Franklin sold everything, my great-grandparents had died. My grandfather worked for Jonathan and he inherited their share. He became wealthy. Very wealthy! That is where my money came from," he added.

The people in the crowd were silent.

"Enough!" Mr. Redkin shouted. "I hope I didn't interrupt too much!"

A man in the crowd looked at his map. "Will you show us where Mr. Harding and his wife Elizabeth are buried?" he asked quietly.

Mr. Redkin shook his head. "No," he answered. "It was the last wish of Jonathan and Elizabeth that they be buried in this section. They wanted no one to know where they were buried. My grandfather helped to move them from the main section to this section. When I was a young boy, he showed me where they rested. I am the only one that knows! When I die, the location will die with me. I will honor the last request of Jonathan and Elizabeth."

The woman, who asked the question, began to sob loudly. Her husband held to her as they walked through the crowd toward the gates. As they neared the light post, the man turned. His eyes were filled with tears. He smiled softly as he and his wife turned and walked slowly toward the parking lot. The people in the crowd could hear their sobs.

Many of the women in the crowd wept.

"Why did your grandfather tell you?" a woman in the crowd asked.

Mr. Redkin laughed. "There are many things my grandfather told me and showed me," he said laughing. "Rumors are often based on fact and facts are often the wishful thinking of many."

He looked at Tommy. "I leave you with a Christmas gift!" Mr. Redkin said as he reached into the breast pocket of his coat. He removed a check and he handed it to Tommy. Tommy looked at the check. The check was addressed to The Homeless Christmas Dinner Fund. Mr. Redkin had signed the check. The amount was blank.

Mr. Redkin looked at the crowd. "For every dollar donated to the Christmas dinner for the homeless, I will match it," he said laughing.

The people in the crowd applauded.

"I leave you with a Christmas gift," he said laughing. "My grandfather told me many things and he showed me many things. When you think of Caroline Brown Harrison remember she was a woman of noble character. Remember, she is buried here!"

Many people in the crowd laughed.

Mr. Redkin bent downward toward the young boy standing in the front of the crowd. "I plan to come next year, if my health is good!" he said smiling. "I will tell more stories about Robert Galloway."

The young boy looked at Mr. Redkin. "Is Daniel Boone buried here?" he asked.

Mr. Redkin's eyes narrowed. He leaned upward and smiled softly at the young boy. "My great-grandfather saw the tombstone placed on the grave of the man named Daniel Boone," he told the people in the crowd. "Daniel Boone was alleged to have taken a hunting trip with one of his friends before his death. There are several stories of how Daniel Boone died. One story is he died alone in the woods. One story is he died in Missouri." Mr. Redkin looked downward at the young boy. "One story is Daniel Boone died in a saloon fight. He killed six men before someone shot him in the back," he added.

The young boy's eyes widened.

"There is debate on the date Daniel Boone died," Mr. Redkin said, as he kneeled toward the young boy. "One story is he died in 1820. One story is he died in 1824." He looked carefully at the young boy. "One story is he died in the year 1827."

Mr. Redkin stood and he looked at the people in the crowd. "The words on the tombstone were simple words. *DANIEL BOONE, FRONTIERSMAN, ADVENTURER, EXPLORER*," he said smiling.

The people in the crowd made an awing sound.

"Before I forget!" Mr. Redkin yelled. "Captain Steven English was a real tough guy! He and his thugs murdered innocent women and children. Many of the people he murdered were elderly and ill! The Chickasaw Indians were peaceful. Their beliefs forbid the act of scalping. There was no Indian attack!"

Many people in the crowd began to whisper to each other.

"I don't fault the young boy," Mr. Redkin said with a sigh. "He just read the garbage he was given to read. Facts are often the wishful thinking of many." Mr. Redkin waved his hands as he walked through the people in the crowd toward the iron gates. Many people in the crowd patted him on the back as he walked past them. He waved goodbye as he walked through the gates of the pauper's section toward the parking lot.

"Where were we?" Tommy asked Barbara.

The people in the crowd laughed and clapped.

Tommy laughed. "Robert Galloway guarded the Mayor for more than three weeks while the militia guarded his house. While the militia guarded the Mayor's house, the Governor cleaned house. He removed every corrupt policeman he could find," he yelled.

The people in the crowd cheered.

Barbara placed her hands on her hips. "In case you haven't guessed it, it seems Mrs. Caroline Brown Harrison didn't control the Governor like she thought!" she shouted. "The Governor didn't send the militia to the home of the Mayor to arrest him; he sent the militia to protect him from the corrupt police."

The people in the crowd laughed and cheered.

Tommy removed the coat and he placed the coat, hat, and the third pistol on the ground. He removed the gun belt and smiled softly. "The story of Caroline Brown Harrison ends here," he said softly. "After the trial she went into seclusion until her death." He pointed toward the main section of the cemetery. The people in the crowd turned to look where he was pointing. "She was buried there beside her husband."

"Or!" Barbara yelled.

The people in the crowd turned to look at Barbara.

Barbara pointed toward the back of the cemetery. "She was buried for more than two years in the grave of the notorious riverboat gambler Blackjack Calhoun. She was buried beside the people she hated and despised."

"Or!" Tommy yelled as he pointed toward the main section of the cemetery. The people in the crowd turned to look where Tommy was pointing. "She is buried in the grave at the rear of the cemetery. The monument inscription reads - *A WOMAN OF NOBLE CHARACTER IS BURIED HERE*."

Many people in the crowd laughed and clapped.

"What about Daniel Boone?" the young boy asked.

The people in the crowd laughed.

Tommy looked at the crowd very seriously. "It's only a rumor and there is no basis of fact," he answered. "Daniel Boone died in the year 1820 at the age of eighty-three. He is buried beside his wife in Missouri. The City Cemetery wasn't opened until 1822. The man buried here was killed in a saloon fight in the year 1827."

The young boy lowered his head.

The people in the crowd grinned at each other as they nodded their heads.

The people buried here are the poor and the unknown," Tommy added.

Barbara looked very solemn. "Many of the graves had no markers and people are still buried here. Twelve people have been buried here in the last two years," she said softly.

The people in the crowd got very quite.

A man in the crowd looked at his map. "Is this the same tour you did last year?" the man asked.

Tommy smiled. "This is the eighth year we have held this tour," he answered.

"Where are the re-enactors?" a woman asked.

"We don't use them," Barbara answered. "We don't believe it is dignified."

"I got my monies worth," a man yelled. "Do you charge five dollars every year?"

Tommy's face was solemn. "We don't charge any money! Our purpose is to bring awareness of the poor in the city and to remember those who have died and are buried here," he answered softly.

"How do you make money?" a woman asked.

Tommy smiled. "We ask for donations to help defray the cost of the Christmas dinner for the homeless at the mission. Every penny is spent on the dinner. If any money is left, it is given to the Big Brothers Association to provide food for the needy. Every penny is spent on food," he answered softly.

"There is a box near the front gate by the parking lot. If you wish to donate, we appreciate any amount you may choose to give," Tommy added.

"Where are the Mayor and the man that hid the records buried? Are they buried here?" a man asked.

Barbara smiled. "No," she answered. "Mrs. Caroline Brown Harrison was one of the last people buried here. The cemetery was closed except for the poor and the unknown. The Mayor and clerk are buried in the Elysian Fields Cemetery on highway forty-two."

"The only people buried here today are poor, homeless, and nameless," Tommy added. "The city pays for the burial. The burial is simple but dignified. Last year, the City Council approved funding to place markers on every grave." Tommy pointed toward the rear of the cemetery. "A large portion of the stone wall had collapsed and it was repaired. Street lights were placed toward the rear."

Barbara smiled. "Follow me and I will take you to the oldest section. You can read some of the markers. Mr. Redkin mentioned some names tonight!" she said excitedly. "We will pass several of them as we walk toward the rear."

A man looked at his map. "Mr. Nathan Clark is buried in the main section," he said as he looked at the people. "He should have been on the list of stops!"

Tommy raised his hands. "Nothing is known about Mr. Nathan Clark," he yelled. "I heard some things tonight I did not know. His wife was from Boston and she is buried in the family cemetery in Boston. He was buried in the main section. All that was known is that he was an attorney and founded the law firm of Clark and Higgins. The law firm was dissolved many years ago." Tommy smiled.

The people in the crowd nodded their heads.

Barbara took a flashlight from her pocket and began walking toward the rear of the cemetery. The people followed. She walked a short distance and stopped. "Many of the graves were unmarked. The City Council placed markers with names and dates on the graves of the people we could identify," she said quietly. "Mr. Redkin mentioned the name Hollis Taylor. He is buried here."

Barbara pointed her flashlight toward one of the graves. HOLLIS HOUSTON TAYLOR BORN 1882 DIED 1948, the marker read. The people looked toward the marker.

"Swing your partner to the left!" Mr. Grimes yelled as Mr. Smith played the fiddle quickly.

Hollis laughed as he swung his wife, Lois, to the left.

"Swing your partner to the right!" Mr. Grimes yelled.

Hollis laughed as he swung Lois to the right.

Mr. Smith played the fiddle quickly, then, he stopped playing.

"Bow to your partner!" Mr. Grimes yelled.

Lois laughed as she stopped dancing and curtsied to her husband. Hollis laughed as he bowed toward her.

Mr. Smith began playing the fiddle quickly.

"Promenade!" Mr. Grimes yelled.

Hollis and Lois laughed as they joined hands and joined the large circle. Mr. Smith played his fiddle loudly as the people began to promenade in the large barn.

Barbara moved the flashlight from the grave and pointed it toward another. "Mr. Redkin mentioned the name Mrs. Mayo," she said loudly. "Her first name is Alice! She is buried here beside her husband Roy." Barbara pointed the flashlight toward one of the markers. ALICE MAY MAYO BORN 1867 DIED 1947, the marker read. The people looked toward the marker.

Alice smiled as she slowly rocked in her rocker. Her hands were sore from the sewing but not sore enough to reach toward her husband and hold his hand.

Roy smiled as she clasped his hand. He leaned backward in his rocker and slowly rocked forward. He smiled as he looked at the night. "Beautiful night!" he said.

Alice nodded. "I love our time together," Alice said softly. "It seems there is so much work to do. I enjoy just sitting on the porch and rocking."

Roy smiled. "Did I tell you I loved you today?" he asked with a solemn look on his face.

Alice smiled. "Only four times," she answered.

"Four times!" Roy said surprised. "I thought it was five!"

"No," Alice said grinning. "I counted them, only four times!"

Roy leaned to his left and gently kissed her on the cheek. "I love you!" he whispered.

"I love you too!" Alice said, as she returned the kiss.

They leaned backward, holding hands, and rocked on the front porch of their home.

"Beautiful night!" Roy said.

"Beautiful night!" Alice said.

Barbara moved the flashlight beam from the grave of Alice Mayo toward the left. "Most of Jonathan Harding's worker's are buried in that section," she said softly. "Up ahead, is the grave of Charlie Glass! Mr. Redkin spoke about him tonight."

The people followed Barbara as she walked four graves forward. She stopped and pointed the flashlight beam to the left. CHARLIE GLASS BORN 1921 DIED 1942, the marker read. The people in the crowd looked toward the marker.

Jonathan slowly stood from his desk and walked toward Charlie. Charlie lowered his head as Elizabeth smiled and placed her arm around his shoulder. "He's very bright!" Elizabeth said.

Jonathan grunted as he approached Charlie. "There is a job available but not anyone can do it!" he said as he folded his arms to his back. "The job requires dedication and strict attention. I have been unable to fill the job because I have not met the right person. I think you are the right person!"

Charlie raised his head and nodded.

Jonathan placed his arm on Charlie's shoulder as he led him toward the machines. He pointed toward the large sewers. "Mr. Glass we have a problem!" he said sternly. "These machines must run, they can not stop! If the spindles of thread get too low, everything stops! It takes thirty minutes to thread the new spindle and restart the sewers. I need someone that can watch the spindles of thread and notify the technician they need to be replaced."

Charlie smiled as he looked at Jonathan. He nodded to Elizabeth.

"Are you currently employed?" Jonathan asked in a stern voice.

Charlie nodded his head no.

"Good!" Jonathan said as he reached into his pants pocket. "I need you to start today, right now! If you can start now, I will give you a signing bonus!"

Jonathan smiled as he removed his hand from his pants pocket and placed two silver dollars in Charlie's hand. "It is a deal?" he asked in a stern voice.

Charlie grasped the two silver dollars and nodded his head.

Jonathan smiled. "Folks!" he yelled to the people on the plant floor. The people stopped working briefly to look at Jonathan, Elizabeth, and Charlie. "I want to introduce the most recent partner of Harding and Associates, Mr. Charlie Glass!"

The people on the plant floor clapped their hands.

"Welcome Charlie!" an elderly woman said.

Charlie smiled as he looked at the people. He smiled to Jonathan and Elizabeth as he grasped the two silver dollars in his hand.

Barbara moved the flashlight beam from the marker of Charlie Glass to the narrow path. "Follow me," she said as she began to walk forward. "We are approaching the main area where almost all of the markers read, UNKNOWN."

Barbara walked toward the rear of the cemetery as the people followed her. She pointed the flashlight beam on the small path as she spoke. "This section has no records that we could find. The graves had no markers until the City Council approved a marker on each grave. We don't know if the person buried is a man, woman, or child. We don't know the date the person died." She stopped and pointed the flashlight beam toward one of the graves. The marker read, UNKNOWN. The people in the crowd looked at the marker.

Elizabeth laughed. "I have an announcement to make!" she said smiling as she placed her arm around her younger brother, Nathan's, shoulder.

Nathan looked upward at the people and smiled.

"Nathan is going to work for Jonathan!" she said proudly. "He won't start for a few years but Jonathan made him a deal!"

"What deal?" Mr. Burgess asked. "Why is he waiting? He finished school!"

Jonathan laughed as he placed his arm around Nathan. "I'm sending Nathan to law school!" he said laughing.

The people in the room laughed and clapped their hands.

"A lawyer? Nathan's going to be a lawyer?" Mr. Burgess asked.

"Yes!" Elizabeth answered proudly. "When Nathan finishes law school he's going to work for Jonathan as the legal attorney."

Nathan smiled as his sister Elizabeth placed her arm around his shoulder.

The flashes of light were bright and intense.

"Mr. Nathan Clark!" Professor Whiteside said as he walked toward the front of the classroom. "Will you please

explain to Mr. Nelson Higgins why if you pass the bar exam, you can practice law in every state except Louisiana!"

Nathan stood very quickly and he looked toward Nelson. "The laws of Louisiana are based on French law," he said. "The base of the law is on property rights. The laws of the other states are based on the Bill of Rights and the Constitution. Those laws are recognized but lower court rulings are based on property rights. In order to practice law in the state of Louisiana, you must first pass a separate bar exam based on property rights." He quickly sat in his chair.

Professor Whiteside walked toward Nathan. "Are you finished?" he asked.

Nathan nodded his head.

"Incomplete and unacceptable!" Professor Whiteside said as he walked toward his desk. He turned quickly toward the class. "If I was a judge and Mr. Nathan Clark came into my courtroom with an answer like that, I would fine him in contempt of my court and throw him out!" he said as he made a motion of throwing someone.

The students lowered their heads.

"In a few weeks, you will each take an exam to graduate from this school," he said frowning. "There is at least one question on the final exam related to French law and the state of Louisiana. If you pass, and that is doubtful, you will then prepare for the bar exam. If you pass, and that is doubtful because there is at least one question on the bar concerning the state of Louisiana, you will become officers of the court."

"As officers of the court, you must prove anything you or your clients say!" he yelled. He looked toward Nathan. "When did property rights become the standard in Louisiana? What legal ruling allows Louisiana to require a separate license to practice law? Which court made that ruling? What are the dates?"

Professor Whiteside looked toward the class. "Mr. Nathan Clark's answer is incomplete and unacceptable because he has not presented any legal evidence that what he said is true!" he yelled. "As an officer of the court you have the duty and obligation to your client to be prepared for any and all questions. You must dot every I and cross every T! One word can make the difference in the interpretation of a contract or provide the basis of an appeal!"

Professor Whiteside walked quickly to his desk and sat in his chair. He looked at the class and pounded his fist on the desk. "You can only argue two points of law in the courtroom!" he yelled. "What the law says and the intent of the law. I want every one of you to go to the library and prepare a legal brief that explains, in legal terms, why the state of Louisiana requires an attorney to pass a separate exam. I want facts, legal rulings, and dates."

Professor Whiteside raised his hand in the air. "I want it on my desk tomorrow morning! Everyone can leave except Mr. Nathan Clark," he added.

The students gathered their books and quickly left. Nathan gathered his books and walked slowly toward Professor Whiteside. As Nathan approached the desk, Professor Whiteside picked up an essay book. "I read your brief concerning the property dispute between two parties. I found parts of it disturbing!" he said softly.

Nathan lowered his head.

"You covered everything but you added a section that no other student covered, the good faith intent of both parties," he added.

Nathan looked upward and narrowed his eyes.

Professor Whiteside placed the essay book on his desk and he pointed to a stack of essay books near the edge. "I read each one of those once, I read your essay four times," he said softly.

"What's wrong with it?" Nathan asked.

Professor Whiteside raised his hands in the air. "Nothing!" he answered. "You covered everything and the end result is the defendant loses."

"Why is it disturbing?" Nathan asked.

Professor Whiteside stood. "The law in this case study is very clear," he said. "There is a contract dispute and the plaintiff has filed suit against the other party for a breech of contract. The plaintiff is right and the defendant is wrong! You added a section where the defendant made good faith intent to correct the problem. If you look at the facts in the case, the good faith attempt was reasonable. The plaintiff made no faith effort to resolve the problem. If he did, the case would never have gone to court."

"Why is that disturbing?" Nathan asked.

"You added a human element to the case," Professor Whiteside answered. "If I was a judge and you presented this brief in my court, I would read it more than once. Because of the facts in the case, I would have no option but to rule in favor of the plaintiff. It is disturbing because I wouldn't feel good about my decision."

Nathan narrowed his eyes. "Why would the judge feel bad about his decision?" he asked.

Professor Whiteside picked up the essay book and placed it in front of Nathan. "If there was a jury in the room, your arguments would have swayed them," he answered. "The defendant would have won even though the law is on the side of the plaintiff."

Professor Whiteside stood and smiled. "The law is very specific in many cases but there are times when many other aspects must be considered," he said as he leaned toward Nathan. "You effectively argued those other aspects that must be considered."

"Is that good?" Nathan asked.

Professor Whiteside sat down. "I read it four times," he answered. "Do you know Mr. Nelson Higgins very well?"

"Yes," Nathan answered. "We have studied together. He is waiting for me in the library."

Professor Whiteside pointed toward the stack of essay books. "I spoke to Mr. Nelson Higgins yesterday concerning his essay. He got everything correct but he added a section no one else added. He effectively argued that the law related to how the boundaries were recorded and approved violated the due process clause in the Constitution. When the defendant discovered an error in the recording of the boundaries, he attempted to correct the error. The law did not allow him the process to correct the error!" Professor Whiteside stood. "His essay was also disturbing. If a jury heard it, they would have been swayed," he said softly.

Nathan narrowed his eyes. "I don't understand? Why are they disturbing if they brought up legal and moral issues?" he asked.

Professor Whiteside smiled. "The exercise is designed to prepare the student for a courtroom confrontation," he said as he leaned toward Nathan. "You both completed the exercise but Mr. Higgins challenged the constitutionality of the law itself and you, Mr. Clark, challenged the morality and intent of the plaintiff. The plaintiff is supposed to win! Your arguments made him lose!"

Nathan narrowed his eyes.

Professor Whiteside laughed. "The plaintiff is supposed to win because the law is on his side but it is not the right thing to do," he giggled. "You did your job! Not only did you represent your clients but you sought justice for the defendant." He leaned closer toward Nathan. "If I was a judge and I was given those two essays, combined, I would rule in favor of the defendant and feel good about my decision. I would feel good because justice had been done."

Professor Whiteside turned toward the chalk board. "The exercise is not about contractual law. It is about morals," he said softly. "The exercise tests the morals of the student."

He turned slowly and looked at Nathan. "I wrote that exercise more than twenty years ago and it is only given prior to graduation. The exercise is a trick! It is designed to see if a student understands that the practice of law is more than written laws but the attempt to seek justice. I have only had two students get both parts correct," he said with a sad look in his eyes.

"I have had many students come through my class that I am proud of and I have had a few students I am not proud of," he added.

Professor Whiteside sat in his chair. "Your essays were shared with the faculty. You got the intent part correct because that is your strength. Mr. Nelson Higgins got the due process part correct because that is his strength. The other students missed both parts," he said smiling. "Your legal arguments demonstrate moral character and a desire to not only follow the law, but seek justice. In the last ten years, I have only had two students to demonstrate such high moral values. Only Clark and Higgins have written such compelling arguments." He grinned. "I read them four times each and Professor Stoke read your essays six times."

"The faculty and I are in agreement!" he added.

"You and the faculty are in agreement about what?" Nathan asked, with a surprised look on his face.

"We have to obey the law and apply it equally to everyone," he said, as he pointed toward the corner of the classroom. In the corner, a statue of Justice stood. The statue was of a woman holding a sword in one hand and a set of scales in the other. A blindfold covered her eyes. "Lady Justice is a symbol of the fair and equal administration of law. The law must be administered without corruption, greed, prejudice, or favor. Justice is blind because she wears a covering over her eyes. The reason she wears the covering is to judge the cases and the people on the merits of law and truthful facts in the case. Laws are made by men and there are times those laws are flawed!"

"The two students that got both parts of the moral exercise correct, held a keen insight of law and the human element of those that come before the court. They will best serve Justice as judges of the law and the merits of those laws and the truthful facts in the case."

"Their legal arguments were impressive!"

Professor Whiteside leaned forward toward Nathan. "The faculty and I compared all four essays. Their legal arguments were impressive but not as impressive as the legal arguments of Clark and Higgins. Mr. Nelson Higgins is very strong on constitutional law and you are strong on contractual law and you add, in simple terms that any judge or jury can understand, the human element. The faculty and I are in agreement, the two of you can make a difference! Mr. Higgins will challenge laws that need to be challenged, and you will bring the human element into his challenge, to guarantee that those laws are changed! If you two combined your talents, the law firm of Clark and Higgins would be a formidable force for Justice in Memphis!"

Nathan narrowed his eyes and smiled.

The flashes of light were fast and furious.

"Your Honor!" Nathan said, as he stood. "The law firm of Clark and Higgins represents the plaintiff Mr. Charles Bowen in the legal suit of Bowen versus Martin Paper Products, in the case of the illegal termination of Mr. Bowen, due to injuries he sustained from defective machinery."

Judge Craig nodded his head.

"Your Honor!" The opposing attorney said, as he stood. "I represent the defendant Martin Paper Products. The law is very clear in this case! The employer is required to present, in writing, the condition or conditions for employment. The conditions for employment at Martin Paper Products are going to church on Sunday and attendance. If you don't go to church or come to work, you're fired! Mr. Bowen signed a contract ten years ago where he agreed to those two conditions. Everybody that works for Martin Paper Products, except the management, signed the contract."

Judge Craig nodded his head and the opposing attorney sat down.

Nathan approached the bench. "We concede that the employment contract Mr. Bowen signed ten years ago was valid and enforceable, at the time he signed it," he said as he placed a document on the judge's bench.

The attorney for Martin Paper Products leaned toward Mr. Martin. "This is going to be fun!" he whispered. "They just got out of law school four months ago and passed the bar exam last month. This is their first case."

"However, if you interpret the contract exactly, there is no exclusion for personal illness!" Nathan added. "If Mr. Bowen died on Wednesday and he was buried on Saturday, his employment would be terminated on Monday, because he failed to show up for work four days in a row, and he didn't attend church Sunday morning."

The people in the courtroom laughed loudly.

Judge Craig looked irritated as he pounded his gavel on the bench to quiet the people in the courtroom. "What is your point? If you concede the employment contract was valid, at the time he signed it, why are we here?" he asked.

Nathan walked to his seat and sat down. Nelson stood. "Your Honor," he said quietly, "the contract Mr. Bowen signed ten years ago was based on Public Law 98-435. Two years ago, in the case of Coppage v. Kansas, 234 U.S 1, 13-15, 20-23 (1924); the Supreme Court of the United States ruled that a similar law was unconstitutional. The court ruled that the law was vague as it related to employer responsibilities and due process for termination. The court's ruling was effective the date the appeal was initiated at the state level. Since Mr. Bowen's contract was based on a similar law, the law that allowed the contract was ruled unconstitutional six years ago. Mr. Bowen's contract was invalid six years ago, his termination was illegal!"

Mr. Martin leaned toward his attorney. "What the hell is he talking about?" he whispered.

The people in the courtroom began to whisper.

"Quiet!" Judge Craig said, as he pounded his gavel on his bench. "What the hell are you talking about?" he asked Nelson.

"The company of Martin Paper Products had the obligation to rewrite the employment contract of Mr. Bowen based upon the decision of the United States Supreme Court," Nelson answered. "To comply with the court's ruling, the new contract would specify exact reasons for termination, include exclusions for personal illness, provide a method where breeches of the contract are discussed with Mr. Bowen, and provide Mr. Bowen an opportunity, to respond, before disciplinary action is taken. Since this was not done, Mr. Bowen's termination was illegal! His termination violated a direct ruling of the United States Supreme Court."

The people in the courtroom whispered loudly.

Judge Craig pounded his gavel on his bench to quiet the people. "Can you prove this?" Judge Craig asked quickly.

Nelson picked up two large stacks of papers from the desk. He walked to the attorney for Martin Paper Products and placed one stack before him. He then walked to Judge Craig's bench and placed a similar stack of papers before the judge. "Your Honor," he said quietly. "I have prepared the brief as released by the Justices of the United States Supreme Court and information related to the law in question." He turned, walked to his chair, and sat down.

The attorney for Martin Paper Products looked at the documents quickly. He whispered to Mr. Martin and he stood. "Your Honor!" he said, in a loud voice. "I have consulted with my client and I request a recess to discuss settlement terms. If you give us thirty minutes, I think we can reach an agreement and the case can be dismissed."

Judge Craig looked at the stack of papers in front of him. "Request denied!" he said softly. "The law firm of Clark and Higgins has introduced several important issues before this court that may affect every worker in Shelby County." He looked at Nelson. "Continue!"

Nathan stood. "The law, in question, was based on the At-Will Employment doctrine adopted by several states based on

Horace G. Wood's 1877 treatise on the master-servant relationship. The law was designed with the intent..."

Barbara pointed the flashlight toward the marker then she quickly pointed the beam toward the path. "Follow me to the oldest section of the cemetery," she said smiling.

Plato's Dream

8:32 P.M. – December 23, 2007

The people in the crowd followed Barbara as she walked toward the rear of the cemetery. She stopped beside one of the graves and she looked downward and pointed to the headstone. "This is perhaps the oldest grave. The person was buried in 1822. This person was one of the first people buried here. We do not know if the person is a male or a female," she said.

Barbara looked upward at the people. They were frozen! No one was moving. Barbara looked toward the rear of the crowd toward Tommy. Tommy seemed frozen! His mouth was opened and he was speaking to a young boy. There were no words. Barbara looked puzzled. No one was speaking. No one was moving. The people were frozen.

She looked toward her left to the stone wall. The new lights were dimmed. The lights, shining on the stone wall, had dimmed! As she looked at the lights, they slowly dimmed. The stone wall was fading! The lights of the street lamps were dimming. As she watched, the stone wall began to darken. The stone wall faded into darkness.

"Aohhhhhhhhhh," a coyote howled.

Barbara looked quickly to her right. She heard a coyote howl. She was frightened! "How did a coyote get into the city?" Barbara asked herself.

Barbara suddenly became very cold. The weather wasn't cold but she shivered. She pulled her coat closer to her. Barbara was cold, so cold! She began to shake from the cold as the people seemed to blur.

Barbara lowered her head. She was cold! She looked upward at the people. They were blurred! The people seemed to be fading into darkness. She looked toward Tommy. She couldn't see him! The crowd had faded into darkness.

"Aohhhhhhhhhh," the coyote howled. Charise shivered from the cold. She pulled the blanket upward, over her head. "Aohhhhhhhh," the coyote howled again.

Charise shivered from the cold. "Mother, father," she said softly.

The canvas of the wagon was pulled slowly backward, as Charise's father looked at her. "It's only a coyote. He won't bother you," her father said, smiling.

Charise held the blanket toward her face. "Father I am very cold and scared," she said.

Charise's father smiled as he reached into the wagon. He picked her, and the blanket, up in his arms and he carried her to the fire. He placed her beside her mother and her brother.

"We are only two days away from Saint Louis," Mr. Sawyer said, as he stood before the large fire. "There is enough land for everyone! It will take several years to completely clear the forest but there is enough land for all the families." He looked at Charise and her brother Samuel and he smiled. "However, the young kids may not like it because the first thing we are going to build is a church and a school," he added.

The people sitting around the fire began to laugh and to clap their hands.

Charise smiled. She held Samuel's hand and hugged her mother. She looked at the people; they had traveled far. The weather was cold and the wagons were difficult to move on the plains. They had been traveling for more than four months. She looked to her right to Mrs. Brice. In her arms, she held her twin daughters. The twins were born two weeks ago. Her mother helped with the delivery. Everyone had made the trip safely, so far.

They sat at the fire listening to Mr. Sawyer tell stories of the new territory named Saint Louis. Mr. Sawyer was a trapper. He organized the group and he led them here. He spoke until the wood had burned. Then, they retired for bed.

She awoke early, before sunrise, and ate breakfast. The meal was bacon and corn cakes. The milk was gone and she drank water. The water tasted stale. It had been more than three days since they filled the water barrels. She and her brother, Samuel, helped to gather the milk cows and they began the trek forward.

They had traveled most of the day when the wagons began to slow. The wagons stopped! She looked outside their wagon to see the men riding forward. The men held their rifles and they rode forward very quickly.

Charise's mother climbed quickly into the back of their wagon. She was driving the wagon. She had stopped the horses and quickly climbed into the back. She held to Charise and Samuel.

She watched the men ride forward. The land was flat and there was about one mile to a ridge. The men rode to the ridge and stopped. They appeared to be speaking to one another. Several of the men rode toward the right and left. The men rode a far distance, looking beyond the ridge. Then, the men rejoined into one group and quickly began riding toward the wagons.

Samuel was frightened. "Mother," he said. "Is something wrong?" Charise's mother held tightly to them. She didn't answer Samuel's question. She reached for the flintlock and pulled the hammer backward. "Quiet," she said softly, as she placed the flintlock on the dropdown.

She watched the men ride from the ridge. The men rode their horses very quickly. When they came to the wagon train, they stopped quickly. Captain Clark rose upward in his stirrups and he pointed toward the ridge. "Were here!" he yelled. "The river is over the ridge! We're in the Saint Louis territory!"

Everyone began to shout and cheer. Charise and her brother hugged their mother as her father rode quickly toward them. He dismounted his horse and hugged them. "It's beautiful!" he said, excited. "The grass is green and there are many trees!"

"Quiet! Quiet!" Reverend Norris said, as he walked toward the wagons. "Everyone gather together for a prayer! The Lord brought us here safe."

The people left the wagons and gathered together in front of Reverend Norris. Everyone kneeled and lowered their heads.

Reverend Norris removed his hat and he lowered his head. "We thank you Lord for the blessings you have given us," Reverend Norris yelled. "Two hundred and twenty-six began the journey and two hundred twenty-eight arrived. This is your land Lord. We come to honor it, not to destroy it. We come to live in peace, not to wage war. We come to praise your name. In your name, we will build a city. In your name, we will build a nation. Amen."

"Amen," the people answered.

Charise was excited; a new land and new adventures. 'What would happen? What new adventures are ahead?" she thought. 'What does my future hold?"

3:22 P.M. – August 4, 2008

"Will you be late?" Mrs. Barkley asked her son.

"No mom. Dad and I won't stay long. When the game is over we will drive straight home," Ray Jr. answered.

"Bye honey," Mrs. Barkley said, as she leaned upward to kiss her husband. She stood at the doorway with the glass door opened.

Ray Sr. smiled as she kissed him. He looked at Ray Jr. "I bet you two dollars the Grizzlies win!" he said excited.

"It's a bet!" Ray Jr. said, excited.

Mrs. Barkley watched her husband Ray and Ray Jr. walk to their Jeep. Ray Sr. opened the door when he froze!

Mrs. Barkley looked at her husband. His hand was on the door handle of their Jeep and he was smiling. He was saying something to Ray Jr. but there were no words. Ray Jr. was walking around the back of the Jeep. He was looking at his father. He was smiling and his mouth was opened but he wasn't speaking. Ray Jr. was frozen!

She looked toward the Jeep, waiting for Ray to enter. He didn't! Ray had his hand on the door handle. The door was partially opened and Ray was standing frozen!

"Ray," she said softly. "Is something wrong?"

Ray didn't answer.

Mrs. Barkley looked closely at the Jeep and her husband. She could see people! There were people standing around the Jeep. The people were looking upward at something. The people were very faint and then they began to become very clear. She looked upward toward the trees. The trees were gone! The trees were not there! The sky was a deep blue.

The people began to become very clear. There were men, women, and children. Her husband and her son were gone! Their jeep was gone! The people were standing in front of the jeep. She couldn't see her husband and her son from the people. The people looked poorly dressed. Their backs were toward her and they were looking upward.

Mrs. Barkley looked upward. Her eyes widened. She saw it! She saw what the people were looking at. "My goodness!" Mrs. Barkley gasped.

She was standing at the door with the door opened as she watched her husband and her son walk to their Jeep. She closed the door and stepped out of the doorway to the porch. The Jeep was gone! She couldn't see it! People! People were standing in their yard. The people were looking upward!

She was frightened! Mrs. Barkley turned quickly. She reached for the door handle but it wasn't there! Her house was gone! Where her house stood, many people were standing. They were looking upward! Mrs. Barkley turned toward the Jeep. As far as she could see, there were people. The houses were gone! The street and the telephone poles were gone!

The people were standing looking upward. There were men, women, and children. They were poorly dressed with their backs toward her. They were looking upward. "It can't be!" Mrs. Barkley said, softly. Her eyes widened as she continued to look upward.

She began to move backward slowly. As she moved backward, she continued to look upward. Suddenly, she screamed! Someone behind her placed their hands on her waist. She screamed as she was slowly lifted upward.

"Can you see?" Bradley laughed as he placed Margaret on his shoulder.

Margaret screamed and laughed. Her eyes were widely opened as she looked upward. She's beautiful!" Margaret said. "How tall is she?"

"I don't know," Bradley answered. "She is the tallest thing I have ever seen. The captain said there is a light in her torch. It is lit at night. At night, you can see the torch from twenty miles away."

"Her torch is the light of freedom," Margaret's father said, as he leaned toward her. "In her left arm she holds a tablet with the date of the Declaration of Independence."

"My turn! My turn!" Victoria yelled, as she pulled on Bradley's pants.

Bradley lowered Margaret to the ship's deck and he picked up Victoria. He placed her on his shoulder. "I can see her dress and the stars in her crown!" Victoria yelled excitedly.

Margaret looked at her mother. She was crying. "Mother don't cry," Margaret said.

Margaret's mother leaned downward toward her. "These are tears of happiness, not sadness," she said softly, as she hugged Margaret. She stood quickly and held to her husband's hand. "We're in America!" she said proudly. Everyone looked upward as the ship slowly approached the statue.

The ship moved slowly toward the docks. As the ship passed the statue, the people began to weep with joy. Margaret looked at her father and her brother Bradley. They were weeping. Everyone was weeping.

The ship docked and everyone stood in line to leave the ship. Margaret's father held to their tickets. As they neared the gate, he turned. "Stay together. We have to go to dock seventeen. The boat leaves for Memphis at five o'clock," he said.

"Father," Margaret said. "I don't want to go to Memphis. I want to stay here! I want to live where I can look at her."

Margaret's mother leaned downward. "We can't stay here," she said smiling. "Your uncle Charles is waiting for us in Memphis. He has a job waiting for your father and brother."

"It's a terrible job!" Bradley said, as he leaned toward Margaret.

Margaret's eyes widened.

"No it's not!" Bradley said. "It is a great job! Father and I will learn how to make clothes. It is a big factory that makes men's clothes. Father will run one of the sewers while I will learn to cut the cloth."

"Where is Memphis?" Victoria asked.

"It is beside a great river," Bradley answered. "The river is almost as wide as the ocean! We will take a boat from Saint Louis to Memphis."

Victoria's eyes widened. "Will we sleep on the deck?" she asked excitedly.

"No," Bradley answered. "We have a room. There are beds."

Victoria lowered her head. "I like sleeping on the deck. I like the smell of the ocean," she said softly.

They walked down the plank toward the dock. At the end was a small gate. As they neared the gate, a man held his hand toward Margaret's father. Margaret's father handed the man their tickets. He looked at the tickets and pointed toward his left. "The dock is about four city blocks. It is on the other side of this dock," the man said.

The man smiled as he held his hand outward toward Margaret's father. "Welcome to America!" he smiled, as he shook her father's hand and handed him the tickets.

They picked up their cases and walked to dock seventeen where they sat on a bench waiting for the boat to begin loading. From where they sat, Margaret could see the statue. She was magnificent! Margaret opened a small bag and she removed her needlework. She was making a Christmas scene with several carolers. She unrolled the cloth and she began to stitch one of the children.

Bradley watched her and he came to sit beside her. "Very nice," he said. "You stitch real well. Perhaps, you can sell it when you are finished."

"No," Margaret said. "I want to keep it. It will remind me of home." She looked upward at the statue. "I would like to stitch her," she said softly.

"That would be nice," Bradley said. "If you could stitch her, you could stitch anything," he laughed.

"Mother!" Margaret said. "Bradley's doing it again!"

"Bradley!" Margaret's mother said sharply. "Leave your sister alone! Stop teasing her!"

Bradley stood. "Mother, I didn't say anything! I just remarked at how well she stitches," he said, with a grin on his face.

"Bradley!" Margaret's father said sternly. "You know what your mother is talking about. Margaret doesn't like being called Stitch!"

"Father," Bradley said. "I didn't call her Stitch. If I did, it was meant as something nice! She stitches real well! Perhaps she can get a job at the factory stitching clothing. I think she has a great talent for a ten year-old girl."

Margaret's mother smiled. "You do have a talent, Stitch!" she laughed.

Margaret's father stood and he smiled at Margaret. "You need to put those up! It is almost time to board the boat, Stitch!" he laughed.

Margaret narrowed her eyes, as she placed the needle and thread in the basket. "This is America," she said, as she pointed toward the statue. Margaret stood and she placed her hands on her hips. "There is Wild Bill and Buffalo Bill. There is Chief Crazy Horse and Standing Bull. I am sure there is room for Stitch O'Brian," she said laughing.

2:32 A.M. – May 19, 2009

Carolyn awakened with a pain in her chest. Her left arm and shoulder were hurting. She slowly stood and walked out of her makeshift tent. She looked toward the river and sat down. The pain in her chest hurt. There was pressure on her chest. It felt like something was pushing her.

She looked to her left to Burris' tent. She started to stand but the pain in her chest hurt. "Ohhh!" Carolyn said slowly.

She sat and took a deep breath. Her left arm and shoulder hurt. The pain in her chest came again. "Ohhh!" Carolyn moaned.

She lowered her head and the pain stopped.

Carolyn was looking at the river. It was very beautiful! The sky was clear and the stars were bright. She looked toward the city. The moon was full. It had risen over the bridge. The water was dark but the light of the moon reflected off the river.

She looked to the trees. They were bare and the leaves were gone. On the branches was a light dusting of snow. She looked toward the ground. The ground was lightly covered with snow. Near her tent, Mason and Gerald were sitting. They were playing checkers by the light of a small fire. Near them, Dottie and Sharon were sitting. They were talking.

Carolyn looked to the river. In the river, she could see the dinner boat at the dock. 'The dinner boat leaves at 9:00 P.M.," Carolyn thought. She looked at Mason and Gerald. She could see Gerald's face from the light of the fire. His face was very intense. Carolyn attempted to smile but her mouth wouldn't move. 'Gerald will lose," Carolyn thought.

She looked at the trees and the light snow on the bare branches. 'It must be cold," she thought. She didn't feel cold. Carolyn didn't feel anything. She looked at the river. It was very beautiful! The sky was clear and it was full of stars. The moon had risen over the bridge.

She waited for the whistle on the dinner boat to sound. Carolyn attempted to listen. She didn't hear anything! 'The dinner boat leaves at 9:00 P.M. Before it leaves, the whistle sounds. It must be running late," Carolyn thought. She looked at Gerald's face. He was concentrating on the game.

The moon was full and very beautiful! It had just risen over the bridge.

3:00 P.M. - March 19

"TA DA!" the trumpet blared.

Leon opened his eyes quickly!

"TA DA!" the trumpet blared.

Leon was standing looking upward toward the sky. The sky was a deep blue and there was a large white cloud in the sky.

"TA DA!" the trumpet blared.

Leon was standing! He was standing on his grave! He looked to his right and left. There were many people standing looking toward the sky. He looked upward to the large white cloud in the sky.

"TA DA!" the trumpet blared.

"Leon!" Leon's mother yelled. The voice came from behind Leon. He looked quickly behind him to see his mother. She was standing on her grave. In her arms, she held his baby sister Cassie. He ran quickly to stand beside his mother.

"TA DA!" the trumpet blared.

"Bark! Bark! Bark!"

Leon heard a dog barking. He looked toward the gates of the cemetery. They were opened! An old dog came running through the gates very quickly.

"Lucky!" a man yelled behind Leon.

The old dog ran quickly past Leon. Leon turned to see twelve people standing on a grave. They were holding hands as the old dog ran quickly toward them. One of the men bent downward as the old dog jumped into his arms. "Lucky!" the man yelled, as he and the others petted the dog.

"TA DA!" the trumpet blared.

Plato's Dream

The people in the cemetery looked upward toward the sky. The white cloud was getting larger. It began to quickly fill the entire sky.

Leon looked to his mother and smiled. He looked at his baby sister Cassie. Leon reached toward her and he gently stroked her hair. He kissed her on the cheek and he placed his arm around his mother's waist. Leon looked to the cemetery. People were standing looking upward. There were men, woman, and children. Many of the men and women held infant children in their arms.

"TA DA! TA DA! TA DA!" the trumpet blared quickly three times then, many trumpets began to blare.

Leon and his mother smiled and looked upward toward the sky. The cloud had expanded to fill the entire sky and a bright, white light began to form in the center. As they watched, the cloud began to part.

"TA DA!" many trumpets, blared.

"Now if death is like this, I say that to die is gain; for eternity is then only a single night." - Plato 360 B.C.

Plato's Dream

Added Bonus – Original Ending

The following section was included in the first draft written in 1986. Edward intended this section to be the original ending but, as he modified the work, the work took a different direction. This ending was cut from the book in 2004 as he believed it distracted from the work and poked fun at several professions: lawyers, politicians, and actors. We agreed!

An author will rewrite their book many times, preparing as many as ten drafts. The goal is to improve the work. During these rewrites, sections are added that improve the work and sections are removed that distract. Many times a section is very good but takes the work in a different direction. Those sections are removed and discarded. We believe some sections should not be discarded completely as they represent the thoughts and ideas of the author. In this section, Mr. Arnold proposes two unique and original concepts: genetic consciousness as a legal defense and the possibility of genetic consciousness having an effect on salvation.

Mr. Arnold didn't want this section added. However, we liked it! As an added bonus, we have included the original ending as written in 1986. It is easy to see that this section does take the work in a different direction. However, it is as relevant today as when it was written, eighteen years ago. We hope you enjoy it as much as we did.

Publisher's Addendum

Epilogue

3:05 P.M. - March 19

Mrs. Caroline Brown Harrison stood looking upward toward the sky; the sky was a deep blue. The large cloud disappeared when she heard many trumpets blare. She stood at the rear of the large cemetery facing west. She didn't know what it all meant. She shrugged her shoulders and turned. Behind her, a large monument stood. A WOMAN OF NOBLE CHARACTER IS BURIED HERE, the inscription read. She shrugged her shoulders. The large monument was placed at the rear of the cemetery. It was very far from the other monuments.

The cemetery was very quiet. There was no one in sight. All she could see were large monuments. She walked to the main gates but they were closed and locked. She looked toward the main section of the cemetery when she noticed a crowd of people standing in front of the gates to the pauper's section. She walked quickly toward the crowd.

"What's going on?" she asked quickly.

"They're gone! They are all gone!" a man in the crowd answered.

"Gone where?" Caroline asked.

"It's the Resurrection!" another man in the crowd said. "Everyone in that section is gone!"

"There has been a mistake!" Caroline said, as she pushed her way through the crowd of people. She stopped before the gates. They were made of metal and locked. "Unlock these gates!" she demanded.

"I don't think there is a key," a man in the crowd answered.

Caroline turned to look at the people in the crowd. The crowd was mainly men. She saw several women in the crowd. "Who are you people?" she asked abruptly.

"We are all that is left," a man in the crowd answered. "I saw the gates close and then people began to disappear. We are all that is left." He turned and looked at the main section of the cemetery. "They are gone too!"

"Let me in!" Caroline shouted as she banged her fists against the iron gates. She looked upward toward the sky. The blue sky had begun to darken. "My name is Mrs. Caroline Brown Harrison! You don't know who you are dealing with!" she shouted, as she shook her right fist upward.

"You don't know who you're dealing with!" a man said softly.

Caroline turned to look behind her. The man that spoke was standing behind her. He was dressed in a black suit wearing a black hat. In his hands, he held a deck of cards. The man was shuffling the cards. "Banging on the gates won't work! I have already tried it," the man said as he shuffled the cards.

"Who are you?" Caroline snapped.

"Does it matter?" the man shuffling the cards asked. "They are all gone!"

"What does this mean?" Caroline asked.

A woman stepped forward. "It's the Resurrection, Carolyn," she answered. "All the believers have been taken. We are what are left."

"My name is not Carolyn!" Caroline said quickly. "My name is Mrs. Caroline Brown Harrison!"

"Oooo!" the man shuffling the cards said, "Cat fight!"

"Who are you?" Caroline snapped at the woman.

"Does it matter?" the woman asked, as she shrugged her shoulders. "I am a real estate agent. I manipulated the points on home loans and created large balloon payments. When the people couldn't pay, I foreclosed and then resold the property." She lowered her head. "I ruined many lives," she said sadly.

"What is this all about?" Caroline asked, with a puzzled look on her face.

"Choices!" the man with the cards answered. "We all made choices. I am a gambler and I cheated innocent people."

"I am a lawyer!" one of the men in the crowd said.

"Me too!" most of the men in the crowd said.

"That is a fine lot!" Caroline snapped. "I am trapped in a cemetery with a bunch of damn lawyers!"

"Not me!" a man in the crowd said loudly. "I'm a politician! Don't insult me by calling me a lawyer."

"I am a politician too!" a man in the crowd yelled. He waved at the politician who had spoken. "Hello Smith! I didn't notice you standing there."

"I'm an actor!" a young man said. He looked at several women standing together and he pointed toward them. "Those are my wives!"

Caroline narrowed her eyes. "You mean I am stuck here with lawyers, politicians, and actors?" she asked with a snarl on her face.

"No we're not stuck. Not really," the real estate agent said. "There are two resurrections. We missed the first one! If I remember my Bible class on Sunday, there is a second Resurrection."

"That's right!" the young actor said. "My first wife spoke about it. It is like a trial! We get to plead our cases." He looked at the people in the crowd. "Marcie is not here! She must have been taken." He smiled as he looked at the people. "I'm set! I played an attorney in two movies."

"That's good!" one if the lawyers said. "I'm real good before a judge and jury. I have gotten most of my clients off by appealing to the jury's sense of fairness and sympathy. Most of my clients were guilty but it didn't matter." He looked at the actor. "What kind of trial is it? Are we allowed to bring witnesses?"

The actor smiled. "There is no jury only one judge," he answered. "There is a book. If your name is in it, you're OK. If your name is not in the book, you get to plead your case."

"Simple!" one of the lawyers said. "When the judge takes a break, we manipulate the book! We add our names while the judge is in his chambers drinking coffee." He moved his hands around his coat pockets looking for a pencil or a pen. "Does anybody have a pencil or a pen? I don't have one."

The lawyers began to look for a pencil or a pen. Their pockets were empty. They nodded their heads no.

"That won't work!" one of the lawyers said. "No body has a pencil or a pen. There is supposed to be some type of scales. If we can mess with the scales, we can make them lean in the right direction."

"I don't think so!" one of the lawyers said. "I think the judge keeps the scales with him at all times. We can't tamper with the evidence. It looks like we are going to have to challenge the law!"

"I am only allowed to practice in Georgia," one lawyer said. "I was disbarred from practicing in Tennessee. I will have to get one of you fellows to represent me."

The real estate agent narrowed her eyes. "I don't think the laws are based on Tennessee law," she said.

"What are they?" one lawyer asked.

The real estate agent narrowed her eyes. "I think we're talking about the Ten Commandments!" she answered. "There are only ten laws."

"That's easy!" one lawyer said loudly, as he looked at the people in the crowd. "I got the Ten Commandments kicked out of every elementary school in Alabama! It was a violation of church and state. Let me go first! I will challenge the laws as being unconstitutional."

The real estate agent narrowed her eyes. "I don't think this court recognizes the Constitution," she said.

"There are only two ways to challenge laws in a court of law," one lawyer yelled. "What the law says and the intent! I will challenge what the laws state and the intent of the Ten Commandments!"

"Sounds good!" one lawyer yelled. "The Ten Commandments were written many years ago! They don't apply today. One Commandment said something about coveting your neighbor's ass. The Commandment clearly refers to a farm animal."

"Do you feel hot?" one lawyer asked, as he wiped his brow.

"It is getting warmer," the actor said, as he began to unbutton his coat. He looked upward toward the sky. The sky appeared to be getting darker.

Several of the lawyers nodded their heads as they unbuttoned their coats.

"I don't remember all of the Ten Commandments but I know one refers to honoring your mother and father," one lawyer yelled. "That is vague! I honored my mother and father until they got old and in the way. I went to court and had them committed! I visited them every Christmas. I honored them!"

"Me too!" several of the lawyers said.

"I'm screwed on that law about adultery!" the actor said. "Every one of my wives except the first one was married! I stole them from their husbands."

"That's OK," one of the lawyers said. "I know that law and I have beaten the adultery charge several times. The law is vague. Unless they have witnesses and movies and still pictures, they can't prove a thing. Deny! Deny! Deny!"

"I think you have to be found guilty on all ten counts!" one lawyer yelled. "If you're innocent of one of the ten, they can't convict you! Take that law on killing. Has anybody here killed anybody?"

"That depends," one of the lawyers answered. "I once sent an innocent man to the electric chair. He was innocent but I framed him to get my client, who was guilty of the crime, off. Technically, I didn't kill him! The state did it! You're right! I never killed anybody!"

"Is it my imagination or is it getting hotter?" one of the lawyers asked, as he removed his coat.

"It is getting hotter!" one of the lawyers answered. They looked upward toward the sky. The sky appeared to have darkened. The lawyers took their coats off.

"That law about false idols is easy to challenge!" one of the lawyers yelled. "People think I worship the dollar. Technically that is incorrect! The dollar is the currency with George Washington's picture on it. I prefer the one with Benjamin Franklin's picture!"

"During the fall, Sunday is football day," one lawyer yelled. "To most Americans, that is a Holy day! I kept the Sabbath! I was glued to my television set watching football. I sent my wife and kids to church while I stayed home." He paused and looked around. "They are not here!"

"Don't forget basketball," one lawyer said. "I watched every game on Sunday. It was the highlight of my week."

"Is it getting hotter?" one of the lawyers asked, as he placed his coat on the ground and wiped his brow.

"Seems so," one lawyer answered. He unbuttoned the top three buttons of his shirt.

"When is this hearing?" one lawyer asked the actor.

"I think it is tomorrow," the actor answered.

"Pretty quick," one lawyer said. "I hope it is in the morning because I want to get everything over with."

"We are screwed on the Commandment on stealing!" one lawyer said.

"No, we are not!" one lawyer answered. "Stealing refers to going into someone's home and taking what is not yours! I have never held a gun to anyone's head and taken what was not mine. I used the courts!"

The lawyers nodded their heads.

The real estate agent narrowed her eyes. "I am not a lawyer but I think the Ten Commandments are pretty specific!" she said. "I don't think you can challenge the laws or their intent. If you remember, they were set in stone. The judge created them! I think he knows what they say and their intent."

The two politicians moved forward. "We will rewrite the law!" one of the politicians said. "We will make the Ten Commandments null and void in Shelby County! It will be back dated to cover everyone here!"

"Great idea!" one lawyer said. "We will make it a good thing to disobey the Ten Commandments. We will make everything we did good! Does anybody have paper?"

The lawyers checked their pockets. They shook their heads no.

"Damn!" one of the politicians said.

"What are we going to do?" one lawyer asked.

"Insanity defense!" one lawyer shouted. "We are all crazy!"

"That doesn't work," one lawyer answered. "I used it three times and in each case, my client was convicted."

"It worked for me!" one lawyer yelled. He pointed toward three men standing near a tree. The people in the crowd looked where he was pointing. There were three men standing near a tree talking. "I defended those three men. Each one of them murdered more than three people each. I used the insanity defense and got them off."

"That's it!" one of the lawyers yelled. "We are all crazy! We didn't understand the Ten Commandments! Therefore, we are innocent of all wrong doing!"

Caroline stood by the gates listening to the lawyers debating. "You are all crazy!" she shouted. "I am not going to plead insanity! I am Mrs. Caroline Brown Harrison! The judge doesn't know who he is dealing with!"

One lawyer leaned toward another. "She is not crazy!" he whispered. "She's a bitch!"

The lawyer leaned toward the other. "Being a bitch is not defensible! If she was younger, we could use that defense about the monthly curse! She's too old for that and she's too old to have a kid. We can't use the defense that she has those post blues or whatever. She's screwed! She's a bitch!"

"Is it getting hotter?" one lawyer yelled, as he wiped his brow.

"I'm hot and thirsty!" one lawyer said. "Is there a water fountain in this cemetery?"

One of the politicians moved closer toward the gates. "There are several water fountains but they don't work," he answered. "We had to decide to paint the new football stadium or cut the water service to the cemeteries and the children's playgrounds. We decided to paint the football stadium."

The lawyers nodded their heads.

"I think you are all missing the point!" the real estate agent said. The lawyers turned to look at her. "We have all been tried, convicted, and sentenced. I don't think there is a reprieve."

"The hearing is tomorrow morning," one lawyer said, as he wiped his brow.

"I don't think so," the real estate agent answered. "Have you considered not offering a defense but simply asking for mercy?"

"Mercy!" Caroline yelled, in a shrill voice. "Mercy for what?"

"For the things you have done," the real estate agent answered.

"Mercy!" Caroline screamed. "What I need is a good lawyer. These lawyers are no good! I need a good lawyer!"

"There were only two good ones here and they are gone," one lawyer said. He pointed toward the locked gates. "Nathan Clark and Nelson Higgins were buried there! They were taken with the others."

"Bring them back!" Caroline ordered. "I want them here to defend me!"

"They aren't coming back," one lawyer said quietly.

Caroline turned toward the locked gates and pulled on them. "Let me in!" she screamed.

"Damn it's hot!" one of the lawyers said. The people looked upward toward the sky. The blue sky had darkened and there was a reddish glow in the sky.

The lawyers looked toward the real estate agent. They were hot and sweating but she wasn't. "Aren't you hot?" one of the lawyers asked.

"No," the real estate agent answered. "I feel fine."

"I'm hot as Hell!" one of the lawyers said. "My tongue is swelled from thirst and I am hungry."

"I feel fine," the real estate agent answered.

"Do you have water?" one lawyer asked as he moved closer to her.

The real estate agent raised her arms to show she was not holding anything. She was wearing a simple pants suit. "No," she answered.

"Why are we hot and you are not?" one lawyer asked in an angry tone.

"I am sorry for everything I have done wrong," the real estate agent answered. "I asked for mercy."

"Mercy!" Caroline screamed, as she turned from the gates. "Mercy from whom? You are a disgrace to every woman that ever lived! I will never ask for mercy! People beg me for mercy!" She held her right fist in the air. "People shook when I was before them! If I had lived longer, I would have crushed every poor person that ever lived!"

One lawyer leaned toward another. "I'm not crazy but if that bitch keeps yelling, I will be crazy!" he whispered.

"I know what you mean!" the lawyer whispered back. "I really don't mind the heat but that bitch is driving me crazy! This is pure torture!"

The lawyer looked at his wrist. His watch was missing! "I don't have the time," he yelled. "It seems I have dropped my Rolex. Does anyone have the time?"

The lawyers looked at their wrists. Their watches were missing also.

"I am real good at telling time!" one lawyer yelled. "We have been here about twelve hours! The hearing should begin at anytime."

Many of the lawyers picked their coats up from the ground and put them on. Then, they adjusted their ties.

Caroline paused to wipe her brow. She was sweating profusely. "It's so hot," she whispered, as she turned toward the iron gates. She was wearing a long dress that was buttoned to her neck. She unbuttoned the top button of her dress. "Let me in!" she screamed as she pulled on the iron gates.

One lawyer leaned toward another. "I hope to hell she keeps that dress on!" he whispered. "Her ranting is driving me crazy! If she keeps unbuttoning that dress, I'll go blind! It's bad enough going before the judge crazy but I don't want to be blind too!"

The other lawyer nodded his head.

"I want to be as far away from her as possible," the lawyer continued. "There is guilt by association! If we are too close to her when the hearing starts, the judge will think we are dating her or something."

"The hearing had better start soon!" one lawyer whispered, as he leaned toward another. "I don't think I can take much more of her! I never killed anybody but I don't think the Commandment on killing referred to bitches."

"Let me in!" Caroline screamed, as she pulled on the iron gates.

The lawyers held their hands to their ears to mask the high, shrill screams of Mrs. Caroline Brown Harrison.

"It is time for me to go," the real estate agent said softly.

"Go where?" one of the lawyers asked.

The real estate agent pointed toward the rear of the cemetery. She pointed toward several large monuments. "I am to go there," she answered.

"What is there?" one of the lawyers asked, as he wiped his brow.

"Forgiveness," the real estate agent answered. She turned and walked toward the large monuments. The lawyers watched her as she walked behind a large monument.

"She's crazy!" one of the lawyers said, as he removed his shirt. His whole body was sweating. He looked upward toward the sky. The darkened sky had a red glow to it.

The lawyers rushed toward the iron gates of the pauper's cemetery. "Let us in!" they screamed, as they pulled on the iron bars.

Blackjack Calhoun stood near the gates watching the people pulling on the gates. He reached into his vest pocket and he removed a large fold of money. He laughed as he dropped the money and the deck of cards to the ground. Blackjack smiled as he looked where the real estate agent had walked.

He wasn't sweating! He stopped sweating shortly after the real estate lady told the people in the crowd that she had asked for mercy. He asked for mercy too!

Blackjack reached into his coat pocket and he removed a small notebook and a pencil. He thumbed through the notebook looking for the end. The notebook pages recorded the amounts of money he had won and lost. He turned to the last page and wrote - All debts paid!

Blackjack replaced the notebook and pencil in his coat pocket as he walked toward the large monuments. He walked toward the tree where the three men stood. As he walked, he removed his watch from his vest pocket. He slowly wound his watch as he approached the three men.

"Are you coming?" he asked.

"We will stay a while," one of the three men said. They weren't sweating.

"When did you figure it out?" Blackjack asked.

"When the first trumpet blew," one of the three men answered. The other two men nodded their heads.

Blackjack turned and looked at the crowd of people pulling on the gates. They were screaming to be let in. "Is it true?" Blackjack asked, as he turned toward the three men.

The three men looked at each other. "I was OK one day and then I snapped," one of the three men answered. "I didn't know what I had done for several years."

"Me too!" one of the three men answered. "I was bullied by several men. One day, I snapped. I knew what I had done but I wasn't sorry." He lowered his head. "I finally realized that what I had done affected innocent people."

"Not me," the last man said. "I was mean from the day I was born. I am the only one that really deserves to be here. I was just plain mean! There were times I could not control myself. It felt like many different people inside of me. I was OK for a few months then, it was like someone took control of my body. My name was Altus! Altus was a Roman soldier who crushed many revolts against Caesar. Altus did things I didn't know about for several days. When the first trumpet blew, I asked for mercy but nothing happened. When the third trumpet blew, Altus asked for mercy!"

"There are degrees of mean," Blackjack said, as he looked at the people screaming at the iron gates. He looked downward to his pocket watch.

"I am real good at telling time too!" one of the three men said. "When the first trumpet blew, I looked at the sun. It was about 3:00 P.M. We have been here about twenty-five minutes."

Blackjack smiled as he looked at his watch. "It was stopped," he said. "I had to set it and wind it. I guessed 3:00 P.M. also."

He looked at his watch. The time was 3:28 P.M. "It was always a little fast," he said, as he moved the second hand backward to 3:25 P.M.

"Are you coming?" Blackjack asked, as he looked at the large monuments.

"In a little while," one of the three men answered. "We were talking to each other about our choices. It helps to talk."

"Don't be too long," Blackjack said smiling.

"We have all the time in the world," one of the three men said. "The judge's forgiveness has no limit or time frame."

Blackjack smiled as he walked toward the large monuments. As he neared the monuments, he stopped and turned toward the pauper's section. The people were yelling and screaming as they pulled on the iron gates.

"Let me in!" Caroline screamed, as she pulled on the iron gates. "My name is Mrs. Caroline Brown Harrison! You don't know who you are dealing with!"

The Author

Edward Ronny Arnold developed the concept of *Plato's Dream,* in the year 1981, as Edward argued with his Psychology instructor concerning Plato's work, *Studying Death.* The class was titled *Death and Dying*. He disagreed with the instructor's interpretation of Plato's work.

Edward abandoned the work twice. He began writing *Plato's Dream* in the year 1986 and he worked on it in the year 2001. Edward abandoned the work in 2001 to complete his first published work, *Rebecca*. In 2001, Edward had completed four hundred sixty-two pages. He drastically cut the work, in 2004, as he believed it was too complicated and the reader would get lost in the various stories.

Plato's Dream is Edward's sixth book and his first attempt at romance. The work is not about physical romance, although it is certainly there, the work is about life and death and how both states are often viewed.

Edward's published books include: *Rebecca*, *The Lepers*, *Rashida*, *The Ram of God*, and *The Tenth Scroll*.

He holds the degrees of B.S. in Psychology and the M.A. in Sociology from Middle Tennessee State University. Edward has completed twenty-seven graduate hours toward the Ed.D in Psychology. He lives in Nashville, Tennessee with his wife Michelle and their two children, Khristine and Khristian.

List of References

Anderson S, Bankier AT, Barrell BG, de Bruijn MHL, Coulson AR, Drouin J, Eperon IC, Nierlich DP, Roe BA, Sanger F, Schreier PH, Smith AJH, Staden R, Young IG. Sequence and organization of the human mitochondrial genome. Nature, 1981, 290- 465.

Aristotle. Generation of Animals, 350 B.C.

Aristotle. God from Metaphysics, 350 B.C.

Barbujani, Guido, Bertorelle, Giorgio. Genetics and the population history of Europe. Proceedings of the National Academy of Sciences of the United States of America , 2001, 98(1), 22-25, 2001.

Cann RL, Stoneking M, Wilson AC. Mitochondrial genome variation and the origin of modern humans. Nature. 1987, 325, 31-36.

Cott, Jonathan (in collaboration with Hanny El Zeini). The Search for Omm Sety - Reincarnation and Eternal Love. New York: Doubleday and Company, Inc., 2001.

Genesis 5:3-4. The King James Version of the Holy Bible authorized in 1611.

Hawthorne, Nathaniel. The House of the Seven Gables, Boston and New York: Houghton Mifflin and Company, 1850.

Mendel, Gregor. Experiments in Plant Hybridization, Read at the February 8th, and March 8th, 1865, meetings of the Brunn Natural History Society, 1865.

Plato. Studying Death, 360 B.C.

Plato. Studying Death:II - Ways to Hades, 360 B.C.

Saint John 11:11. The King James Version of the Holy Bible authorized in 1611.

Saint Matthew 9:24. The King James Version of the Holy Bible authorized in 1611.

Sykes, Brian. The Seven Daughters of Eve, New York, NY:W.W. Norton & Company, Inc., 2001.

Watson, James D., Crick, Francis. A Structure for Deoxyribose Nucleic Acid, Nature, 1953, 171, 737.

Watson, James D. The Double Helix: A Personal Account of the Discovery of the Structure of DNA, New York: Atheneum, 1968.

Plato's Dream

www.ingramcontent.com/pod-product-compliance
Lightning Source LLC
LaVergne TN
LVHW101321110826
845152LV00011B/23